GAIA REBORN

—·—

A NOVEL

J.R. WALCUTT

SPIRIT WARRIOR PRESS

ALSO BY J.R. WALCUTT

Gaia Hunted

2023 Spirit Warrior Press Trade Paperback Edition

Copyright © 2023 by Jason Walcutt

jrwalcutt.com

Cover Illustration © 2023 by Abigail Drapkin

abigaildrapkin.com

Cover Design by James, GoOnWrite.com

LIBRARY OF CONGRESS CATALOGING-IN-PUBLICATION DATA

Gaia Reborn: a novel / Jason Walcutt

ISBN 978-1-7327583-2-2

eBook ISBN: 978-1-7327583-3-9

1. Urban Fantasy—Fiction.   2. Legends and Mythology—Fiction.   3. International Thriller—Fiction.

Subscribe to the newsletter to get a free story as well as stay up to date with all the latest news, sales, and promotions!

If you're interested in the other books in the Ascended Prophecies Series visit jrwalcutt.com.

Printed in the United States of America

To Anna, Lilah and Ori

CHAPTER ONE

RED SKY AT MORNING

My life is a lie. But this truth, like many others, is easy to forget while lounging on a tropical island. As my best friend and I sit on a high cliff overlooking the ocean, the bright Hawaiian sun burns away my usual preoccupations and worries. My zen-like peace is suddenly interrupted by a loud pop beside me.

I turn my head to see that Jessie's entire chin is engulfed in pink bubble gum. "Wow," she says, "that was a big one."

"Keep it there. You look good."

Jessie snorts and turns on her side to face me. "Can we chat about something?"

"Sure, shoot."

"Don't take this the wrong way, Marie, but you're too timid."

I grin to mask my unease. Despite two years of using that name, it's still weird to hear it said in conversation. It's not my real name, and real names are like tattoos—they stay with you your entire life. Even if you remove it, there'll always be a scar. "My timidity is cute," I say, batting my eyes.

"Well, that's undeniable, but what I'm saying is you're too cautious." When she sees the confusion on my face, she adds, "Last night was a perfect example. Despite my many valid arguments about why we should go out dancing, you refused to leave the house."

"Yeah, no shit. It was three in the morning."

"Exactly. Too cautious."

"Caution keeps you out of trouble."

Jessie raises her bug-eyed sunglasses. "Trouble is what keeps life interesting." She fumbles through her canvas bag beside her chair, looking for tanning oil.

Trouble is the last thing I want. I take a deep breath and gaze out at the white caps. The Pacific Ocean extends forever into the distance. Despite the sea's constantly changing nature, it's always made me feel serene. The peaceful scene is only disturbed by the music of a small party of teenagers cliff jumping a few hundred yards away from us. "Sometimes I think that without my caution, you'd never actually sleep."

She squirts some oil into her hand. "Speaking of sleeping, I heard you screaming right before you got up."

I force myself not to jolt. I feel as if a cinder block has been dropped onto my chest. *Don't make a big deal out of it*, I tell myself. "Yeah, I had a bad dream."

"You were crying out a word. A name? Sounded like 'Guy Ah.' Who is he? An old fling?"

"Don't know."

"What was the dream about?" she presses.

I now know why she's interested. "Doesn't matter. Nothing in dreams makes sense. They're the vomit of our subconscious," I say, hoping that puts an end to it.

"At least you have dreams."

To any other person, this might sound ridiculous. But I know the truth. I should tell her why she doesn't dream; why she doesn't know who she truly is. I should tell her that her true name isn't Jessie Rodriguez. But I don't. Because I understand the consequences, and how everything will change, and how there's no putting the truth back into the bottle after it comes squirting out. Instead, I say, "I envy you. Dreams are so annoying. They get your heart pounding and your blood pumping and fill you with terror in the middle of the night."

"Says the girl who has hookups in a dream. Now that's the type of adventures I want."

My face burns. I shouldn't have told her about that, but when you're having a secret tryst with Casanova, well, it's a fun conversation starter. "You have those nightly romps."

"Hey, I'm proud that I have a healthy sex drive." Jessie takes a clip out of her hair, letting her thick black mane spill down. "Anyways, I'd be willing to share."

"I'm OK, but thanks," I reply, focusing my attention on the swooping sea birds snatching up fish from the waves.

"You need to get over that guy."

"I am over him, actually," I say, too quickly.

"What was his name—Josh, Jeremy, Jake?"

"Jared." Just saying his name is like tearing open a fresh wound. How many times a day do I think about him, regret what I did to him, even though I did it for his own protection? At least that's what I tell myself. "I'll never see him again, and we're both better for it."

"Gosh, your insides are in a twist." She pops another bubble and smiles. "All I'm saying is that you should be bolder. Once you realize your true potential, you'll blow everyone away."

"I'm sorry that I'm inadequate."

"You're not inadequate," she replies, wincing. "Sorry I brought it up. I know I should keep some of my opinions to myself. Do you forgive me?"

"Jessie, I like you how you are. You push me in a good way. Don't change a thing."

Under the scorching sun, I close my eyes and retreat to that place in my mind where I go when I think of Jared Stone. It's a wall. A towering, brick structure that I've created in my imagination. The barrier keeps me from learning the truths on the other side, protects me from the thousands of voices that could easily invade.

I hear them cry out to me. They want to own me. The wall is the only thing separating me from a destiny that will destroy Jared and me.

The sun disappears, and I shiver in the sudden shade. Opening my eyes, I expect to find a cloud blocking the sun. Instead, a figure looms over me—a shirtless, muscular, board-shorted surfer.

"Hi ladies, you look lonely," says the guy, who pushes a lock of blond hair out of his eyes.

I choke back a laugh. The man is a walking stereotype.

Jessie pushes her shades down, and her eyes glide over him as though she's a rancher appraising a bull. Apparently, she sees things differently. "Marie. Are you ready to throw caution to the wind?"

He stares straight at me, and I can't say I mind the attention. The guy could be Mr. November in Men of Hawaii calendar. I suddenly remember him from evenings at Lush, the bar we work at. "Your name is . . . Troy, right?"

He nods but doesn't appear pleased to be recognized. His forced smile makes my stomach churn, as does his penetrating gaze. Then Troy peeks down at his palm and back up at me. I frown in confusion as he does this two more times without saying a thing.

That's when I notice the photograph in his hand. The realization crystallizes. Goosebumps spread across my skin.

I don't hear anyone.

Gone are the crowds of cliff jumping kids. Gone are the sounds of pickup trucks and blaring reggae. I hear only surf breaking on the cliffs and the screams of distant seabirds.

"You did well," says a voice behind us.

When I hear that voice, I know we're screwed. Troy takes a step back, and as he retreats, I get up from my chair—heart thumping, skin itching. As I turn, I pray that it isn't so.

But it is.

Surrounding us, blocking our escape, are five unlikely people. The two heavy-set men and one woman in billowy Hawaiian shirts could easily pass for orderlies; it's the lead individuals who arrest my attention. To anyone else, they'd appear as identical silver-haired old men in matching knitted cardigans and rubber-heeled slippers. But I know what they truly are.

Jessie stands up beside me. "Troy, I didn't know you volunteered at the nursing home. That's so sweet."

She has no clue how much trouble we're in.

One of the old men wears a red scarf; the other wears a blue one.

Red Scarf reaches into his sweater pocket, takes out a roll of bills, tosses it to Troy, and jerks his head as if to say *scram*.

"Nothing personal, ladies," Troy says, "but tomorrow is rent day." He winks and runs off. The bastard.

They found me. How is it possible? I changed my name, my identity, cut off all forms of communication. I didn't contact anyone from my former life. How did they track me down?

Blue Scarf tilts his head, reminding me of a lizard. "We found two of them."

"Then we will be rewarded doubly," says Red Scarf.

"Hi," Jessie says sweetly. "Did you come here to watch the birds?"

"No, they didn't," I reply, taking a step back and pulling Jessie with me. We're only a few feet away from a forty-foot cliff that ends with jagged lava stones.

Red Scarf opens his cardigan, and the metal of his gun glints in the afternoon sun. "Alive is preferable," he says, his face as expressionless as a sphinx. "But dead will do as well."

CHAPTER TWO

Paradise Lost

Jessie tugs at my arm. "Do you know these people?" she asks, the first inkling of concern lacing her voice.

I shake my head. While Jessie sees only two old men, I see two swirling brownish-red auras, underneath which are reptilian olive-hued faces composed of jagged teeth, wrinkled skin, and unblinking yellow eyes.

"Why the fuck does he have a gun?"

I know exactly why, but to explain that right now would be like explaining the physics of steam locomotion while staring at an oncoming train.

"Get them," says Red Scarf.

We both take another step back as the large orderlies advance, but behind us, there's nowhere to go—unless we plan to swan dive onto the rocks below.

"What are we going to do?" Jessie asks, her voice liquid fear.

The truth is, I know what I have to do. The problem is, it scares the hell out of me. Once I go down that road, who's to say that I can turn back?

The orderlies come at us. In a few seconds, we'll be theirs.

"Stay close," I whisper to Jessie. "I'm trying something," She gapes, but before she can say anything, I'm gone. In a place in my mind.

Time slows to a halt.

I'm at the wall, its cold red bricks high above me. I stare at it, terrified of the voices it holds back—my past lives. I have to do something that scares me to the core.

It's checkmate. They forced my hand. I know what these people represent, and the things they'll do to Jessie and me. I shouldn't have gotten her into this. I never should have befriended her.

I'm a danger to everyone around me.

The voices behind the wall cry out to me. In my mind, I clench my fingers tight and pull back my arm. I throw a punch, and my fist slams into the bricks. Cracks form. I reach back and punch again. Chunks of mortar and brick crumble down.

I pull back my fist one last time and pray: Please, help me—don't kill me.

My clenched hand plows a hole through the wall. Immediately, ethereal wisps of light come flowing through. They're my past lives, and I have no idea how to control them or summon them. I just hope that whichever one comes into me knows how to fight.

One of the wisps circles my arm and wraps around my shoulder. An instant later, it slithers like a serpent up my neck and then enters me through my mouth and eyes. The light blinds me, and my whole body convulses as the past life invades my mind and takes possession of my body.

Blurry shadows transform into images of people, places, and times. A life, long dead, streams into my consciousness . . .

The evergreens waver in a light wind. Somewhere close by, a crow caws. Up above, clouds blanket the sky, and the first drops of rain plop on my plumed helmet.

A storm is coming.

My hand—small but muscled—grips a wooden shaft with a spear tip stained red. I pound the spear against my shield and let loose a roar.

What I thought was tall grass, is an oncoming wave of invaders armed with broad-blade axes and swords.

Shoulder to shoulder I stand with the men I trained. It doesn't matter that I was born a woman. They have treated me as if I were a brother. Together, we've ridden over mountains and plains. We've forded rivers and crossed oceans. Through sickness, fighting, pain, injuries, we've never stopped spreading the power of our tribe to the farthest reaches of this dark world.

Fear fills the invaders' faces, and for good reason. We will have no mercy on them.

We kick our horses into a gallop and ride toward the first wave of the soldiers, our spears crashing into their ranks—

I'm back on the cliff in Hawaii, where no time has passed. One of the orderlies is about to tackle us. Beside me, Jessie is frozen in terror.

But I'm no longer Mattie Fisher; my name is Manu. No retreat, no surrender. Now is the time for battle. Now is the time for blood.

Right as the woman is about to tackle me, I shove Jessie to the ground, then duck and scrunch into a ball.

The woman's huge arms embrace open air. As her frame looms over me, I use her forward momentum to her disadvantage. I grab and pull her backward, propelling her as if she's a rock launched out of a sling.

She vaults over me, and her massive frame tumbles over the precipice. Her echoing screams end with a distant splash, followed by silence. I pivot away from the cliff as another orderly advances; the third is almost on Jessie. I cry out to warn her as she fumbles through her canvas bag.

The man grabs her shoulder, but she whips around with her arm extended and a face lit with fury. He sees the stun gun a half-second too late. White lightning electrifies his chest. His body spasms, and he collapses to the ground. Jessie doesn't hesitate before stomping her heel into the orderly's face.

Impressed by her actions, I quickly turn to the last orderly, who's throwing a punch aimed at my face. I crouch and drive my knee into his gut; he doubles over clutching his mid-section and gasping for air.

The lizard men, who have yet to move, appear annoyed. "We were told she had not mastered her abilities," says Red Scarf.

"The information was false," Blue Scarf replies. "I'll get Gaia. You get the other." Then he pulls a long knife from his sweatpants and shuffles toward me.

I grab a beach chair.

We circle each other, waiting for the other to make the first move. The lizard man feints left and then thrusts the knife toward my stomach.

I sidestep the knife like a matador guiding a rushing bull and swing the chair in front of the oncoming blade. The point pierces the thick material. Before he can pull back his hand, I spin the chair, and the knife pinwheels from the lizard man's hand.

Immediately, his foot swings through the air in a high, fast roundhouse aimed for my head. I turn and dodge the kick, but he slivers behind me and wraps his thin arms around my neck in a deathly tight choke hold. I struggle to free myself, yet a burst of pain arrests my attempt for freedom.

I throw my elbow into his stomach. He grunts, and I temporarily break his hold. But then something I expected happens.

A thousand voices reverberate through my skull. A deafening chorus. My past lives—still gushing through the crack in the wall—rise in rebellion. They rush inside my mind, taking control.

I try pushing back against them, but they're a tidal wave swallowing everything. I can't withstand their force.

I heave, sucking for air, which is blocked by the lizard man tightening his arms like a vise around my throat. Manu fights to stay with me. I need her now, and she knows it, but her essence seeps away.

The man squeezes harder, and I see stars.

My breathing stops.

As her parting gift, Manu takes hold one last time. With my last ounce of awareness, I sink my teeth into the man's arm until I taste blood. He cries out and loosens his grip, and I slip out of his arms, rolling away.

I waver in and out of consciousness. Red Scarf lands a hard punch to Jessie's head, and she crumples to the ground.

"No!" I gasp, but there's nothing I can do.

I struggle to my knees, but the voices invade me like angry wasps around a hive.

I grip my skull, rocking back and forth. Hundreds of wisps of light jockey to take control. Right as I repulse one, another replaces it.

I'm a queen in Sumer. I'm draped in furs and hunting wooly rhinoceros across frozen tundras. I'm on a tropical island living in the trees, cooking a meal of sago and taro root. I stream through lives as if they're revolutions on a carousel. None last for more than a moment, but in that instant, I know everything about them. Where I lived. What I cared about. Whom I loved.

I can't control them or concentrate. The voices are in control, and their rule is anarchy.

I scream, shake, and convulse. I want it to end. Why won't they leave?

Blue scarf rises to his feet, blood dripping from his arm. He reaches into his coat, takes out the gun.

I'm helpless.

There's a long pause as he aims the barrel of the gun at my temple. There's nothing I can do to stop him.

He pulls back the gun's hammer. I wait for the explosion, but at the last moment, he raises his hand and slams the butt of the gun against the side of my head. All falls silent.

Blessedly silent.

CHAPTER THREE

HAWAIIAN BARBECUE

The sweet, noxious aroma of gasoline floods my nostrils. My head throbs like an open wound. I'm going to be sick. A deep breath does little to quell the nausea.

I look around, but everything is pitch black. My body trembles in the cool, moist air. The only sound I recognize is that of the coqui frogs, whose song has kept me up many nights.

I'm lying on my side. Moving proves impossible. My arms and legs are tightly bound to something hard. Someone stirs behind me.

"Marie." It's Jessie. She's alive. A wave of relief passes through me. "Are you OK?" she asks.

I realize that the heavy thing I'm bound to is her. We're positioned back-to-back, and our hands are tied together. I clear my throat and fight down my headache's heavy beat. "Hurty. Very hurty, and incredibly freaked out. What about you?"

She snorts. "He hit like my sister."

Yet I hear the underlying fear in her tone. "Where are we?"

"I don't think you want to know." Intertwined with mine, her fingers provide a modicum of comfort. "They threw us into the back of a car and drove us up the volcano. We're in one of the old lava tubes."

Once on a drunken dare, I'd explored a lava tube, one of the caves that run below the surface of the island formed by flowing magma. Taking a deep breath, I gag. "Let me guess. We're covered in gasoline?"

"Pretty much."

"Have you tried twisting out of the restraints?" I ask, shifting my head around. "You like to play with handcuffs."

"Neither the time nor place," she warns. "I've been struggling to get us loose for twenty minutes."

"Let's work together. Maybe we can slip out."

We undulate our bodies together as if dancing a horizontal worm, but all we succeed in doing is creating a low, circular berm around us.

I've been in worse situations, I think, seeking to reassure myself. I have to get Jessie out of here. I pulled her into this, and I have to get her out.

There's only one solution: one of my past lives.

Hesitating, I remember what happened on the cliff. The overwhelming waves of voices swallowing me. That was exactly what I'd been afraid of, and if I hadn't been knocked out, I fear my brain would have melted.

But what choice do we have? Maybe one of them can escape from handcuffs?

The wall in my mind is still there. Not only that, but the breach I created has completely re-sealed. I'm not surprised; it was one of the first things I taught myself after my Ascension. A psychologist would call it repression, but I call it not going insane. It's a defense mechanism that assures me that while I'm asleep or not concentrating, one of my past lives won't suddenly invade my brain.

I go back to the imaginary wall and visualize breaking open a hole, but the wall doesn't change. Not even a crack. I will myself to open it. No effect. I imagine pounding my fists against it. Nothing. I listen, and I don't even hear any of my past lives. It's as if they've all disappeared.

Great. Isn't this perfect? The times I don't want them, they're always there, but when I need them, they go on a lunch break.

"We're stuck," Jessie says, interrupting my mental calisthenics. "Why did they leave us here?"

"I don't know."

"What the hell happened back there?"

"What do you mean?"

"Excuse me? I've known you for two years. We've lived and worked together the entire time. You were a different person back on the cliff. The way you moved and acted."

There's no reason not to tell her. She has a right to know. It's her birthright as well as mine. "Jessie, there are things you should know. You and me, well, we're different—"

"You can say that again." The new voice cuts like a cleaver through the cave. Chills run down my spine.

A light leaps up from the lava tube's entrance, illuminating the smooth walls. I hear the click-clack of familiar high-heeled boots.

Tatiana Williams emerges, carrying a kerosene lamp that casts monstrous shadows. She wears a fur coat and leather pants. The silver streak in her thick, dark hair shines in the yellow light. "Gaia. I am so happy to see you again."

I swallow my fear. "I can't say the same."

"Marie, who is this Victorian Goth?" Jessie asks.

Tatiana grins. "Is that the name you're using now?" She takes a few steps closer to inspect us. "Little good it did you." Her eyes flash hate in the fiery light. "Remember what I promised. Time to eat what you grew."

"Why don't you untie us and say that right to her face?"

Despite Jessie's bluster, I feel Tatiana's words hit their mark. Not long before coming to Hawaii, Tatiana and the god she serves hunted me. In their violent wake they left a trail of dead including Patrick, my best friend, and Gertrude, Jared's mother. Even after I destroyed one of the gods who pursued me, they wouldn't stop chasing me. I knew they wouldn't. I just didn't think they'd find me now.

"No, I'd rather hear your screams as you burn." Tatiana turns to leave but pauses and spins back around. "Oh, by the way, Gaia, thank you for finding Pele. We've been searching for her almost as long as we've been searching for you. Two birds, one stone. That's the way I like to kill Mother Goddesses."

"Why do you serve him, Tatiana?" I ask, fear roiling my stomach. "He doesn't represent anything good for you."

Anger ripples across her face, wrinkling her flawless skin and twisting her red lips. "Don't assume for a second that you know anything about me." She spits on the ground. "I've waited a long time for this." She walks toward the entrance then pivots and hurls the kerosene lamp. It smashes against the wall of the lava tube, and flames shoot across the floor, igniting the gasoline. A wave of fire engulfs the space.

"Bye-bye," Tatiana says.

It takes all of two seconds for the entire floor to be immersed in flames. But to my surprise, the small berm we created keeps the fire at bay.

Jessie struggles against our restraints, and her legs kick out toward the fire. The flames lick at our skin.

"Don't do that. You'll light your foot on fire."

Jessie tries to respond but coughs violently. She clears her throat. "That may be the least of our concerns."

She's right. Each breath is like inhaling from the tailpipe of a semi-trailer truck; the smoke will kill us before the fire.

The flames rise higher as the cave's detritus ignites. I gasp as the fire eats up all the oxygen.

Then I hear an explosion outside our lava-tube tomb.

No, a gunshot. It's followed by three more blasts.

A man screams, followed by a muffled command from Tatiana. Several more gunshots ring out.

"Jessie," I say, shaking my arms. "Stay with me."

No response.

"Are you OK?" I wiggle my fingers but her hand barely responds.

I've got to get her out of here, but I can't stop sucking back the heavy smoke.

There's one last gunshot, like a warning, then the sound of crumbling rocks and a painful grunt. An interminable silence ensues. I fight to stay conscious. At any second, a spark could land on us, and we'll light up like a Christmas tree.

My vision blurs. A pit opens in my stomach as I realize that we're not getting out of here. Is this really how it ends? I feel so disappointed and sad.

A tremor of movement comes from Jessie, who suddenly exclaims, "Got it!" The next moment, she pulls one of her hands free. "You're right. I *do* like to play with handcuffs. Now let's get out of here."

We pull ourselves up and manage to find a fire-free path edging along the tunnel's side.

I fully expect Tatiana to be waiting for us when we exit coughing and hacking. Instead, we find a single person lying knocked out at the opening. When I turn him over, I think the smoke is playing tricks on my eyes. It can't be him.

Jared Stone. The man I love but swore I'd never see again.

CHAPTER FOUR

L'OMELETTE

I smell like a truck stop—gasoline fumes, burnt ash, and despair. Staring into my bathroom mirror, I barely recognize my face through all the grime smudged over my freckles. My tangled chestnut-colored hair contains a fine collection of dirt, leaves, and other souvenirs from the lava tube.

I step into the shower and let the spray of high-pressure hot water massage my sore body. As it wipes away the filth, I try to sort out my racing thoughts. I still can't believe that Jared is in our house.

Two years ago, he and I survived horrors that stretched the imagination. After our ordeal, I cut him out of my life. I burned that bridge to my past. It's as if I'm meeting a ghost, and I prayed that I wouldn't see him again.

I shut off the water feeling as if I'm a new person. I twist my hair into a towel and wrap myself in a thick bathrobe. I almost look normal again, except for my eyes. Usually a vibrant green, they're dull and tired in the glare of the fluorescent light. I sigh and put in contact lenses, changing my eyes to brown.

When I exit the bathroom, I find Jessie waiting in the hallway with crossed arms and a stern expression. She helped me carry Jared down from the lava tube along a winding path that ended at a small parking area. In Jared's pocket, we found a key which unlocked a pickup truck and hefted him into the cargo bed and drove home.

"Are you going to tell me what this is all about?" she asks.

I avoid her eyes and walk to my bedroom. It's as messy as I left it this morning, with dirty piles of clothes and overdue library books about mythology and religion stacked in mini-mountains. Before we left to sunbathe on the cliff, I'd promised myself that I'd clean it today. That promise seems years in the past.

Jessie follows me and closes the door behind us. She's all dressed up for her shift at Lush—a lacy black top, a pair of knock-off Gucci jeans, and pink pumps. I wear sneakers on the job, but Jessie always insists on heels.

"Don't give me the silent treatment. I was nearly murdered this afternoon." Her eyes flash. Hands on her hips, she leans forward. "I don't want to call the police, but I will if it'll keep us safe."

Jessie grew up in Chicago. From the few fragments of stories she'd told me about her upbringing, I gathered it didn't sound like the police were the people she called when she was in trouble.

"No, don't. That'll just bring more problems." I rummage through my closet and take out my last two clean shirts.

"I don't want some thug sucker punching me while I'm working." She reaches into her purse and takes out a tube of mascara.

"No one will bother us."

Jessie and I debated buying plane tickets and leaving the island as soon as possible on our drive back from the lava tube, but with Jared knocked out, I couldn't in good conscience leave him. And we agreed that it would be better to go to work than sit around the whole night freaking out about being attacked. At the bar, at least we could drink for free and freak out.

"What about the asshole with the nice shoes?" she asks, inspecting her honey-brown eyes in a pocket mirror.

"Tatiana escaped."

"So, we're not safe for the long term."

"We're safe for now. That's all that matters," I say, trying to convince myself. To distract myself, I debate between the two blouses. The gray one has a bateau neckline and longer sleeves, like the old shirts I wore as a school teacher. The other is black and tight—a sleeveless U-neck that Jessie nicknamed my "screw me, I'm single" shirt.

"By the way, he woke up a half hour ago."

I jerk to attention. "What?"

"Is he *the* Jared Stone?" she asks, eyes narrowing. "The guy who broke your heart?"

"He didn't break my heart, and it's complicated," I say, quickly deciding on the black blouse.

"Everything's complicated with you. It's the same guy, right?"

"Yeah."

"How did he find you?"

"Jared has a way of tracking people down." Noticing my frantic, searching eyes, Jessie sighs, and retrieves the dark-gray thigh-length circle skirt hanging over my bed's headboard. It's the one that I was searching for. "Thanks."

"My pleasure, and you should consider your pair of black-heeled sandals. They show off your legs."

"I'll take it into consideration."

Jessie shakes her head. "Is your name even Marie Tudor?" She leans forward in a challenge. "Because now that I think about it, the name sounds fake."

My head drops, and I avoid her eyes. "It's not my real name."

"Well, what is it?" she says, tapping her foot.

"Mattie Fisher."

Jessie snorts. "OK, Mattie Fisher, pleasure meeting you."

"Don't be that way, Jessie. I'm still the same person. I changed my name to avoid what happened today. I did it to disappear."

Jessie doesn't respond right away. "That woman called me Pele. What did she mean?"

I freeze then let my shoulders slouch. Now is the time to lay out the truth. "I should have told you before."

"Told me what?"

"It was what I was saying in the cave. We're . . . different."

"What do you mean?"

"Well, it's hard to explain, but—"

Jessie's cell phone rings. She takes it out of her purse and reads the number. "Shit," she says. "It's Tom. I'm an hour late." She puts the ringer on silent, drops the phone into her bag, and points at me. "This conversation isn't over. When you get to work later, you're telling me everything, and I don't care how personal it gets." She draws back and inspects me. "Borrow my blush and put a little color on your cheeks. You're whiter than a polar bear."

"Are you sure you don't want to take the night off? It's been a hell of an afternoon."

"Girl, I won't be working. I'm going to get a stiff drink, and I'll have one waiting for you when you arrive. I'll tell Tom you'll be in soon." She kisses both my cheeks, spins around, and leaves the room.

I change and check the mirror. I don't have Jessie's curves, but I also don't look half bad in the skirt and blouse. As per Jessie's suggestion, I add a little make-up and put on the sandals. Right before I leave the room, I give myself a quick spray of a fruity perfume, then take a deep breath and steel myself for what's to come.

Jared Stone is waiting in our kitchen, and appears to have fully recovered. He's leaning over the sink eating kidney beans straight from the can with a teaspoon. I don't know if I necessarily have a "type," but if I did, Jared would win the prize. He's put on a little weight since I last saw him, which is good, because he was too skinny. His brownish copper hair, which used to hang in his eyes, is nicely cropped back.

His gaze lands on me. His blue eyes go wide and his jaw drops, revealing white teeth.

I wish I could have posted that reaction on Instagram. I hold back a smile. "Come on, Jared, you can do better than that." I walk past him toward the pantry.

He recovers, and his face assumes a cool slate expression. "I was never much of a cook."

"Allow me?" I ask, donning a striped apron.

"Sounds fine to me," he says. He puts the can of beans in the sink and leans against the counter with his arms crossed.

"To what do I owe the pleasure, Jared?"

"Small talk? Really?"

I flash a smile that would make a housewife from the 1950s proud. "You gotta start somewhere." I take our biggest knife out of a drawer and ram it into a cutting board on the counter. The blade sticks up vertically, wobbling. "I told you that I never wanted to see you again."

"I guess I'm not much at following directions." Looking cheeky and proud, he returns my smile. "It's great to see you again. You look good."

That smile melts my insides, and I spin away and open the refrigerator to hide my blushing cheeks. Just hearing his voice tears open my heart. I want to apologize, I want to say that I never wanted to hurt him. I want him to know that I really want to be with him. But I can't.

The fridge is depressingly empty. Jessie and I tend to order takeout Chinese food more often than not. I get a sinking feeling that the can of beans might be better than what I can offer.

That's when I hear the whisper: *Eggs, bacon, milk.* It's one of my past lives speaking from behind the wall in my mind. I don't question the voice. Instead, I rummage around, and am surprised to discover all the ingredients.

"I missed you," he says after a minute.

Fighting to stay in control, I feel blood rush to my head. I slam the fridge harder than I meant to. It shakes, and an unripened mango falls off the top and rolls across the peeling linoleum floor. "How did you find me?" I ask, avoiding his eyes.

He reaches down for the mango and offers it to me. "I've been searching for you."

"Thanks," I reply, my hands shaking. "But that doesn't answer my question."

"I was following Tatiana," he says nonchalantly.

"Seems she got the better of you."

"Actually, I scared off her guards and was almost able to capture her, but she slipped away."

"She knocked you out?" I ask, while putting a pan on the stovetop and adding some slices of bacon.

"She didn't. When I was walking down into the lava tube, I slipped and hit my head. Still, lucky I found you when I did."

"It's lucky that we found you when we did," I shoot back.

"Yeah, really lucky." He pauses. "Now that I've found you. I hate to be the bearer of bad news."

"What do you mean?"

"It's about the Father Gods."

My hands jerk, and I drop the egg I'm holding. It breaks on the floor. "Shit," I say under my breath.

Jared grabs some napkins from the table and crouches beside me to mop up the broken yoke. I'm painfully aware that his body is inches from mine.

"What is it?" I ask.

"Massacres every week," he says, his voice growing dark. "Mostly women, some men. Murders buried in newspapers and on the internet. Weird that they're all connected to some cult." He reaches inside his leather jacket, takes out a phone, and offers it to me. "Take a look, but it's not pretty." My eyes slide over the gruesome headlines and photos. Killing after killing. Hundreds of deaths. "Do you see a pattern?"

I gulp as my skin turns cold. "It's him, isn't it?"

Jared's unblinking eyes spook me a bit. "The Shadow, Gurzil's maker, has begun the Purging. He's killing Mother Goddesses. Targeting both Ascended and Descended gods and everyone who has a connection with them. Priests, priestesses, sympathizers, friends, family members. The murders will continue until someone stops him."

The war between the Mother Goddesses and Father Gods has been fought for millennia. In fact, it's not really a war; it's more like a genocide. There was a Purging two thousand years ago, and most of the Mother Goddesses were murdered. During the Purging, one of my past lives, my last Ascended life, was murdered, and until two years ago, I had no clue about any of this.

"Is that why you're here? To convince me that I'm the solution. Am I really the secret weapon that will save the world?" I whisk the eggs violently at the counter. "You're deluding yourself Jared. I can't do anything to stop this."

He shakes his head, his face soft and sympathetic. "I know Mattie. You're not ready."

It's my turn to pause. "What do you mean?"

"You don't have control over your past lives."

His comment sends shivers down my spine. "How do you know that?"

"Because no god has the ability to channel when they first Ascend."

"I'm not a god." My body tenses. "The Ascended aren't gods. They're just normal humans with the ability to remember their past lives."

"Call yourself whatever you want, but it takes years of training to master channeling."

"I have no idea what you're talking about." I turn to the pan with the sizzling bacon. "What is channeling?"

"I wish you hadn't left," he says, exasperation in his tone. "There was so much you didn't know."

"OK!" I say, throwing down my spatula. "It was mean to leave you in the hospital, and I still regret it to this day. But I had my reasons, and they were good ones."

To my surprise, he takes my hand in his, and pulls me closer. My breath catches and I can't help but look up into his eyes. Throat dry and skin on fire, I feel as though I'm falling. "Are you ready to tell me what those reasons are?" he asks.

Should I tell him about the prophecy? About his destiny? No, I can't. It's a burden for me to bear. I love him too much to heap that wagon-load of trouble onto his shoulders. I drop his hand and turn back to the stove. "What were we talking about?"

"Channeling," he replies, his voice sadder. "It's the process that allows one of your past lives to occupy your body."

"I thought I was supposed to naturally get those abilities."

"No, you have to learn how to do it."

I pour the whisked eggs into the hot pan with the bacon in it, and the mixture pops and bubbles. "Just tell me why you're here."

"I can take you to a place where you can master your powers. Where you can learn how to channel."

It's all too much. I know I haven't learned how to control my past lives—it's like a shouting match in my head. But I can't get involved with the Ascended. And I especially can't get involved with Jared, despite every part of my body, except my brain, wanting him. "I thought I was clear with you before. I don't want you to come after me."

"You can't leave the world of the Ascended, Mattie. You're in it forever."

"I'm happy where I'm at. I don't want things to change."

Jared stares at me for a length of time, quiet, and finally asks, "Is your friend a Mother Goddess?"

I don't know how he guessed that, but I nod begrudgingly. "Yes, she's Pele." I met Jessie the day my plane landed in Hawaii. She too was on a one-way ticket. I knew the instant I saw her that she was like me. Every Ascended god can identify another Ascended god. In my eyes, she has black hair, skin the color of dried lava, passionate eyes, and a fiery orange aura. Her deistic form. Her true god form.

"If you have the ability to Descend gods, then you also have the power to Ascend them."

I don't know how I Descended Gurzil, a Father God who'd been hunting me. When I Descended him—taking away his ability to remember his past lives—I basically rendered him comatose. I would have felt bad about it if he weren't a sociopath who tortured Jared and murdered my best friend.

"I don't want her to Ascend," I reply.

"You can learn how to Ascend gods at the place I'll take you."

"Didn't you hear me? I don't want her knowing. It's safer that way."

"She has the right to know her true self."

"Just like I had the right to know? There are times that I wish I was actually given the choice—instead of being tricked into it."

I drop the frying pan in front of him on a trivet. The French omelet is black. "Turns out I'm not much of one."

"Much of what?"

"A cook—nor a housewife for that matter." I strip off the apron and throw it to the side. A quick glance at the clock shows that I'm now late for my shift. "I gotta go to work. You can keep the beans and the spoon." I head for the door, and Jared follows. "Where are you going?" I ask.

"I'm not letting you out of my sight. I'm your Protector. It's my job to keep you safe. I'll follow you wherever you go."

"Suit yourself."

But secretly I'm praying that he'll turn around and leave. I remember the prophecy, which I learned within the first moment of my Ascension. It's three-fold: I will Ascend in the City of Peace. I will bring balance back to the world. I will kill the person I love most.

Ergo, I'm destined to murder Jared.

CHAPTER FIVE

CONFESSIONS

A s soon as Jared and I arrive at Lush, a man stumbles out the front door tenderly clutching a nose pouring blood. Thick rivulets of it stream down his arms. His eyes are red and pulpy, and distressingly, his nose is bent in the wrong direction. He's already limped to his car before I realize that it's Troy, the one who betrayed us to Tatiana.

As I push open the hefty wooden doors, Taylor Swift's crooning spills over me. Lush is the only decent bar in Hilo, a mishmash town of new and old set among crumbling architecture from the 1960s. Half dive bar and half gastro-pub, the place attracts residents from every subset culture on the island ranging from itinerant day laborers to doomsday preppers, ethnic Hawaiians, and aristocrat haoles. Lush is the one place where everyone comes together to drink cheap Kona beer.

Jessie stands behind the bar, a napkin full of ice pressed against her knuckles. She nods to me and pours two shots of tequila. When I come up beside her, she slides a shot over. She raises her glass, and I clink mine to hers. "*Cheers.*"

I choke and cough as the alcohol hits the back of my throat.

"You brought him?" she asks, glancing toward Jared, who has taken a seat below a giant stuffed tiger shark mounted to the wall.

"I didn't invite him. He goes where he wants."

"He's cute."

"Come on, Jessie."

"What? It's a compliment."

"Sure," I say, "really flattered." It takes all my self-control not to look over at him. Why do I hate to admit that I'm secretly happy that he's here? That I feel safer and more complete? I take a hand towel and wipe away imagined smudges on the bar top. "I saw you had a chat with Troy."

She grimaces as if biting into a lime. "The little prick thought he could waltz in and wink his way through an apology. We'll see how far his good looks take him with a broken nose."

Lush is sparse for a weekend night. A group of farmers share a pitcher of IPA. Some elderly bikers attempt to look tough while drinking fruit-filled cocktails.

I scan the bar for more psycho grandpas then I remember that Jared has that covered. I keep telling myself not to glance in his direction, but in the end, I can't help myself. He's still staring at us, and he gives me a small smile that makes my cheeks burn.

Jessie pulls me to the side. "So tell me what you mean by us being different."

I push Jared from my mind, reach into the fridge, take out two beers, and hand one to her. Thankfully, Lush has a really relaxed policy for drinking on the job. "You'll need this." I don't know the best way to begin, so I come out with it. "You're a goddess."

Jessie flashes a quick smile. "That's not much of a secret," she says, fluttering her eyes and running her hand through her hair.

"No, that's not what I mean. You are literally a goddess. You were—are—a mythological deity. Pele to be exact."

"Sweet," she says with a laugh. "What are my powers? Super strength? X-ray vision? Wait, am I succubus?"

"It's not like that. You don't have any powers."

"Kinda lame. What's so great about being a goddess?"

"You've heard about reincarnation?"

She frowns slightly and nods.

"You're capable of remembering past lives."

She stares at me as if I'm an eighty-year-old flasher—with more concern than shock. Finally, she places her hand on my arm. "Oh honey. They hit you hard on your head."

I brush away her hand. "No, this is real." I'm regretting telling her this way. I should have thought about this beforehand, but it's not as if there's a doctor's pamphlet titled "Congratulations You're an Immortal God." I just have to wing it. "You're called a Descended Goddess."

"OK," she replies, seemingly taken aback by the force in my voice and takes a pull from her beer.

"This means that although you have the ability to remember all your past lives, you currently can't."

"Why not?"

"You have to undergo a ceremony."

Jessie sighs and shakes her head. "What you're saying is completely bonkers."

I look away, taking a sip of beer, forcing down my frustration. I knew this wouldn't be easy. It took me weeks to accept my true nature, and the entire time I was hunted by a serial killer. I'm approaching the subject wrong. Suddenly, an idea comes. "Why do you think you never dream?"

The question cuts right to the bone, and Jessie shudders. I've struck a nerve.

"I used to be like you," I continue. "I couldn't remember my dreams, but I knew that I dreamed. It was this really weird feeling. I thought something was wrong with me, but nobody thought it was strange, except me, because I knew I was different. In those dreams, my lost dreams, I went to places. I knew that I was greater in my dreams than when I was awake. Those dreams turned out to be visions of my past lives. You've always wondered why you don't dream. Well, here's the reason."

Jessie's face narrows suspiciously. "I thought you said that dreams were the 'vomit of our subconscious.'"

"Maybe for most people, but not for us."

"So we're the same? You never remember your dreams either?"

"I used to be like you. I went through this ceremony, and I Ascended. Now, for better or worse, I remember every past life, every memory."

One of the bikers hails us for another round of drinks. I leave Jessie to stew and deliver the order. I'm not sure if I'm getting through to her. We've never really talked about spiritual beliefs before, so it feels like I'm throwing her into the deep end.

When I return, Jessie's expression is one part confused and two parts skeptical. "You can remember past lives?"

"Yes and no. I can remember them, but I don't have any control over what I access. It's like a heavy metal concert in my head. They overwhelm me and take control of my body. That's what happened on the cliff and why I could fight. I channeled a past life."

She takes a drink from her beer and then smirks. "You're messing with me. What past life?"

I shrug. "I don't know. I only saw fragments of her. I think she was some soldier from ancient times."

Jessie's face breaks into a grin. "Let me get this straight. You kicked the asses of several people twice your size because you became a warrior."

"Well, I didn't *become* her—it's like her mind came into mine, and she had control of my body, but it doesn't matter because it didn't last. I didn't have control."

Despite my desire to do the opposite, my eyes find Jared in the corner. He smiles, and I smile back, feeling suddenly lightheaded.

After a long pause, Jessie takes my hand. "You're serious about this."

"This is the reason I came to Hawaii. I came here to escape."

"So, there are other gods, like you and me?" she asks, her tone slightly less skeptical. "Other people who can remember their past lives?"

"Many. Some of them are good, and as you've seen, some are bad. Very bad."

"It sounds so impossible."

"I know it does, and I'm sorry that there isn't an easier way to explain it. I didn't believe it at first either. I thought it was all bullshit. But after the things I've seen and experienced, it's undeniable."

"How do you know for sure I'm one of these gods?"

"You look different in my eyes. From the moment we met, I've known what you truly are."

"Why didn't you tell me sooner?"

I grimace and finish my beer in a long pull. Jessie has already finished hers. "I was planning to, but we became friends." Even though my head swims, I crack open two more beers and hand one to her. "I didn't want you to be scared or afraid. I also knew the dangers and didn't want to bring you into harm."

She puts her hands on her head and exhales. "I'm sorry, Marie. Shit, I mean . . . Mattie?" she replies hesitantly. "This is too much to take in. How can I possibly believe this?"

My stomach lurches. I'm losing her. "I'm afraid you're just going to have to trust me. There's no way for me to prove it otherwise. In retrospect, maybe I should have avoided you the moment I saw you at the airport. I should have walked in the other direction. But I needed a friend after what I went through. I'm sorry now I've put you into danger, but you should know that my main concern is keeping you safe."

"You're really not bullshitting me?" she asks, still eyeing me warily.

"This is real."

After taking a sip, she puts down the beer bottle, falls silent, and looks into her palms. Maybe searching for the answer. After a long pause, a glint of a smirk emerges on her face. "You know, I like how that sounds. Jessie the Goddess."

"Yeah . . ." I concede, uncertain about her reaction. I'm not sure I've convinced her. At that moment, one of the farmers accidentally spills a pitcher onto the floor. "Let me take care of this."

When I get back, Jessie shakes her head, and says, "Fuck it." She drinks the rest of her beer and slams the bottle down. "For my entire life, it's like I've been running. I've always known I was different, and it's scared the hell out of me. I was in a bad place in Chicago. I was hanging with the wrong people and doing the wrong things. It felt like my life was heading off a cliff. Fast. A big part of that was that I didn't understand who I was. I've never understood who I am. One day, I got an urge. I had to get on a plane to Hawaii. I had to get out. I think the reason I had to leave was because I had to meet you. It was fate. Now, you're telling me there's a reason why I'm different. As strange as it sounds, I actually believe you."

I empathize. I had the same type of urge.

"I've started a journey, and this is the next step."

This wasn't the response that I was expecting, nor was it the one I wanted. "But we have a good life here. We live in paradise and take care of each other. Are you prepared to leave this?"

Jessie wraps an arm around my shoulders and pulls me closer. "It has been good here, and we both needed this. Hawaii has been a place where we could heal. Bad things have happened to us. But we can't grow here. You need to figure out how to use your powers and I need to finally learn the truth about myself."

An image of Patrick flashes through my mind, and I fight the urge to cry. Father Gods murdered him. I can't put Jessie at risk. I can't lose her. "You don't have any clue how dangerous these people are. They're killers. They'll murder anyone in their way."

She runs her hand through my hair. "I understand it's dangerous. That's why I'm relying on you. You'll look after me. Anyways, we're not safe here. They know who I am, where we are, and they'll be back. You know that."

A cold lump forms in my throat. She's right; Tatiana now knows about Pele. I can't let them hurt her. "That's true," I agree reluctantly.

"So, what do we do now?"

I swallow to push down the lump. "Jared can take us to a place where they can teach me how to control my Ascended powers. You can conduct the Ascension ceremony there." I stare into my friend's eyes. "I'm giving you the choice that I never had. If you want, we can go, and you can Ascend. Otherwise, we'll both run, and I won't stay with you. I'm too much of a danger. I'll give you all the money I have, and you can disappear." My life is about to change drastically, no matter what choice she makes. I close my eyes, take a deep breath, and ask shakily, "What do you want?"

"When does Jared want to leave?" she asks. "I'm ready."

I'm taken aback by her eagerness. "Are you sure about this? There's no turning back after the ceremony."

"Are you trying to convince me or yourself?"

I laugh and rub my shoulders to relieve the tension. Jessie knows me too well. "May the gods help us. Heaven knows we'll need it."

"Where're you going?" she asks, as I turn away.

I point toward Jared, and she nods.

When I arrive at his table, I pull out a chair and sit across from him. "Here are some ground rules."

"OK," he replies, voice neutral.

"Number one: I'm in charge. That means you do what I tell you to do, no matter what. If I tell you to bark like a dog, you do it. No debate, no bullshit. You just do it. Understand?"

"OK."

"Number two: You have to protect Jessie over me. We're going to this place not for me but for her. She isn't Ascended, and she doesn't understand the true danger she's in. What this means is that if both our lives are in danger, you have to put Jessie's safety first."

"I can't guarantee that."

"Oh, yes. You will."

"Mattie, I'm your Protector, not hers."

"Jared, do you remember rule one?"

He nods.

"So promise me."

"OK, I promise."

"Number three: You have to be completely honest with me. This can't be like last time, when you withheld the truth thinking that you were protecting me. I don't want anymore lies—do you understand?"

His eyes flicker for a second. "Yes, I do."

"Finally, number four: we're not in a relationship, and I don't love you. You got that?"

His eyes widen and he swallows hard. "Crystal clear."

"Perfect. We're ready to go whenever you are."

I swallow hard. Everything is happening way too fast. This morning I could have never imagined I'd be sucked back into this world, and I certainly hadn't imagined I'd see Jared again.

My only hope is that he believes my lies.

CHAPTER SIX

FOOLS AND FOES

Three hours from Albuquerque, Jared slams down on the brake and we screech off the road. Smoke spews from under the hood of the rented sedan. A few seconds later, the inside fills with exhaust, and the three of us jump from the air-conditioned car. The noon-day sun's scorching rays hit my skin like a sledgehammer.

Jessie unfolds a Spanish fan from her purse and vigorously waves it in front of her face. "I told you this piece of junk would break down."

"Yes, I recall," says Jared, equally frustrated. He brushes lingering fumes away from his face. "Well, something is wrong with the engine."

"You think?"

"Give him a break, Jessie."

"I was willing to use my credit card to rent a real car," Jessie adds.

"If we'd done that, the Father Gods would know exactly where we are," Jared replies, while attempting to lift the hood. Up until this point, I'd been impressed by his preparedness. The fake IDs he'd provided for the flight back to the mainland hadn't raised a single eyebrow.

I stare out at the bleak yet beautiful desert. In the distance, a chain of mountains edges the horizon. "We have to get out of this heat," I say, wrapping a shawl over my head.

"How far away are we?" Jessie asks.

"Not too far," Jared says.

Jessie and I exchange worried expressions.

"That's a little too vague, given that it feels like it's five hundred degrees out," Jessie says.

"Yeah," I say, "where are we headed?"

Jared investigates the smoking engine, not saying a thing.

That's when it hits me. "You don't know where we're going!"

His body jerks and then becomes rigid.

"Holy crap." Jessie says, astonished. "You really don't know, do you?"

As Jared turns around, I see his cheeks are bright red. "No. They never told me the exact location."

"Whoa, back up," she replies. "How did you even find out about this place?"

Jared glances away, arms crossed. "An email I got six months ago."

"Who was it from?"

"An anonymous sender."

"What did it say?" I ask.

"It told me to take you to Navajo Nation to complete your training at a school for the Ascended, where your teacher, Coyote, would be waiting for you."

I wait for him to say more, but he doesn't. "Let me get this straight. You got a random email six months ago telling you to take me to the middle of the desert. That's it?"

"They said we'd find a school here."

"Jared, look around. Navajo Nation is the size of Maine. How are we supposed to find anything here?"

"Do you do everything that random emails tell you?" Jessie asks, a thin smile on her lips. "How much cash have you sent that Nigerian prince?"

"Come on. Let's get out of the sun," says Jared. "I saw a gas station a few miles back." He pops the trunk and gets out our bags.

"Did you ever think that this could be a trap set by the Father Gods?" I ask.

"No, they mentioned things in the email. It was clear they were Mother Goddesses."

"What things?"

He turns without a word and walks back in the direction we came. I'm stunned. This feeling of being misled dredges up memories of him—other moments of deception that still hurt to this day. It's a dash of cold reality on my fantasized version of him.

We walk down the highway, rolling our suitcases behind us, the desert enveloping us. The earth—painted hues of yellow, red and orange—is cracked and blistered from the sun's fury, and the sparse dusty grass and scraggly bushes attest to a daily battle for life. The horizon stretches on forever, intermittently broken by mesas, which remind me of massive sand castles.

Two hours later, having not seen a single vehicle, we drag ourselves into the solitary gas station, which also appears to serve as the local super market, pharmacy, VHS pornography rental store, bar, restaurant, and center of government.

Three locals stand at the back of the building watching NASCAR on a small TV and drinking Bud Light. They cast suspicious stares as we enter.

"Water and lots of it," Jessie says to the beanpole clerk in a camo shirt.

We each buy a gallon of water, and I spill about half of mine down my shirt as I chug the water.

"Woohoo!" yells one of the locals, now grinning.

I glance down. My blue T-shirt is soaked. "Real classy," I reply.

They hee-haw and turn back to their race as the three of us collapse under the shade of the gas station's awning to continue rehydrating.

"So who's this Coyote guy?" I ask, turning to Jared.

"He's a legendary warrior. He's been teaching and training Ascended gods for centuries."

"Coyote," Jessie says. "Sweet name."

"He's one of the most important gods in the pantheon of New World Mother Goddesses."

"I just hope we can find this school."

Jared takes a gulp of water and wipes his arm across his mouth. "Mattie, you're the one who can see the deistic form of gods. Keep your eyes open and look for them."

"OK, I'll do what I can." I thumb back toward the yokels. "By the way, none of them are Ascended."

After ten minutes of staring out at the empty, dusty road, Jared stands and turns to go back into the gas station. "I'll ask about a new car."

"Good plan. I'll continue my stakeout."

"I'll help her," Jessie adds.

We sit on the porch for an hour. During that time, we see three people: a woman missing most of her front teeth, an elderly man babbling incoherently, and a guy who leers at us before joining his buddies to watch the race.

When Jared returns, he announces he was unable to find a replacement car. "The gas station clerk said we could sleep on the floor."

"We either catch a ride or we're stuck here?" I ask.

"Pretty much."

"I can give you a ride home, darling," interjects one of the locals, who's been eavesdropping while smoking.

"We'll think about it," says Jessie. The local grins and goes back inside. After he leaves, she adds, "I'm not going anywhere with those creeps."

Another hour later, our hopes of getting out of the place fall as the sun slowly sets on the horizon.

Our boredom is finally interrupted when an old VW Bug pulls into the gas station. From the tiny car emerges an enormous man wearing a food-stained purple-striped muumuu and furry moccasins. He has no discernible neck, and his pencil thin mustache twitches like a small animal above his smiling mouth. He maneuvers his gigantic body to the gas station's entrance—an oil tanker entering a small port.

He pauses, and his doll-like brown eyes focus on us. "Hello!"

I shoot a skeptical glance at Jessie, whose eyebrows arch with impressiveness.

"Hi," I reply.

"How are you?" he asks, with a child's curiosity.

"I'm good."

"That's nice." He doesn't move. For an awkward ten seconds, he stares at us and then asks, "What are you doing?"

I glance at Jared, who shrugs.

"We're searching for someone," I say.

"Who are you looking for?"

"A friend."

"Oh, friends are nice. I have lots of friends." He smiles, revealing perfect white teeth. "Would you like a bag of Cheetos?"

"I'm OK," I reply.

"I'm buying some Cheetos."

"Sounds like a plan."

"You look nice. I'll share them with you."

"That's kind of you."

He waddles past us into the store, and Jared looks at me with a question written on his face.

"Yeah, Jared. That guy is totally Ascended. Did you see those food stains? Total giveaway that he's an immortal god."

"I'm taking that as a no."

"That would be a good guess."

After a few minutes, the man returns carrying the largest bag of Cheetos I've ever seen in my life. His arm is stretched halfway into the bag, and he already has orange powder smeared across his lips. "Delicious," he murmurs, stuffing a handful into his mouth. He stops in front of us again and, in between bites, asks, "Have you found your friend yet?"

"Nope."

"Who is he?"

"He's—you know, just a friend," I say, seeking to end the conversation.

"Why are you looking for him?"

"Um, he'll teach us some stuff."

"Oh, he's a teacher! I've had a lot of nice teachers. They taught me many things. What will your friend teach you?" Once again, I glance at Jessie, who performs a dramatic eye roll.

"Spiritual stuff."

"Ooohhhh! You need a spiritual teacher! Maybe you're searching for me—I'm a Navajo shaman."

I stare pointedly at the cheese dust mustache around his mouth. "You are?"

"Yeah, I've taught many nice people."

"You have?" I ask skeptically. I can't help but feel a little sorry for the man.

"Uh huh. Would you like me to teach you?"

"No, we're fine," I reply, trying to be polite.

"Really? That's too bad," the man says, genuinely sad. He turns and heads back to his car but then turns around and adds, "because I know where to find the gods."

The three of us do a double take at the same time.

"Wait!" I yell, standing and rushing over to him. "What do you know about them?" I grab the man's arm.

"I know where they live," he says cheerily. "If you want, I can take you to them."

The same local as before, pops his head out from the doorway and says, "Come on, darling. Stop talking with that freak. He's in here every other day talking nonsense. Why don't you come party with us?"

"What's your name?" I ask the large man.

"I'm Hank."

It's a long shot, but it's the only shot we currently have. "Hank, we're coming with you. Jared, grab the bags."

We pile into Hank's ancient VW Bug and find it littered with empty food containers. Jared sits up front while we're in the back. The car smells like pine freshener and, of course, Cheetos.

We're driving when he asks, "Which god are you seeking?"

"Coyote."

Hank shakes his head. "I haven't seen him in a long time. Maybe you'd rather meet Raven or Wolf or Corn?"

"No, we have to find Coyote," I reply.

He grimaces. "That's too bad. The gods of this land have much knowledge." Distractedly, he pokes his finger at a plastic Hawaiian hula girl on the dashboard and giggles as the figure rocks back and forth.

"Where are we headed, Hank?" Jessie asks.

Ignoring the question, Hank squints at me in the rear-view mirror. "What do you want to learn from Coyote?"

"Um, it's a little complicated," I finally say.

"Nothing is too complicated to explain," Hank replies. "Unless you're afraid of the knowledge. If you fear the truth, everything is complicated. It's because you're afraid of confronting the inevitable. Cheetos?" he asks, offering me the jumbo-sized bag.

I shake my head, perplexed, as he stuffs another handful into his mouth.

Hank, who drives as if he's ninety, takes us up a dusty gravel road that climbs toward a cluster of mountains sprouting out of the flat wilderness like mushrooms. Over the course of three hours, we zigzag through a series of dangerous hairpin turns, which nearly give me a heart attack. The entire time, Hank asks simple questions, and we provide him simple answers. All the while, I'm losing faith that this was the right decision.

Jessie falls asleep. Jared tries to remain vigilant and attentive, but after a while, even he zones out staring at the unchanging desert vista. I mostly tune out Hank and respond with yes or no or maybe to his never-ending queries. He doesn't notice my lack of attention. His bright, elementary demeanor seems impervious to any slight.

It's nighttime when the road ends at two massive boulders blocking the road.

Hank stops the car. "We're here!" he gleefully exclaims.

I'm a little confused until we walk around the boulders and find a trailer home hidden behind them, pressed against a rock face.

As soon as Hank opens the trailer home's door, a ball of black fur rushes out. The Boston terrier bolts straight at me and stops at my feet to stare up with adorable eyes.

"I think you found a friend," says Jessie.

I reach down and scratch her neck. The dog flips onto her back, legs splayed and tongue hanging out the side of her mouth in rapture, as I scratch her belly.

"Poppy, you're embarrassing yourself!" says Hank.

"Ah, nice puppy," I say.

The inside of the trailer smells like gas-station nachos and is a mess. The TV blares court shows.

Once we're all inside, Hank furrows his brow. "Do you really want to talk to the gods?"

"Yes," I say. "We do."

"Okey dokey. Come this way." He leads us to the back of the trailer and throws open the door to a closet. Inside is a small shrine filled with colorful dolls representing different Native American gods. "I carved them all," Hank says proudly. "There's Hastsehogan and Nohoilpi. That one is Tonenili. Oh, and that one in the back is Tsohanoai, but he's usually very quiet. Go ahead. You can talk with them. They'll answer your questions."

That's when we realize that Hank is not mentally stable. I drop my head into my hands and groan.

"What a waste of time," Jessie says.

"I'm sorry," I say to her. "We should have stayed at the gas station."

Only Jared continues to stare at the figures, his mind seemingly processing something.

"Come on," I say, "we have a long trek back."

We turn to go, but Hank grabs my arm, his grip like iron. "Do you really want to talk with the gods?" His tone is different—sterner.

A sudden surge of fear flows through me. "Yes," I reply, but my voice lacks the confidence it once possessed.

Hank's previously soft eyes are now penetrating, calculating. "Fine," he says, "I'll take you to them." He lets go of me, reaches into the shrine, and pulls down on the closet rod.

There's a loud pop, and Hank pushes the false wall inward; it swings to the side, revealing a dark passage.

A shiver of anxiety runs down my spine. Hank isn't the simpleton I'd assumed he was.

"Hell no, we ain't going through there," says Jessie, thinking the same thing as I am. We'd had enough fun in tunnels for the rest of our lives after our experience in the lava tube.

"This is the way to the gods," Hank says, as he walks into the darkness, leaving us alone in the trailer.

The tunnel goes straight into the mountain. We all look at one another, mentally debating our options.

Jared breaks the silence. "This is the only way," he says firmly, before following Hank.

"Ah, shit," says Jessie. "This isn't going to be any fun."

The weight of the mountain presses down on us. We can't see a thing in the tunnel, and several times I step on Jessie's heels as we scramble along. All the while, a drumming beat of nervousness pounds in my chest. Something tells me that we're not going to find what we want at the end of this tunnel.

After what feels like forever, a pinprick of light appears in the distance. The light grows brighter with each step.

My breath catches when we finally emerge into an open corridor lined with red colonnades. I share an expression of open-mouth awe with Jessie. Where are we?

Arched passageways fringed with potted blooming flowers run off in various directions. Exquisite ceramic tiles covered in a strange, flowing language I don't recognize adorn the walls. Beyond is an open courtyard lit by torches, and under an awning sit several children dressed in turquoise tracksuits staring up at a woman.

All of them are Ascended gods judging by their deistic forms, which range from animals to grown adults to calm-faced Buddhas. Each has a flickering aura. Their teacher, an Ascended goddess with a blue aura and the head of a white crane, is reading them a story from a book.

We follow Hank across the courtyard, passing the children, none of whom notice us, and enter a room that has a high ceiling and is decorated with paintings of deer, corn, cacti and eagles along the walls. The entire structure is built into the side of a cliff. It's like an ant colony—more expansive on the inside than the outside.

As we navigate the compound, we pass a cafeteria crowded with both teenager and adult gods eating dinner. It's the first time I've ever seen so many gods my own age.

One of them looks up—a good-looking guy in his mid-twenties with black hair and almond-colored eyes. Our eyes lock for a moment, and he smiles. I can't help but smile back.

Hank waves us along. "Come. The gods await."

We arrive at a large wooden door, where Hank pauses. "Behind this door are the Elder Gods. They will determine your fate."

Jared shoots me a worried glance, which I return. I'm not particularly fond of other people determining my fate. I briefly think about suggesting to Jessie that she leave, but it's too late for that.

Inside, we find a regal room with heavy tapestries hanging from the walls. On a raised platform are three chairs. In each one sits a god. There's one with a crescent moon on his forehead and a full-moon for a mouth, a woman whose face is half red and half blue, and a wrinkled crone with wings sprouting from her back.

Ten feet from them, Hank halts and raises his fist. "Elders," he declares. His simple voice has been replaced with a flat, indignant tone. Hank has also changed. He's no longer a bumbling guide; he's stronger, confident, forceful.

That's when I realize that Hank is a god. How did I miss his deistic form? He has a canine face, wolf-like fur covers his muscular body, and his aura is bright purple.

With scornful, leaden eyes, he stares at us and says, "Here are the petitioners: Gaia and Pele. I have judged them to be unworthy for training. I offer them up for sacrifice."

CHAPTER SEVEN

Judgment

Hank transforms before us. His paunch tightens to hard muscle, and disdain flashes in his green eyes. He straightens from his stooped posture until he looms over us.

"Three times tested, three times failed," he says, through a sneer. "They are disrespectful, ignorant, and afraid. Unworthy of the gift of Ascension. For gods so immature, so unenlightened, sacrifice is the only logical course."

My jaw drops, and a cold mass sits heavy in my stomach. "Wait!" The heaviness of the Elder Gods' scrutiny shifts toward me. I gulp hard, my mouth dry. "You never tested us."

"I asked you many questions, and your answers proved to be alarmingly dissatisfactory," Hank says impassively. "Do you not remember?"

My knees wobble as I recall that the entire time we'd been with him, he'd been questioning us—and evaluating our responses and judging whether we should be allowed at the school.

Hank turns back to the Elders. "They have no respect for their gifts. They block their minds." Hank's barrel chest puffs outwards, his physique domineering. "They build walls where there should be bridges. They protect their own egos. In short, they fear their true selves."

He's right. I'm guilty of everything he's accusing me. But if I admit this, then we'll be in deeper trouble. "I only Ascended two years ago," I reply, thinking it a reasonable explanation. "No one trained me to control my past lives."

"It is pointless to train you. You will inevitably fail."

"How do you know?" I ask, turning back to the Elder Gods. "Give us a chance to prove ourselves."

"I've spent lifetimes training the Ascended," Hank says, "and I know your type. Both of you are too old, yet also too immature. How am I supposed to reverse years of repression and ignorance? No god has ever mastered channeling at your age."

My stomach swirls as I realize that Hank is our teacher, and the pieces snap into place as I gaze on his canine-like deistic form. Hank is Coyote.

"You are a lost cause," he continues. "The sooner we sacrifice you, the sooner we can truly begin your training. You, Gaia, should be supporting this decision," he adds with distressing calmness.

"Excuse me," Jessie interjects, raising her hand. "What do you mean by sacrifice exactly?"

"We will destroy your current bodies, and Ascend your souls into new bodies. Younger bodies," he says, in a matter-of-fact tone. "Children are better vessels. Their new minds are much more malleable, more receptive to new knowledge."

"So you'll murder us?" I clarify, disbelief and anger tumbling inside me.

"Murder doesn't exist for the Ascended," he replies nonchalantly. "We are immortal beings."

"Nope, I'm done here," Jessie says, brushing off her hands and turning to me. "Let's get out of here. These people are insane."

I agree, but doubt quickly invades my mind. We're not halfway to the exit when two guards, dressed in desert camouflage and carrying assault rifles, materialize in front of us and block our way, their grim, tight faces unyielding.

"We have a right to go," I say.

"You have no such right," Coyote replies. "Gaia is too important a goddess to be locked away in a body that doesn't respect her.

Your mind contains some of the most powerful past lives in the history of the world. You keep them trapped, and it's not fair to them. They deserve a mind that will allow them to flourish, not be imprisoned."

"Let me get this straight," Jessie says. "We traveled all the way here just for you to kill us."

"You're too selfish to understand your true potential. To the Mother Goddesses, Gaia is the most important goddess. She is the key to the prophecy, but she is trapped inside of you." He points a thick finger at me. "The only way to free her is to give her a body with a more progressive and open mind."

I spin back to the Elder Gods. "Give us a chance," I plead. "We can change."

Coyote bends down and picks up Poppy, who has followed us all the way here. He scratches behind her ear. "What is it they say?" he asks himself. "Oh yes, you can't teach an old dog new tricks. It's the same for gods. The older the soul, the harder it is to channel all those voices, all those past lives. You already have too many attachments to this world. Your family and friends. The very concept of yourself is a construct so complex and integrated into your psychology that it's impossible to replace it with the new identity that we seek to teach here at the Lyceum."

"But we can master our past lives—just give us a chance," I say again, urgently.

"We do not teach you to *master* past lives!" Coyote yells, slamming his foot to the ground. "That is the opposite of what we seek. Your past lives can never be mastered. You haven't even realized a basic tenet of the Ascended. You see," he says, turning to the Elder Gods, "they are unteachable."

This entire time, the Elder Gods have been sitting like statues listening to us. I search for a shred of sympathy in their eyes but I see none. A decision has already been made. Our fate is sealed.

Finally, the crone, who'd been staring blankly forward like a statue, focuses on me, unblinking, and then turns her head and nods at Coyote.

The realization slams me like a sack of bricks: they're actually going to murder us.

Coyote bares a thin, satisfied grin. "Once both of you Ascend into new bodies, you'll understand that this was the right decision."

The guards grab us by the arms and wrench us toward the door.

"Jared, help!" I scream, but two other guards have their rifles aimed at him. His eyes are wild, his jaw tight.

We struggle with the guards, fighting to rip free, but they're too strong. As they drag us away, a chasm opens inside my chest, and I squeeze my eyes shut, wishing this to be a nightmare, wishing to wake up.

"Wait," says someone who appears from a side entrance, "we should give them a chance."

When I open my eyes, I see a beaming yellow aura surrounding two diametrically opposed images: a tiny Indian girl of about nine years old, black hair braided into pigtails, a sari wrapped artfully around her small body, her earth-colored eyes filled with everlasting love; and an elephant with enormous ears, ivory tusks, and a twisted trunk.

I met Ganesha when Jared and I were being hunted by Gurzil, the god of war. The Ganesha I knew was an elderly man, and he helped me on my journey to complete my Ascension. But I witnessed his murder. I'd thought I'd never see him again.

"With all due respect, Ganesha, you have not mastered your own abilities," Coyote argues. "As someone who has guided many through the process, you should attest that it's easier to teach the young."

"This is true," Ganesha says, nodding. "But in my penultimate life, I had the pleasure of meeting Mattie Fisher, Gaia's current incarnation. She displayed great strength and bravery under extreme stress." Ganesha walks up to me, takes my hand, and squeezes it. "We should give her a chance," she says directly to the beast of a man who towers over her.

"No!" Coyote booms. "I will not train someone so old and immature. She is destined to fail."

"You know," Ganesha says, "she reminds me of you, Coyote. When I first trained you, it could be said that you were immature, selfish, and disrespectful. I could have petitioned the Elders to sacrifice you, and I'd be lying if I said I didn't think about the possibility. Yet I believed in you—the same way that I believe that one day Mattie will fully embrace Gaia and her past lives."

"Times were different," Coyote snarls. "We didn't have the luxury that we do now. They hunted us more fiercely. We had to do whatever we could to survive, and we couldn't wait."

"We don't have the luxury of time," Ganesha chides, with a dismissive shake of her head. "We all know about the murders that happen every day. They are hunting us again, and the Purging has begun anew. We can't wait for Gaia to come to us as a clean slate. We must work with what we have and that means training both Pele and her."

Nostrils flaring and eyes ablaze, Coyote appears to struggle for a response. Finally, he gives us a stony stare. "I yield to the Elders. They shall decide their fates."

Every eye in the room turns toward the three gods. The Elders quietly speak among themselves, and as the minutes tick by, their conversation grows heated, though I can't hear what they're saying. The crone, sitting in the middle, has a neutral, referee-esque expression, while the pleading hand gestures and emotion-filled demeanor of the red-and-blue-faced woman starkly contrasts with the metallic gaze and clipped gestures of the man with the crescent moon on his forehead.

Finally, the crone slices her hand through the air, cutting off further debate, and focuses on me. "Gaia alone is more precious to our cause than any other," she declares in a deep, prophetic voice.

"It is she for whom the prophecy has been written. We can not risk losing her. She must master her abilities above all else."

I wish I could sink into the floor. I don't like where this is headed one bit.

"Therefore, we agree with Master Coyote's assessment; however, based upon the testimony of Ganesha, we will allow Gaia one week to demonstrate progress with her abilities. If she is unable to learn in the allotted time, she will be sacrificed, and her soul will be Ascended into a new vessel. This decision is final." She turns toward Jessie. "Gaia's first test will be the Ascension of the goddess Pele. If Gaia fails to Ascend Pele, both will be sacrificed. If Gaia succeeds, then Pele will also be given one week to show progress. If she fails to absorb Master Coyote's training and teachings, she too will be sacrificed."

A loud gong chimes from some unseen location, rattling my insides. The Elders nod in unison, stand, and exit out a side door. Jared, pulled by the guards, is brought in after them.

It's as if I'm in a black hole being sucked from the inside out. I glance at Coyote. Our eyes meet. His gaze is fiery, and I'm pushed back by his radiating anger. He spins around and follows Jared into the adjoining room.

My life is in the hands of a man who wants me dead.

Ganesha squeezes my hand and brings me out of my cocoon of worries. "It's not as I would have hoped, but it is enough," she says. "I have full faith that you will demonstrate your abilities."

"I don't have any control over my past lives," I confess.

"From the moment I saw you, you reminded me of the woman I knew millennia ago. You are strong and powerful, but you must discover these things for yourself."

"How is it even possible that you're here? I witnessed your murder."

Ganesha guides me out of the room. Her actions don't match that of a nine-year-old. "After an Ascended god dies, their soul resides on the physical plane for a short period. In classical Tibetan

Buddhism, this is called the bardo. You rescued my priestesses the day you escaped. Together they made one of the ultimate sacrifices and Ascended my soul into a child of one of the priestesses."

"And you came here?"

"Unless the Ascension occurs right at birth, the Lyceum is where every new god goes to learn channeling."

"I really appreciate your help, but I don't have much hope."

"Mattie, I believe the things I said. You do have the potential to harness your powers. Prove me right. Prove to me that you are the same as the woman I loved."

Ganesha squeezes my hand again and walks away. Fear shudders through me as she leaves. I have one week to prove myself, or Jessie and I are dead.

CHAPTER EIGHT

RELAX AND DON'T SCREW UP

"Get your hands off me!" Jessie screams, kicking and struggling as two guards drag her out of the room.

"Stop!" I rush over, but before I can take another step, someone grabs my arm painfully and yanks me backward.

When I turn, I'm greeted by a scarred face and bulbous eyes. Down the center of the god's skull runs a black mohawk. A thick, metal-studded collar, like one for a Rottweiler, is looped around his neck. A deep, menacing purple aura pulses around him.

He throws me against the wall. Pain radiates across my shoulders as I hit stone.

"Welcome, Gaia," he says, spitting the syllables. "It's wonderful to see you again."

We must have had some interaction in a past life. Likely not a positive one. "I can't say the same, and if you touch me like that again, you'll regret it." I make a move to get around him, but his hand slams into the wall, trapping me in place.

His deistic form fades to reveal a man a little older than I am in his mid-twenties. His clean-shaven face is boxy with a jaw as sharp as a framing square. His blonde hair is buzzed short. Muscles bulge beneath his turquoise tracksuit. He reminds me of the jocks I knew in high school. Popular, handsome, one-hundred-percent asshole.

"Threats won't get you far here," says the man.

"Is that right?" My hands clench into fists. "Threats got us stuck here. Maybe they'll get us out."

New anger bursts into his eyes, and the muscles across his arms tighten. "Do you even remember what you did to me?"

Damn it. My past lives carry a lot of baggage, and I never lack for enemies. "Gaia from two thousand years ago might have slighted you in some way, but I'm not her. So, leave me alone!"

His bear claw of a hand seizes my arm. "I will never forget how you betrayed me, and I will never forgive you." He snaps and locks a black metallic band around my wrist. "This will show us where you are at all times. Don't think for a second that you'll be walking out of here alive."

I rip my arm free from his grasp and shove him away. "If you hate me so much, kill me." Hesitation flickers across his expression. "Come on, don't be a coward. You're so sure of yourself. You're so righteous. Stop making threats and do something."

His hand drops, and for the first time, I notice the long knife sheathed in his belt. Fresh sweat materializes on my brow as his hand grabs the knife's handle. Perhaps it wasn't the best idea to antagonize him.

The man's eyes beam with intensity as he draws the knife from the sheath and aims it at my stomach. He could easily plunge the blade into me.

"Whoa, slow down you two," says an unfamiliar voice. I turn away, taking a breath as the tension dissipates. The man holding the knife eases his arm away. "That's right, let's step away from this precipice and consider our options for a second."

I risk a glance toward the new person. My first thought is that I've never seen anything like this before—and I've seen a lot of really weird shit.

He's part man, part goat, and part fish. He wears a conical hat adorned with several vertical horns that bear a disturbing resemblance to erect penises. Also disconcerting is the fact that there appears to be a stream of running water, complete with fish, flowing up and around his shoulders.

"Don't get in my way, Enki," says the man, knife still poised near my gut. "I'm teaching her a lesson."

Enki places a hand on his arm and guides the blade away. "Daichsun, buddy. First, thanks so much for helping. I see you put on her tracking bracelet. That's great, but I'll take over from here."

Rage lingers in Daichsun's expression. "She insulted me and must pay a price."

"Sure, sure, sure. She will definitely pay the price, but the problem is that the Elders asked me to prep her."

A shadow of uncertainty passes over Daichsun's face. "They asked you? But I'm first ranked. I should have that responsibility."

"This isn't personal, Daichsun. We all know you're the best," Enki says, patting the man on the back, "but you have a history with Gaia."

Daichsun's eyes, still brimming with anger, return to me, but in the end, he sheathes the knife. "Good luck with her," he says as he leaves. "She won't last the week."

Speechless and drenched in cold sweat, I turn to the god named Enki, whose deistic form has melted away. Tall, lean and muscular, he's the god I saw earlier in the cafeteria. He also wears a turquoise tracksuit, which I suspect is a uniform. Enki is clean-shaven, but he seems like the type who would have to shave only once a month. His face is the first friendly one I've encountered at this new place.

He smiles as if the whole world is one big joke. "Welcome to the Lyceum," he says merrily. "I hope your experiences so far have been generally positive."

I still haven't fully recovered from the confrontation with Daichsun, yet there's something disarmingly relaxing about Enki. His presence puts me at ease. He exudes a calm and optimistic nature, which I'm completely jealous of. Trying to steady my shaky breath, I brandish my best fake smile. "Oh, yes! Murder threats and assault. Lovely!"

"Don't take it too personally. You'll get used to it. Come on. Let me show you around." He heads for the exit.

"Who are you?"

He stops and extends his hand. "My apologies. I have horrible manners. I'm Enki." He brushes his shoulder. "I'm kind of a big deal here."

"Why?"

"Come on, you should know."

"Never heard of you."

"Unbelievable! I'm the creator of life and you've never heard of me?"

I can't help but smile. "I missed that memo."

"You'd think that given the amount of cuneiform the Sumerians wasted writing about me, I'd have a little more street cred."

"Well, Enki, creator of life. I'm Mattie."

"Obviously you are," he replies. "But as a matter of policy, you're actually Gaia here."

"Oh, so you've heard of me?"

"Duh. You're supposed to save the world."

"I can't believe I have a reputation already. I haven't been at this school for more than an hour, and I'm already labeled the Messiah girl."

"It's better than being the mean girl." He glances down at the metallic band on his wrist, which lights up to display the time. "Crap, we're late. Come on, there's a lot to explain."

I follow him into an atrium and through a maze of hallways, passing what could only be described as classrooms with chairs and desks and maps on the walls. Ascended gods, running past us, cast wide-eyed stares at me, which I return in kind. Along the way, Enki cracks stupid jokes and points out the bathrooms, dorms, and training rooms. We climb a set of spiraling stone stairs up several stories and emerge on a balcony that overlooks a deep canyon. Along the canyon's walls are dwellings and rooms: a few armed Protectors are stationed on various levels.

"As you've probably guessed, we're in one of the Native American cliff-dwelling civilizations. This one was originally built by Mogollon people, who were devotees of the Mother Goddesses, around the 1300s. Since the 1600s, this has been the Lyceum. There's nothing and no one around for two hundred miles, and you can only find it if you know what you're looking for."

"Yeah, question," I interject, rubbing my forehead. "How does this place even exist in the middle of the desert? I mean, presumably everyone here is eating food, right? How do they get it here?"

"You haven't heard of Amazon Prime?"

"Ha," I deadpan. "No, really. How do they make this place work?"

He levels his gaze at me. "The Lyceum is run by reincarnated gods who have lived hundreds, maybe thousands of past lives. They have been prophets, generals, kings, and queens. They're more than capable of figuring out how to get toilet paper delivered."

"Duly noted," I reply, turning away and looking out on the incredible hidden world. "The Lyceum. That's what this place is called?"

"Bingo. It's like Harvard for Mother Goddesses."

"I'm really impressed."

"Oh," he says, "I get it. That's sarcasm."

"Less than thirty minutes ago, I was told I have one week here to prove myself. Otherwise, I'm going to be murdered."

"Yeah, they don't make life easy."

"This place reminds me of an ant colony," I say, gazing out on the tall cliffs.

"I can see that." He clasps his hands in front of him. "So, do you have any questions?"

"Of course I do. Where should I start?"

He points to a massive set of double doors behind us. "Well, here, for one," Enki says, expectantly.

"Where is here?"

"This is where you'll Ascend your friend."

My eyes widen. "What, like now?"

"I thought you knew," he says, with not a hint of concern in his voice.

"No one told me."

He smiles. "This is why I'm here with you," he says proudly. "I'm to assist you with the Ascension."

"You?" I ask, not hiding my incredulity stemming from his light-hearted demeanor. "What are you supposed to do?"

"I'm one of the oldest Mother Goddesses at the Lyceum, and the Elders asked me to help you."

"OK, great," I say, a little relieved. "I need all the help I can get. How do I Ascend Jessie?"

"That's where it gets tricky—although I know the ceremony, I don't actually have the ability to Ascend your friend. Only you do."

I release a frustrated sigh. "Great. You're not helpful at all."

"Yeah, I tried to explain this to the Elder Gods."

"You're also not inspiring a huge degree of confidence. Who usually conducts Ascensions at the Lyceum?"

"The priests and priestesses. Wait." He pauses, "Haven't you Ascended a god before?"

"No, never."

"How did you Ascend?"

"I Ascended myself."

A new grin breaks upon his face. "Oh, OK, so that's one at least."

"I don't think that counts."

"Sure it does. Don't worry, just follow my lead and we'll get through this together." He walks to the door then turns to me and adds, "Oh wait! I do have one piece of advice."

"What is it?" I ask eagerly.

"Don't kill your friend," he replies, pushing open the doors.

I grab his shoulder and pull him back. "Excuse me! What do you mean?"

"Well, the Ascension is . . . how would I put it? A delicate ceremony. If you don't do it correctly, you could kill your friend or yourself."

"Please explain."

"You're dealing with her soul. It's more sensitive than brain surgery. If you force her soul to Ascend too fast, her body won't be able to deal with the stress, and she'll die. If you do it too slowly, her soul won't want to Ascend, and in the process, you'll end up dragging yourself into a Descended state, which means you'll end up in a coma and likely die."

"And if she doesn't Ascend, they'll kill me."

"Pretty much."

"This sucks."

"Relax and don't screw up."

"Thanks!" I reply, my mind doing somersaults. "You're super helpful, you know that?"

"Listen, I know the steps in the ceremony, and I can guide you along, but ultimately, it's you who has the ability to Ascend your friend. I know you'll do fine. Remember, relax. Now, come on," he says, walking through the doors. "They're expecting us."

We enter a large chamber, and I have the sudden impulse to walk right out.

The room is a naturally formed cave; the stalactites have been chiseled away and the walls polished down to a smooth finish. Upon this arching canvas is a painted nighttime sky with all its stars. Hundreds of candles illuminate the constellations.

But the room isn't the thing causing the flight of sparrows in my stomach.

It's the hundred or so beings staring at me—a menagerie of animals, angels, and mythic creatures whose auras blaze with every color of the rainbow. I've never seen so many gods in one place.

As we approach, the masses part to make way for us. Their deistic forms fade; most of the gods are children and adolescents, all dressed in the same turquoise tracksuits and black sneakers.

Our footsteps crack the silence. I hate the feeling of hundreds of strangers' eyes on me. When I was a teacher, I had no problem being in the front of the class, but this situation is on par with drowning in a pool of liquid anxiety.

Someone has drawn a pentagram in the middle of the room, and there's a lit candle at each of the points. Jessie stands in the center looking freaked out.

Gone are her high heels, short dress, and jewelry. She wears a simple white gown that exposes her shoulders. Her thick, wavy black hair cascades down her back.

"What the hell?" she asks in a whisper, her eyes wide.

I take her clammy hand and squeeze it. "It'll be fine. Don't worry."

"I don't believe you for a second."

"Gaia, stand next to me," Enki says, "and do what I do."

Despite Ascending myself, I have no idea how to Ascend another person. A chill streaks across my skin, releasing an army of goose bumps.

"Take hands," Enki whispers. We all grab each other's hands and form a triangle.

Silence ensues, and it presses down like a boulder on my chest. I wait, but nothing happens. "What do we do next?"

Enki shushes me, and I follow his gaze to the Elder Gods.

The crone hobbles forward. "Tonight, we welcome the birth of our sister, Pele. We celebrate her return and Ascension. May her knowledge and past lives help us in our continued struggle to exist and to resist the Father Gods. We pray for the day when balance is restored to the world."

"Amen," the assembled gods reply in one voice.

"Let the Ascension ceremony begin," she says. Then staring at me, she adds, "We pray that it will be successful."

Chills shoot down my spine.

A girl no older than ten walks forward and offers Enki a massive bronze goblet. He picks it up, takes a sip, and passes it to me. The wine tastes as if someone dumped a cup of white sugar into it. I pass the goblet to Jessie.

Her eyes jump from the goblet to me. "Are they drugging me?"

"You bet your sweet ass they are."

"And I suppose there's really no way to get out of this?"

"Nope."

"Well, bombs away." She swallows several large gulps.

Enki hums a song. Unpleasant memories of my own Ascension come back to me. The ceremony ended in a bloodbath—literally everyone died. I force myself to repress the memory and focus on the current ceremony.

I match Enki's hum, tone for tone. Jessie gets the idea and hums as well. Eventually, everyone in the room hums along.

The hum transforms into a song. Somehow I know the lyrics, but I don't know the language. Pele's song is different from the one for my Ascension. It's full of joy and intensity. After a few minutes, I hear my past lives whispering behind the wall in my mind.

We sing for a long time, and the energy of the room flows through me like the current of a river—brisk, strong, unrelenting. The song's pitch rises to a sound that is pure and flawless.

Jessie falls into a trance. Her half-closed eyes flutter.

I'm reminded that her life is in my hands, and my skin feels hot. But as the song continues, my whole body tingles and a complete calm envelops me, washing away my anxieties. When I close my eyes, I'm at the wall in my mind. It soars into the infinite sky, protecting me from my past lives.

Then, the next instant, the wall disappears.

For a moment, I'm exposed and terrified. There's nothing standing in the way to stop my past lives from taking control of me.

Arrayed like a tsunami is a sea of lights representing my past lives, but instead of drowning me, they're frozen in place. A single light emerges from the lives and floats toward me.

It wavers, dips, bobs and hovers like a dragonfly. The light pauses right before my eyes, and in a sudden rush, it shoots into me. Pure, satisfying heat ignites inside my chest.

Everything transforms into a blinding white.

A brilliant sun warms my skin. As I inhale, my nose fills with the smell of dust, jasmine, and horse dung. Across the street, a group of country farmers, dressed in rough tunics, shout out fig prices. Next to them is a young woman selling vegetables out of wicker baskets.

I'm in the chaos of a city I've never seen before.

The stone and brick buildings are old yet well taken care of. Some of them are painted gaudy hues of red.

A donkey-drawn cart nearly runs me over. I jump to the side of the street to avoid the massive wooden wheels. The driver curses and throws a hand gesture at me that I know means something along the lines of "go impregnate a thorn bush." The cart continues along the deep crevices of the stone avenue, along with many others.

I don't have any control over my body. Someone else is walking and directing me. It's as if I'm viewing their life, but it's more than watching. I sense the person's emotions—a dark stew of worry and urgency. And their inner thoughts center on one question: how could he betray me?

The street narrows, and armies of vendors selling baskets of cinnamon, peppercorns, and fresh herbs overflow from the surrounding buildings.

We take a turn off the street into a large square bathed in hot light. To the left, glistening with white paint, is a large arch adorned with stone statues.

Hundreds of people, seemingly from every part of the known world, have gathered to talk, negotiate, complain, and laugh. We pass a couple quarreling about their son. Not far away, two senators in pristine white togas debate the need for new taxes on the outer provinces.

My host pauses in front of a jewelry vendor. In a small lead-framed hand mirror, I see a young woman with dark brown wavy hair and pale, freckled skin. Her green eyes burn with a familiar intensity.

It's my own reflection—my body, my face, my expressions, even the jagged-crescent moon birthmark on the side of my face. But it's all been placed on a woman wearing a white tunic and a purple silk shawl.

How am I seeing myself? This is a past life, some vignette from two thousand years ago, but why does the woman appear exactly as I do in the present?

She continues toward one of the forum's looming temples. The tall marble colonnades reach up to the sky. In bronze basins, the offerings of the faithful are burned. Before the entrance is a small statue of a pregnant woman. A symbol of the Mother Goddesses.

Inside the temple, two women bicker. When they notice me, they rush forward with anxious expressions.

"Goddess," says the plump older woman with a bow, her face flushed, "we've been waiting for you." Voice jagged with fear, she shakes her head and clasps her quivering hands. "What should we do?"

"Of course we know what to do, Nerthus," says the younger woman. "We have only one recourse." She is skinny but sinewy; a deep frown besmirches her otherwise pretty face. "We must fight back."

"I will decide if we go to war." I'm surprised by the person's voice. It's the same as mine but carries more authority and power than I could ever muster.

Nerthus tears up and nervously fiddles with the big round stones of her necklace. "If the reports are true, there will only be more bloodshed."

"We don't yet know all the details. Now repeat to me exactly what you saw, Camilla."

"On your orders, Gaia, I went to Carthage to check upon our efforts to provide relief to the indigent of that city. When I arrived, I found

the temple had been defiled and vandalized. The priestesses were murdered. Their deaths must have been recent because no one had yet disposed of the bodies, and I found no sign of our sister goddesses. After witnessing the destruction, I slipped out of the city on the first ship returning to Rome."

"So this could be a singular act?" I ask. "It could be disconnected to the Father Gods?"

Camilla flashes a bitter grimace. "Except, on the ship, I overheard the sailors talking. Before Carthage, they had been in Tarraco. They talked about a public execution they saw. The supposed criminals were all women. Twelve women to be exact."

A rancid sickness spreads through my stomach. Twelve is the number of priestesses assigned to one goddess temple.

"Oh, dear . . ." says Nerthus. "This can't be happening."

"While we still have our strength, we must attack," Camilla declares. "With our alliances with the Praetorian Guard, we could take the city within a week."

"And how much blood would that cost?" I ask. "The facts are not conclusive. You saw our priestesses murdered, but what evidence do you have that it was the Father Gods? None. It could have been a singular act by that minor desert god who has been chafing under the power of Rome."

"I agree with you. I suspect it was Gurzil who committed the crime, and I believe that the Father Gods sanctioned it."

"That is quite the accusation to make," replies Nerthus, regaining her composure.

"Yes, it is. I want more evidence."

"What about the murdered priestesses in Hispania?"

"It could have been hearsay or exaggeration. Sailors have more tales than gods."

"Gaia, can't you see? A Purging has begun."

"Child," I reply, tempering the fear growing inside me. "I was alive during the last Purging. I was there when Mother Goddesses murdered thousands of Father Gods and their supporters. Their *screams still haunt me at night. You are young and thirst for war. I'm old and yearn for peace. I will discover the truth before I don my armor."*

"What should we do, Goddess?" she says, scoffing. "Should we wait until we feel the knife at our throats before we act?"

"Watch your tone!" Nerthus commands. "Have some respect for our goddess."

Camilla opens her mouth for a rebuttal, but I raise my hand to silence both of them. "I am no fool. Just because I desire the truth doesn't mean I don't see the danger." I turn to Nerthus. "We have prepared and trained for this scenario. Send out messengers to all parts of the empire and beyond. Use our contacts along the trade routes and spread the word. All goddesses, priestesses and allies will go into hiding until I decree otherwise. Begin immediately and wait for my next message."

"Yes, as you wish," Nerthus replies, casting one last reproachful look at Comilla before leaving.

"You realize," says Camilla, "that we may only get one chance to send out messengers. It will be weeks before the goddesses in the outer provinces receive the message. It could be months or a year before the message is delivered to the goddesses in the Far East. By that time, they could already be dead."

"If that is the case, and this assault is as planned as you fear, the war is already lost for us. We will have no choice but to hide and wait out the storm."

"Why do you doubt these attacks? They are as plain as daylight."

"Because there is no sense to them. We have lived in peace with the Father Gods for five hundred years. Why break the truce now?"

"They are Father Gods. All they desire is power and control."

"That is not true. Yes, authority. But what about logic, intellect, and the search for truth? These too are qualities of the Father Gods. You forget, Camilla—we are meant to share power with the Father Gods. Domination will only result in our mutual destruction."

"Gaia, are you confusing your own feelings for an individual with that of a group? We all know your husband's position and status. Do you forget where your loyalties should lie?"

I slap her hard across the face. Camilla releases a sharp cry and backs away. "I am Gaia. Supreme Mother Goddess. I live and breathe the fate of our kind. Do not forget that, child."

Camilla raises her head, touching the place where I hit her, and pushes back her shoulders in defiance. "How will you save your people?"

"I'll find the truth from Caishen, the emissary of the Father Gods. He is less duplicitous than the other gods in Rome."

"You are our leader and without you, our ranks will surely suffer a severe blow." She raises her fist. "Let me go in your place."

Ah, I now understand. "Do not fear for me. Instead, let your fears be mine. However, you may accompany me. There is always safety in numbers."

She's about to reply, but at that moment, yellow rays of light shoot from her eyes and mouth. The light overwhelms. Her face splinters into cracks and in an instant, explodes in a blinding fire.

I'm yanked forward by invisible lines; a rush of wind blasts my face. The world spins and tumbles as though in a cyclone as I barrel through the air toward a pulsating white light. The next moment, I plunge into it, and it's as though I'm in a pool of warm water.

When my eyes open, I'm back in the Lyceum. The silence is so thick it could be cut. The assembled gods stare at me in awe.

The past life I channeled has filled me with indescribable fear and despair. It's like I woke up from a nightmare only to realize my reality is way worse.

This lingering feeling leads me to one dreadful conclusion. I must have failed the test. I survived the Ascension, but I killed Jessie.

The pressure of tears builds behind my eyes until they come flowing down my cheeks. How could I do this to her?

I can't make myself look at her. I don't want to see what I've done to her.

Someone touches my shoulders. Through my tears, I see Enki staring at me in shock. I turn slowly. I have to witness the result of my failure, my friend's lifeless body.

But when I focus my gaze in Jessie's direction, I find her smiling. Her brown eyes are round and wide as she stares at her hands. She looks like a newborn staring at the world for the first time. Our eyes meet, and relief floods through me as we rush toward each other and embrace.

Gaia of Rome is the only reason Jessie and I are alive. I don't know how it happened, but when I channeled her, she helped me Ascend Jessie. However, in exchange, she gave me a glimpse into her past—a taste of a larger story that I still don't know. I feel she's trying to tell me something.

All I know for certain is that she's at the center of everything, and her fate and mine are intertwined.

CHAPTER NINE

CLASS BEGINS

W hen I wake up, I have no idea where I am. Given the way my head throbs, I wonder if it was kicked down a flight of stairs. This is to be expected. Channeling past lives requires the mental fortitude that would be needed to complete the *New York Times* Sunday Crossword while juggling five cats in heat.

Turning on the bedside light, I survey my room. I would describe it as prison-cell chic. Concrete walls. No windows. A bedside table and small dresser bolted in place.

Super-duper.

Well, technically, I am a prisoner here, so I guess it's only fitting.

I'm sitting up in bed when a knock at the door startles me. The door opens, and Enki pops his head inside. "Morning, sunshine."

I groan. "Oh, you're back."

He comes into the room and leaves the door open. "You think you can get rid of me that easily?"

"I really don't have the energy nor inclination to engage in repartee." Shotgunning a bottle of ibuprofen sounds much more appealing.

"Too bad. I was looking forward to bantering." He flips on the overhead lights. "We gotta get you moving."

Shielding my eyes from the fluorescent brightness, I make no effort to get up. "How did I get into the room last night?"

"You were a little out of it after the Ascension, so I tucked you in."

"That's creepy."

"I'm like that sometimes."

I swing my legs out of the bed but come to an awkward realization. "Where are my clothes?" I'm wearing one of the turquoise track suits. "Please don't tell me you changed me while I was asleep. That would pretty much win you creep of the year."

"I haven't graduated to that level yet. It was the priestesses." He stands back and admires me as I slouch sleepily. "You look good in it."

"No, I look like a middle-school kid at sleep-away camp."

"Funny." He checks his watch. "OK, we've got to go."

"Where?" I ask, rubbing my eyes.

"Training."

"Already?"

"Yeah, wake-up time is five."

The blinking digital numbers of my tracking bracelet read 7:24. "Crap! No one told me that."

"Yeah, that was my bad."

"Thanks a lot, Enki. They'll kill me at the end of this week if I can't channel properly."

"Hey, I'm sorry," he says earnestly, "but I brought you breakfast." From a bag, he pulls a napkin with two warm biscuits inside. "Come on. You're already in big trouble."

I swing my legs over the side of the bed and slip my feet into the black sneakers on the floor. "What's on the menu today for training?"

He pulls me up and out the door. "We'll walk and talk."

I munch on the biscuit. "This is delicious," I say, after taking a bite.

"They try to break us during training, but at the very least, they feed us well."

I stare at him, stunned, not sure if he's joking, but he just laughs and continues leading me through the labyrinthine halls whose rock walls are etched with spirals. In a long hallway, I pause outside one of the rooms. Inside, there are a dozen children, all of them Ascended gods, listening to an Elder God read a story.

"Is this how you teach them to be gods? Story time?"

"Yes." Enki nods and pulls me along. "For the Younglings."

"Who?"

"Oh, yeah, I meant to tell you this yesterday."

"Seems like there was a lot you should have told me."

"Chit chatting was way more fun," he says, walking fast. "The Lyceum is broken up into two different schools. Younglings are the Mother Goddesses who Ascend anywhere between birth and sixteen years old."

"I'm assuming that you and I aren't Younglings."

"Bingo. We're Agelings."

"What I don't understand is why the gods are being treated like kids?"

He pauses. "Did you see them? They are kids. To work with their past lives, they have to develop their own character and personality."

"I don't get it. I saw Ganesha. She didn't need training."

"She might have seemed that way, but you can't deny biology. They're still children. Although Ganesha appeared in control, she has a way to go. Unless the Ascension occurs right at birth, a god's body and mind need time to develop," Enki explains, turning down a narrow hallway.

"It seems silly to have story time for gods."

"How else would you teach a child to be a person?"

I'm about to tell him he's wrong, but I remember that storytime is a staple for kids in elementary school. "OK, you win this round."

"We must teach them to be moral and righteous early because the alternative is worse."

"Why?"

"All our past lives are different. Some are passive. Others are more aggressive."

Each of my own past lives—ranging from soldier to nun to farmer and queen has had a unique influence on me. Some of them I'm afraid of; if I'm not careful, they might completely control me. Others are more subtle, more collaborative. "What are you getting at?"

"The fear is that one past life could grow too strong and dominate the others. Each past life has its own strengths and weaknesses. The goal at the Lyceum is to teach you to be a leader of past lives, not just a master of one. When one past life dominates, it will control, manipulate and influence other lives. That isn't a good thing."

The realization hits me. "That's what happened to the Father Gods."

"Yeah," Enki confirms. "Many of the most powerful Ascended Father Gods are dominated by one past life. Usually a very old one. This past life has a corrupting influence over succeeding lives. This is why the education of Younglings is so important. It's crucial to teach them empathy and kindness."

"That's a lot for a four-year-old to take in."

"If they can learn a language in a matter of months, then learning to be Ascended is a cakewalk. Come on. We're really late." He takes my hand again and pulls me along faster.

"What about us? How do they teach Agelings?"

"It's no different from any other school. We have classes to learn the basics. There are things that make channeling easier."

"Like what?"

"Darling, you're going to find out right now."

He pushes open a big wooden door, and the rising sun pours over my face. It feels delicious. It's still early, so the heat of the desert isn't unbearable. We're in a large open-air courtyard that's cut into the cliff-side. The cloudless sky stretches out like an infinite sea.

"Impressive, right?" says Enki.

The twenty or so Agelings sparring with wooden swords have flushed faces. Sweat soaks through their tracksuits. The gods strike, retreat, and attack in a dance of combat.

"The view, yes. Not really the sweating people. I've been to Zumba classes before—definitely unimpressive."

But their deistic forms *are* cool. Some I recognize: a cherub-faced boy could be Cupid; a blue-faced, golden-crowned man could be an incarnation of Krishna. Others are harder to place: a goddess with the head of a house cat; a green-and-black-faced god with a flowing headdress of feathers.

Their forms fade, and I can see that the gods range in age from late teens to a woman in her mid-twenties. They come from all the continents. Light skinned and dark. Tall and short. Woman and man.

I'm ripped back to the present by a sharp cry of pain that cuts through the clamor of dueling couples. My shoulders tighten and my head spins. I recognize that voice. It's Jessie. She clutches her shoulder, pain warping her face. Her opponent, a man twice her size, strikes relentlessly.

A sudden realization rocks me on my heels. Her sparring partner is Daichsun. He presses fiercely, taking advantage of her injuries, but despite the flurry of blows, Jessie deflects every attack.

As he slices and chops, she parries and blocks. He presses harder, but she retreats strategically.

"Looks like Pele is doing just fine after her Ascension," Enki remarks.

"Yeah." How the heck is she moving like that? After Jessie's Ascension, the priestesses rushed her off, so we never got a chance to talk. I have no idea how she's handling her transformation. There's something different about the way she moves—she's more confident now. "Who is Daichsun?"

"A Mongolian war god."

I do a double take. "I didn't know war gods could be Mother Goddesses."

"Yeah, it's rare. But Daichsun is as much a Mother Goddess as you are."

The man's face is a Picasso-like painting of anger and ferocity. "I'm having trouble seeing him as someone who embodies the ethos of kindness, empathy, and love."

"Maybe it's his lack of those qualities that makes him such an exceptional student at the Lyceum."

Right as Enki says this, Daichsun feints right and swings his sword around. It strikes Jessie in the stomach. She grunts as her breath is whacked right out of her and collapses backward.

Daichsun doesn't hesitate. He raises the sword, readying a blow to her head. A knockout shot.

In an instant, I'm running toward him. Before he can hit her, I slam my body into his. It's like throwing myself against a brick wall, but he stumbles to the ground. Somehow I stay on my feet.

The war god glares at me with eyes filled with fury. "How dare you take away the glory of a victory."

All the fighting around us stops, and there's a tense energy in the air. The other Agelings stare at us, waiting.

"How about you take a breather and think about the series of bad choices that led you to this one moment?" I retort.

He jumps to his feet and advances. "Out of my way, you pathetic creature," he hisses, in the same arrogant tone I've heard from Father Gods.

"No," I say, voice filled with my own contempt.

Daichsun runs his hand along the length of the wooden sword. "I'll teach you a lesson about respecting your superiors."

The next moment, he's charging me.

This will hurt a crap-load, so I do the only thing I have time to do: close my eyes and raise my hands.

"Stop!" someone shouts right when I expect the sword to crash into me.

When I open my eyes, Daichsun's sword is a mere inch away from shattering my nose.

Coyote strolls toward us, clapping, a smile on his lips. He pats Daichsun on the back. "Excellent form and masterful feint."

He turns to Jessie. "You would have been disemboweled, Pele. Learn this lesson: always protect your flank." Then he asks me, "So, you finally decided to join us, Gaia. Have you gotten enough beauty sleep?"

"I didn't know we had a wake-up time," I say, casting an accusing glare at Enki.

"Excuses will not get you far here." He glances at the sun and checks his watch. "Now that you're rested, how about we get your heart thumping?" Coyote turns to the other Agelings and yells, "Five-minute rest! Then we run the course."

He walks away. I have no idea what the course is, but I assume I won't like it. I pull Jessie up from the ground.

"Thanks," she says, and then focuses her gaze on the person behind me. "I saw you last night. You're Enki?"

"That's right."

"You're the reason Mattie is in trouble this morning?"

"Well, it wasn't intentional."

"Your bullshit excuses might get my friend killed. Is that also not your intention?"

Enki's face pales. There'll be only one winner of this fight, and the loser will probably have a broken ego and a bloody nose. "It's OK, Jessie. He already apologized."

"I'll go get you some water," he says, running off. Smart guy.

Jessie shakes her head. "Sumerian gods are idiots."

"You already know about him?"

"A past life told me about Enki."

"Wait, you've already talked with your past lives?" It had taken me weeks to do that.

"Yeah," she says. "This is super weird, but really cool. I didn't sleep at all last night. I was having these conversations with them."

"So you're not freaking out?"

"No. Not at all. Why?"

"When I Ascended, it was terrifying."

"I do feel different, but not in a bad way."

"What do you mean?"

"My mind feels open for the first time in my life. I see things clearly."

A clear, open mind. What happened to the Jessie I knew? "Have your past lives tried to control you?"

She steps back, her eyebrows high. "No. They would never do that."

How is it so easy for her? My past lives tear me apart. Apparently noticing the frightened-little-girl expression I'm wearing, Jessie cautiously asks. "How are you doing?"

"You know me. . ." I lean close and ask, "Have you seen Jared? He can help us escape this place. I don't belong."

"No, I haven't seen him since yesterday. Anyways, we're not going anywhere." She holds up her arm to reveal a tracking bracelet around her wrist. "But you completed the ceremony last night. You passed the first test. How did you do that?"

"Beats me." No way am I telling her about the Roman version of Gaia when I don't even fully understand what it means.

"We have one week to learn to channel. It's as simple as that."

"That's easy to say, but our lives are on the line. If we screw up, we're dead."

"If we leave the Lyceum, the Father Gods will hunt us down." She pulls me into a hug. "Mattie, you need to have more faith in yourself. Focus and work hard. You'll show them that you're Gaia."

Enki returns from wherever he was hiding, a bit humbler, and says, "We should stretch. The obstacle course is a little tough."

CHAPTER TEN

RACE TIME

When I heard "five-mile run," I thought: piece of cake. Every morning in Hawaii, Jessie and I ran for miles up the volcano. The pain of those runs burned away our collective worries. For me, they were a balm I placed over the fear I had of my past lives and my longing for Jared. Jessie ran to forget about the things she'd left behind in Chicago.

But this "obstacle course" has been no leisure run—razor-wire-edged walls, rope swings and steep hills. Now we're climbing a cliff face. Despite the obstacles and probably thanks to those volcano runs, I'm in the front of the pack.

My fingers ache, and I dare not glance down as I dangle from the thick braided rope one hundred feet off the ground. A single slip of my hands, and the rocks below will finish me.

Two ropes over climbs another Ageling, a girl who looks like she would still be in high school, skinny as a straw with short, spiky black hair. I'd usually be annoyed to be neck and neck with someone, but her deistic form is an orca, which is pretty cool. Above me, Daichsun is in the lead and almost to the top of the cliff. Enki is in third, on Jessie's heels. Below me, the rest of the Agelings scramble up dozens of ropes.

A puff of wind blows, and my heart seizes as the rope sways. As I clench it tighter, a blister on my hand pops. Pain radiates through my palm, and sweat drips off my skin.

I pull upwards, the raw flesh on my hands screaming. I pray for no foot cramps. In elementary school, I hated the rope climb in gym class because my foot always cramped, leaving me stranded at the top of the rope. That would kill me now.

Daichsun reaches the top of the cliff, followed closely by Jessie, who hates to be second. For a brief moment, the war god's eyes, filled with unfiltered hatred, meet mine.

Another puff of wind swings me to the side; my foot goes numb and cramps. Pain streaks up my leg. I'm officially screwed.

The orca girl climbs ahead of me. It's as if someone has thrust a knife into the bottom of my foot, and it takes all my self-control not to let go of the rope. I hang, helpless, forcing myself not to look down.

As I contemplate my screwedness, I hear a loud snap. The orca girl stops climbing. A second later, she drops an inch and gasps. Terror replaces the determination in her face.

Her rope frays at the top, and one by one, the fibers snap. A thin strand is the only thing keeping her from plunging. The girl freezes like a rabbit staring at an oncoming car. The slightest movement could snap the rope.

If she falls, she's dead. My muscles tighten, and a thought hyper-focuses in my mind: I will not be a bystander to her death.

With throbbing palms grasping the rope, I bite down on my lip and pull myself up. Come on, I think. You can do this. My useless feet continue to dangle freely; it's only my arms and shoulders that lift me up.

Pure adrenaline helps me ignore the searing pain in my hand as I climb the remaining section of rope.

A moment after I haul myself onto the cliff, the girl's rope snaps, and she falls. I dive, my elbows taking the brunt of my impact, and catch the end of the rope with one hand before it slips away.

The weight of the girl yanks me toward the cliff. With my free hand, I scramble for anything to halt my free fall but grab only a palmful of dry dirt. In less than a second, I'm dragged over the cliff's ledge.

Right as I go over the side, I snag a desert shrub studded with thorns. The sharp barbs dig deep into my skin, and fresh blood runs down my hands, but my grip remains firm.

It's as though I'm on some medieval torture machine designed to rip off my arms. I attempt to pull her up, but find I don't have the strength, and I can barely hold myself at this point.

I can't let her fall.

One by one, the shrub's roots rip out of the ground.

I search for aid, but none comes. My eyes meet those of the desperate girl's. She hangs helplessly, terror dilating her pupils. I can't let go of her, but I can't hold onto her either.

A root snaps, and I slide a few inches down the cliff. This is it. I freeze, trying not to think about smashing into the ground.

The plant pops out, and we plummet.

Before I have a chance to scream, someone grabs my arm and halts our descent. Enki smiles down, holding my blood-soaked hand. A minute later, another Ageling reaches the top of the cliff and holds him in place, then another joins. They make a human chain that keeps us from falling.

Working together, they pull us up. I want to kiss the ground. The orca girl is in rough shape; she grips her arms and shakes.

We've barely recovered from the incident when Enki says, "Come on. We still have another mile."

I can't possibly continue, but Enki and the other Agelings run off without a backward glance.

After a minute, the girl rises to her feet unsteadily. She touches my shoulders, and says, "Thank you." With nothing more than that, she limps off as well. I can't believe that nobody is making a big deal out of an incident that could have killed two people.

I pick myself up from the ground and brush the dirt off my shirt. I'm about to continue the course, now in last place, when something rumbles inside of me. A warm glow spreads throughout my body; my skin tingles as if fingertips caress it. The heat within me builds until it's about to explode.

I realize too late what's happening. The light blinds me, and it's as if my mind is being sucked through a tube.

The ocean—blue and wide—stretches in all directions. Rough salt stings the cuts in my hands, making me wince. I curl the fishing lines because Hartz tells me to. The word fear doesn't come close to describing my dread of the man. I'm already regretting signing up to sail with him. I care not how much the man has promised to pay, an amount which, no doubt, he will not pay.

While at port, I watched him nearly drown a merchant who tried to renege on an agreement. Over a difference of a few pennies, he almost killed the man. "Give them a pulgada, and they'll take your boat," he muttered to himself.

His temper does not improve once we are out at sea. He works us hard for the first week, and even harder the second. There is no real work to be done, but he makes us weave new lines and mend the nets, which don't need mending.

One morning, when I awake late, Hartz drags me off my hammock and hangs me upside down by my ankle over the side of the boat. He promises that I'll dine with fish if I ever oversleep again.

I now do as he says. The crew lives in terror of him.

The wooden cog creaks under the slow roll of the waves as the square white sail billows out, pushing the boat across the never-ending water. We have been at sea for a month and are traveling to the fishing shoals where the bacalhau are more numerous than grains of sand on a beach.

Hartz's anger only increases. Today it breaks like a gale. He usually allows Endika to sing his songs. Endika's voice carries over the waves and improves the spirits of the crew. The song he sings is about mermaids and sea monsters. I can barely understand his accent. He comes from the mountains where Basque sounds as if it's spoken by the tongue of elves.

But as he sings, an unexplained anger takes over Hartz. He pummels poor Endika, meaning to kill the man.

I can't stand idly, so I rush Hartz and shove him hard. I hadn't meant to push him into the sea. Before he falls though, he grabs the halyard and holds tight.

We drag him behind us, and fury is in the man's eyes as he pulls himself hand over hand back into the boat. Both Endika and I know that Hartz will take his revenge on us if he pulls himself back onto the boat.

So Endika cuts the rope, and I do not stop him.

Hartz curses us as the cog sails away, and his words will haunt my dreams.

I stare a long time at the cut end of the rope. Cutting the rope was as good as cutting the man's throat.

There's an explosion of light, and I'm back on the cliff. My head spins, and I fight back dizziness and nausea. I drop to my knees; my hands press against the dirt, preventing me from falling back over the ledge.

The rope lies on the ground like a dead snake. A cold shiver runs across my skin as my mind processes the realization.

The rope didn't break. It was cut.

CHAPTER ELEVEN

Surprise Visit

As a former teacher, it's weird being back in a cafeteria. Some things are the same: the low tables, uncomfortable stools, stringent smell of industrial cleaning agents. But the assortment of gods eating really good Tex-Mex reminds me that this is no middle-school mess hall.

Like all the rooms in the Lyceum, the cafeteria has been sculpted out of the rock. Red colonnades buttress the natural stone ceiling. Half the room stands open to the cliff, and a cool breeze blows through, soothing my aching body. Trying to distract myself, I half focus on one of the televisions mounted to the walls. They're tuned to CNN.

My life can't get any more complicated until Jared sits down across from me. He smiles, leans forward, and asks, "How are you?"

It's as though the air has been knocked out of me, and I've forgotten how to speak. I suddenly realize that I haven't really thought about Jared since I last saw him. For some reason this makes me feel guilty. On one hand, I can't stop loving Jared, but on the other hand, I know that letting him in would mean his death. Tempering my swirling emotions, I regain my poker face. "Splendid. Having the time of my life."

"I'm taking that to mean you're not enjoying yourself."

"Ha." My whole body feels as if it's been put through a meat grinder. I devote the next few seconds to pushing around the tamales on my plate with a fork and not making eye contact. "They're going to kill me if I don't learn how to channel properly."

"Obviously I wouldn't have brought you here if I thought your life would be at risk," Jared replies. "Like you, I have to do what the Elder Gods say. They run this place."

"Jared, do you know what I've been through so far? These people are dangerous. I nearly died climbing a cliff. If this is all part of the 'training,' then I don't feel confident I'm going to survive this week."

"It was only your first day. You can do it. I know you can."

"Perhaps I wasn't clear with you. I can not channel properly. Every time I try, it feels like I lose control of my body and mind. I'm afraid of my past lives. I'm afraid to channel them. They expect me to overcome this fear in a week? Impossible." I lower my voice to a whisper. "You have to help Jessie and me escape."

"You know I can't do that."

"Damn it, Jared," I reply, fists clenched. "I'm asking for help. Something isn't right here."

"What do you mean?"

I shoot a wary glance over my shoulder and then explain what happened during the obstacle course. "I think Daichsun did it on purpose."

Jared recoils, shaking his head. "No, that can't be right."

"Why not?" I ask. "He's already threatened and almost cracked my head open."

"Because if he tried to kill you, it would amount to treason. The Elders' decree must be respected."

"So you're saying that if he were to go against the Elders, he'd be betraying the Mother Goddess' cause. He would, in essence, be helping the Father Gods?"

"No, I didn't say that."

"You implied it."

He lets out a long breath, and rubs his eyes with his palms. "What do you want from me?"

"I want you to protect me from someone I think is trying to hurt me. I want you to do your job."

"My job? How can I possibly be your Protector if every time I get close to you, you push me away?" His body shakes, and exasperation mounts in his eyes. "I'm trying to do everything you ask of me, and I think I'm doing the best I can, but I'm struggling to understand your mixed messages."

I look down at my plate, avoiding his eyes, "I'm sorry, Jared. I wish that everything could be black-and-white. I wish it could be simple and clear."

"Why can't it be?" he asks, voice getting louder. "What are you afraid of? Why won't you be honest with me?"

My shoulders slump, and my whole body feels numb. There's no point in keeping him in the dark anymore. I'll probably die soon anyways. "You want to know the reason, Jared? Fine," I reply, my body tensing. "You remember the prophecy that says that I'm supposed to die, be reborn and save the world? Well, there was one more part to it." An acute pain strikes inside my chest. I feel the pain, hold it one last time, and let it go. "I'm destined to kill the man I love, and I'm sorry to say that it's you."

The words shock him into silence. A look of pure confusion spreads across his face. "I'm sorry, Mattie. I didn't know," he says, his voice stilted.

When he doesn't say anything else, I press on. "The problem is that I wouldn't be able to live with myself if I did that." Tears start falling from my eyes. "And the hard truth is, we can't be together. I can't have these feelings for you knowing that one day, I'll be the person who kills you," I say, finally looking him in his eyes. "Don't you understand, Jared? I'm trying to save you."

He turns away, and his expression takes on an almost cadaver-like stillness. He stares off into nothing, and the silence stretches for an almost-unbearable length of time. Why isn't he saying anything?

"Jared?" I ask. "Do you have anything to say?"

My words shake him from stillness. Still not looking at me, he asks, "So what do we do now?"

"I don't know. This is why I ran away to Hawaii. I thought that if I could cut you from my life, maybe I could save you. But then you came back, and I don't know what to do at this point." I brush away the tears from my cheeks and sniffle. "So I'm going to leave the decision to you. You can stay or you can go. It's your choice."

He's quiet again for a moment. "I don't know," he finally says. "I'm sorry that you've had to live with this."

I give him a minute before I reply, "Well, what's your choice?"

"I don't have a choice. The Elder Gods have already assigned me a mission. I have to leave and do what they asked."

I grab his hand and pull him toward me. "Don't use someone else as an excuse. We all have a choice. If you leave, then I know what choice you've made."

He focuses on me. "You're right, Mattie. We all have a choice, but please understand that this is a lot for me to take in—I didn't realize that the price of my love for you would be my own life. I want to give you an answer right now, but I can't. I need time to process my emotions and thoughts."

"So you're leaving me?"

"Not for good. I'll be back soon. Stay safe." He turns and leaves quickly.

More tears well up in my eyes, but I stop myself from crying. He left. He made a decision, and now it feels as if I have no one. I'm all alone. I take a deep breath to calm my racing heart. I'm not the person I once was, I remind myself. I don't need to feel depressed and dependent; I can rely on myself.

Enki and Jessie sit down across from me.

"Was that Jared who just left?" Jessie asks, looking over her shoulder.

I nod, returning my focus to my now-mashed-up tamale.

"Where is he headed?"

"I don't know. Some mission."

"Who's Jared?" Enki asks.

There's an awkward pause. "It's complicated," I say.

Thankfully, Jessie comes to the rescue. "What happened to your hands?" She gestures to the bandages around my palms.

"Oh, yeah." I turn to Enki. "Thank you for saving me."

He shrugs, shooting me a carefree smile. "I prefer to see you without broken legs."

"Wait," interrupts Jessie. "What happened?"

For a moment, I consider whether I can trust Enki. He isn't Jared or Jessie. He isn't someone I have complete faith and confidence in. The rational part of my brain tells me to trust no one, yet my gut says that Enki is fine. He did save me after all. So I say, "Someone tried to kill one of the Agelings during the race."

They both freeze, and look at me wide-eyed. "Really?" Jessie asks.

My stomach twists into hard knots as I tell her about how the rope was cut. "I think Daichsun was the one who did it," I say. "But he meant to cut my rope."

Jessie jolts up, her back straightening like an iron rod as her grip tightens on a butter knife. "That bastard," she says, rising to her feet, the butter knife now held like a dagger. I reach across the table and shove her back into her seat.

"Whoa, slow down," Enki says. "Why would he do that?"

"Why would he do that?" I ask, cocking my head to the side. "Have you not seen how he's acted toward me? The guy hates my guts. He's already threatened me twice."

Enki runs his hands through his hair. "Something doesn't make sense. I know Daichsun. He's competitive, but I've never suspected him of maliciously hurting anyone."

I clench my fists. "He hates me for something I did to him in a past life. He's made that abundantly clear."

"Enki," Jessie adds. "Don't be naive. I wouldn't be surprised if he tried to attack Mattie. He's an arrogant asshole."

"Every god here meets that description," Enki says. "They all think they know better than everyone else. Also, how sure are you that he cut the rope?"

I hesitate for a second. "Well, not a hundred percent."

"Unless you have irrefutable proof, Coyote won't believe you."

I turn away, shaking my head. If my only option is to convince Coyote, then I don't have any chance at all. "We're prisoners, you realize that, don't you?" I ask, surreptitiously pointing at one of the armed Protectors in the cafeteria. "We should be working together, not against one another. We're all Mother Goddesses. Why doesn't anyone at the Lyceum treat anyone with respect and love? Isn't that what we're all about? I'm having a real problem connecting our mission with how they're educating us."

I expect Enki to debate me, but his attention is fixed on something behind me. "What's happening?" I ask, realizing that the entire cafeteria has fallen silent.

Enki's face has gone white. A chill clambers up my spine. When I turn, I see a muted television, displaying a headline.

Strange Murders Continue Worldwide.

One of the Agelings unmutes the TV.

A reporter stands in front of a burned down house outside of Detroit, Michigan. "... this is the most recent incident in a series of killings that target alternative religions," the reporter says. Behind her, groups of policemen string up caution tape. Black-suited men duck in and out of the scorched building. The scene brings back the gut wrenching memory of what happened after my Ascension, when the priestesses were massacred. I was saved, but only because of Jared. "The twelve victims were all women between the ages of twenty and eighty. Police say that they were part of a cult or a religious order. All were found with mutilated bodies. Authorities are still baffled by the string of similar murders that have been happening around the world. Experts suspect that the perpetrators are a terrorist organization—"

Someone switches off the TV; the air in the cafeteria is deathly cold.

"This is the reason why they're teaching us this way," says Enki. "It's life or death, and we're the only hope of stopping these killings."

I push away my uneaten plate of tamales, no longer hungry. I press my palms into my eyes as I struggle to figure out my emotions. Despite everything—the murders, the threats to my life and Jessie's, my fear of channeling—the person I can't stop thinking about is Jared. He left me, and I can't blame him. It's his life, and I should be glad that he chose to save himself. So why do I feel so sad?

CHAPTER TWELVE

VULCAN'S WRATH

I'm perched with the rest of the Agelings on top of the Lyceum overlooking the canyon. The sun peaks over the horizon, illuminating the desert with bursts of saffron, maroon, and chocolate. It's breathtaking.

"It's way too early," Jessie says, her eyes drooping.

"Better than climbing cliffs."

Jessie unleashes a huge yawn. "No, I'd rather be moving. I'll fall asleep if we keep sitting."

To be fair, we've been sitting here, "practicing our breathing," for over thirty minutes.

My experiences with meditation have been limited to the last five minutes of every yoga video on YouTube—a calm, soothing voice instructs us internet acolytes to clear our minds and be mindful. I don't think I've ever succeeded in doing either.

"Is she really our teacher?" Jessie asks, under her breath.

At the front of the class, Manat, a middle-aged woman shaped like a praying mantis, sits with a calm, placid expression. When we arrived, she had both her legs wrapped around her neck in a position that looked both impossible and excruciating.

"She did kind of freak me out at first," I acknowledge, remembering her deistic form—a white crane with black Cambrian eyes. "But I really don't mind sitting here."

Manat clears her throat. After giving us a reprimanding stare, she says, "The key to channeling is clearing your mind. On a daily basis, your mind is littered with garbage. Relationships, responsibilities, worries—these clutter your mind like flotsam on the ocean."

Jessie groans and whispers, "This is such a waste of time. We're not even supposed to channel here. It's all about meditation."

But Manat has nailed me spot-on. My mind rolls through fears as if they're infomercials on late-night television, one after another, never-ending.

"You must clear your mind of the trash," she continues. "Once it is blank and your ego is subdued, only then will you be able to channel and become one with a past life." She pauses, takes a deep breath, and closes her eyes. "This is why we meditate. Meditation will help you to rid yourself of the unnecessary thoughts plaguing your subconscious."

Jessie sighs. This is a waste of time for her, but she's lucky. Inexplicably, channeling comes naturally to her. It's never been like that for me.

I always thought that meditation was more useful to monks than normal people, so there's a certain appeal to Manat's message.

"A true channeling is not about controlling a past life," Manat says. "It's a partnership. A merger of two identities. As in a marriage, it's not healthy to bring in your baggage to this union."

Every time I channel, my fears and insecurities distract me. When I can't focus, I lose balance, and the past life overwhelms me—which was the case on the cliff in Hawaii.

"Through meditation, we will foster self-awareness." Manat reaches to her side, picks up a square picture, and shows it to us. "Take out your Eternal Divine Wisdom Yantra."

I pick up the laminated picture. The Eternal Divine Wisdom Yantra is composed of an outline of a body. Radiating out from its center is a series of overlapping red, pink, and green triangles. Two painted open eyes stare back at me.

Until now, I'd never heard of yantras, the various pictures and diagrams that are supposed to help with meditation.

"Focus on the divine awareness reflected in the god's eyes,"
Manat advises.

A snort erupts beside me.

Manat—face like a marble bust—either ignores or doesn't hear
Jessie's outburst. "After you have captured the wisdom of the
god in your memory, close your eyes while continuing to focus
on the yantra. Once we have all reached the second plane of
consciousness, we'll begin our exploration of our sub-egos."

Usually, my mind is like a pinball in an arcade game, bouncing
between different fears, but something is different this time.

I've blocked out Manat's voice and Jessie's smirks. My eyes close
but not from tiredness. As my mind relaxes and my breathing
slows, a strange thing occurs.

The image of the yantra appears in my mind's eye as if it were
always waiting there. The outline of the human stands and then, to
my alarm, walks toward me. In my mind, I run from the figure, but
there is no escape. My eyes feel glued shut. The figure approaches
with arms extended. Its fingers reach out to grasp my head and pull
me into an embrace. Blood pounds against my temples. A wave of
fear surges inside me as I realize I'm channeling, and again, I have
no control.

The figure's index finger taps my forehead; a pure silence
consumes my mind.

The next moment, an explosion of light blinds me. Yellow
brightness cuts like a sword through my mind, creating a blank
canvas. Without warning, images paint themselves on it.

*There's no clear boundary between the man's wild, curling beard
and tangled, greasy hair. His robes—stained the color of dung—are
ripped and disheveled. Eyes bulging with fervor and madness, he
points a bent, broken finger toward Vesuvius, and declares, "Offer
your praise and devotion to Vulcan, for only when you prostrate
yourselves to the god of the mountain, will he give mercy."*

One of the Pompeiians tosses a rotten cabbage, and it splatters on the man's face.

"Old fool!" someone shouts.

"You commit sacrilege against greater gods!"

"Shut y' mouth y' pig's ass!"

The old mystic wipes green slime from his beard. His mouth opens, revealing as many teeth as a foot has toes. He raises his fist and shakes it defiantly. "Mark my words!" he screams. "You will suffer his fury and burn in his fire. It will rain down on you. It will clean away this depraved and wicked city from the face of the earth. Nothing will remain, and history will forget you. Your destruction is nigh!" White foam seeps from his mouth.

A child flings a stone, and it smacks his nose, drawing blood. The mob cheers, and more stones fly. Soon the man is curled up on the ground unconscious.

"Come, Camilla, we have no time for prophets," I say, pulling her away from the crowd.

She reluctantly follows. "Is it true, Goddess?" she asks, twisting the gold rings on her slender fingers. "Will Vulcan destroy the city?"

I glance at the mountain. A thin, perilous bead of black smoke rises from the summit. "Child, you know as well as I that death and rebirth are two sides of the same coin. If the city should burn, it is not because of its denizens. It is because nature and fate are fickle in their whims." I point to the sweating round man looming behind me. "Pay the merchant."

She does so, and I take the small golden calf sculpture, and walk back toward the chariot.

Camilla races after me. "Why do you buy a gift for the Father God?" she asks, her face bunching in on itself. "He could be our enemy—the one who ordered the murder of our priestesses."

"You are young, so let me give you a lesson," I say, while walking. "Courtesy in combat is a rare thing and something to be appreciated. We do not yet know if he is our enemy, so for the time being, we treat him as a friend."

But her expression is still blank and slack as she points to the gift. "But why the golden calf? Is that not a symbol of a false religion?"

I let out a loud laugh. "All religions are false, child. I know this god well. He's a collector, and he has nostalgia for old faiths and traditions." We arrive at our chariot outside the city gates. "Now come, drive the horses fast. I wish to arrive at his estate before sundown."

As directed, Camilla whips the horses hard, and we speed down the stone-paved road. Grape vineyards and fields spread out far into the distance. This land has always been fertile. The shadow of Vesuvius casts a somber dimness that adds to the heavy miasma of dread washing over my skin.

The sun is fading fast. We round a bend and the country estate, sprawling on a hill, comes into view. Camilla pulls back on the reins and the horses neigh under the strain as we arrive at the entrance, barricaded by heavy logs.

My mouth goes dry, and I take a deep breath to calm my pulse. There is an unnatural silence. I detect no sign of opposition or movement near the white villa at the top of the hill, yet a trickle of fear scampers down my spine.

I turn to Camilla, who has already unshouldered her bow. "Wait here. I will go alone."

She stops me mid-stride, shoulders drooping. "Are you sure, Goddess? Do you doubt my abilities? I was first in my class in combat."

In a gentler voice, I explain, "I have no doubts about your abilities. You are my personal attendant because of your skills, but I must meet with this god alone."

She looks to the ground and lowers her bow. "As you wish, Goddess."

I touch her cheek with my palm. "Take heart and do not let your vigilance slip. If you feel threatened, draw first and ask questions later. The air is bad here."

She replies with a stiff nod then nocks an arrow into her bow and takes up guard on the chariot.

With the golden calf in one hand, I climb around the wooden logs and proceed up the hill. On the ground are many boot prints. Soldiers passed this way recently. As I climb the road, no birds chirp. In the distance, a cow munches on lush grass. The fields sway under a gentle breeze. Chickens scramble past me unattended.

I am halfway up the hill when they spring their trap.

A contubernium of armored legionaries—eight in total—emerges from the tall grass. By the look of their steely eyes under their helmets, as well as their scarred skin and enormous muscles, they are battle hardened. The soldiers take up positions around me: two in front, two in back, and two on each side. Each man carries the normal armament: shield, javelin, and short-bladed gladius.

My only weapon is a golden calf.

"You shouldn't have come here," says a familiar voice, "yet he knew you would."

Beyond the legionaries is the speaker. He is as tall as a plum tree and as lanky as a giraffe. He sweeps his senatorial toga over his shoulder as he approaches. His face painted ochre and indigo, the colors of the Far East. Caishen has always enjoyed luxury and showmanship more than most Romans—if that was possible.

"Is this how you treat an honored guest?" I ask.

The liaison between the Mother and Father Gods bridges his fingers and bows his head. "My deepest apologies, Gaia, but you should not take this personally. I received your execution orders only this morning." He runs his disapproving eyes over the soldiers. "Violence is so inelegant."

"Will you do me the courtesy of telling me who signed these execution orders?"

He shrugs and inspects his fingernails, which are painted purple. "There was no signature. Simply the Black Mark and your name. It could be any one of the members of the Ancient Council who ordered it."

My fists clench. "But for what purpose? Why start a war?"

Caishen, his face sympathetic, walks backward toward his villa. He raises his hands in a gesture of futility. "These answers you'll not learn in this lifetime." He turns his head to one of the soldiers, and says, "When you are done with her, remember to kill her servant."

"Caishen!" I yell, "I'm giving you one last chance. Give me the answers I seek, and I will let you and these men live."

His face breaks into a wide smile. "Be careful with her. The legends say she is incredibly dangerous." He spins around, heading back to his villa.

The Decanus—commander of the legionaries—rolls his eyes at the warning. "I will make this one my whore tonight. Dead or alive, I care not." His men laugh.

A tinge of sadness for the fools sprouts in my chest. They should have sent triple the men.

The soldiers tighten their circle with their spears held ready and shields poised. The golden calf drops from my hand and lands with a dull thud. Despite Caishen's warning, they approach me as if I'm only an unarmed woman. They will pay for this mistake.

I reach into my mind and channel Eurotas, champion among the Spartans and scourge of Xerxes. A hero whose feats are still sung today. One of the legendary three hundred who fell at the Battle of Thermopylae. A beast so wild and deadly that I rarely channel him. Yet, my opponents give me no choice.

His soul and mine merge into a perfect union. Eurotas's power infuses every part of my body. His memories, training, passions and strength—they flood through me.

I am Eurotas. Body and soul. Mind and muscle.

The soldier to my right is first to attack. Armed with a weighted net, like a retiarius gladiator, he tosses it at me.

I spin out of its path, grab its edge while it still flies, and redirect the net toward a man in front of me. It wraps around him and his weaponry. With a hard yank, I pull him toward me. The man, off-balance, tumbles into my arms. I hold his head as if to coddle him but instead twist it sharply. The soldier's body becomes limp and lifeless in my arms. I let him drop to the ground.

The legionaries stare stunned at their first casualty. Barely a moment later, a war cry erupts behind me. Sensing him behind me, aiming for my back, a soldier thrusts his spear, abandoning any attempt to take me alive.

I bow forward, letting the spear plunge through empty space. Then I spin around to face the man, grasp the spear, and yank it forward. The spear slips out of the soldier's hands, and I send it flying. It sinks into the neck of the remaining man in front of me.

At this point, all the soldiers fall onto me with weapons raised, trying their hardest to slay me.

I dance among the blades, a step Eurotas knows too well. From one of the soldiers, I gain a gladius. I hack off an arm and then thrust the blade into the stomach of another.

Sensing a rush of movement to my left, I duck as a blade slices the air where my head would have been. I spin, and the decanus launches himself toward me. He's faster than I thought, and his blade grazes my robes.

I retreat, picking up a shield from the ground, and I turn to face him.

He grins, lifts the blade to his mouth, and kisses it. "I'm going to stick your head on a spike."

"Decanus, if you retreat now, I'll spare you."

His lips curl like a rabid dog's. He charges, his sword poised over his head, ready to strike. I wait until he's three feet away before slamming the shield into the earth at an angle. His foot catches on the shield, and he stumbles. As he falls, I spin and bring the sword down swiftly. The head of the decanus rolls off and bounces down the hill.

There are three soldiers still alive. "Come now, if you wish to die." I beckon with a raised hand.

Making the wisest decision of their lives, they turn and take flight down the hill. If they're smart, they will avoid the main entrance, and Camilla's deadly aim. If not, I pray they will be reborn as better people.

I see Caishen running for the safety of his villa. I drop the sword and reach down to retrieve a pilum, a long javelin. I estimate the distance, sprint forward, and fling it. The pilum flies high into the air, arching gracefully, and finds its mark, plunging through Caishen's right shoulder. He staggers forward, nearly collapsing, before disappearing into the villa.

Having no more use for Eurotas, I release him from our union.

When I arrive at the villa, I follow the trail of Caishen's blood along the marble floor to the atrium. He's halfway to death. Blood leaks into the pool in the middle of the room. Gasping for breath, he will not be long on this earth. His eyes grow large when I enter, but then a smile emerges. "I should have believed the stories about you. I doubt three contubernium would have been enough."

"Maybe in another lifetime you will be able to rectify the error."

"I doubt I'll Ascend again. My luck has finally run out."

"Tell me what you know. Why are they killing off the priestesses and Mother Goddesses?"

Caishen coughs, and blood sputters down his chin. "I want assurances."

"You're hardly in a position to negotiate."

He laughs, and more blood spills down his chin. "This is the best time to bargain because I have nothing to lose," he says, his voice weak and raspy. "If I die, I'm Descended for eternity, and you lose your precious answers. If I Ascend, we both win."

"So you want me to Ascend you?" I ask. "Impossible. We are alone here. The Ascension requires a vessel."

Caishen grins painfully. "Marcia, come forward," he says, grimacing.

A pretty woman looking as scared as a young fawn appears in the shadows of a doorway. Swaddled in her arms is a quiet infant. Head bowed, she shuffles over and places the infant next to Caishen on the ground. "He is my infant son still within the Ascension period, and *his identity has not yet formed. There will be no robbery of the soul, I assure you."*

"Your assurances are not worth a grain of salt."

An anguished expression streaks across Caishen's face. "What do you say? I have little time left. Do you want to know? Or do you want my death to be in vain?"

I swat at a buzzing fly, and my neck stiffens. I should have known that Caishen would seek to haggle even on his deathbed.

My options are limited. He is one of my few trusted contacts among the Father Gods. If he dies, I have few leads to follow. Decision made, I take a step toward him. "Fine, I will Ascend you, but you must tell me the reason for the breaking of the holy truce."

Caishen nods and grins again. "Promise on the oath, Goddess."

My eyes roll, but I make the oath. "I promise on the reincarnated soul of Gaia that I will fulfill my pledge. Now talk, while you still have strength."

"Speak with the Oracle. He has the answers you want."

When he doesn't say anything else, my anger flares. "Is that it? Go speak with the Oracle? This is not an answer to my question."

"The truth is I do not know who ordered the Purging. Nor do I know the reason for this war. It was only this morning that I received an order with the Black Seal. But I have heard a rumor that the Oracle has a prophecy for you."

"What is this new prophecy? I was not told of this."

"Now you understand. There were reasons why you were not informed. Go to the Oracle and get your answers."

"This information is hardly worth your Ascension."

"That may be, but you promised," he replies nervously, from between gritted teeth.

My eyes narrow. "Caishen, you did not deliver your end of the bargain." His face drops, but I have an idea. "I will complete your Ascension on one condition."

"What is it?"

"You owe me, Caishen. It might be in a year. It might be in five millennia. But you will pay me back for the service I do for you today. Never forget the debt you owe—because Gaia always collects her debts. Now you promise."

His face blanches; his smile wanes as does his life. "Fine, I promise on the reincarnated soul of Caishen. Now Ascend me before I pass."

I calm my mind and prepare myself for the Ascension, but suddenly the sky erupts into thousands of orange and yellow shards. It's as if it's on fire. Loud gongs send my mind spinning.

My eyes snap open, and I'm back at the Lyceum. Above me, white and brown blobs block out the blue sky. As my vision clears, I see the concerned faces of Jessie, Enki, and Manat staring down at me.

Jessie sighs with relief. "She's waking up."

"What happened?" I groan.

"You blacked out and fell flat on your back," Enki explains, the concern in his face also ebbing.

"Ouch. My head hurts like hell." I sit up and the world spins. I notice we're alone. "Where is everybody?"

"They went to the next class," Enki says.

Manat's eyebrows draw together, and she stoops toward me. "Gaia, tell me what you saw. You entered a trance and were reliving a past life. Which one was it?"

I'm about to answer when an impulse tells me to keep my mouth shut. "I don't remember."

Manat narrows her eyes. "It is incredibly rare to enter a trance. I will have to inform the Elders. You two"—she gestures to Jessie and Enki—"take her back to her quarters. She needs rest." She looks at me. "I excuse you from classes for the rest of the day."

Jessie and Enki pick me up and lead me back inside.

Gaia's vision echoes in my mind. Some things make more sense—like why Caishen helped me two years ago when I was being chased by Gurzil. But now I have so many more questions. Who ordered the Purging, for instance?

Now I know for sure that Gaia is telling me something; her search for answers is somehow connected to my own experience. I rub my hands, stiff and tight, against my tracksuit. I must wash them, especially my fingers. They feel as if they're covered in blood.

CHAPTER THIRTEEN

Penultimate Life

Coyote enters the classroom and slams the door behind him. He pauses, and a sliver of a smile creases his face. We all jerk to attention. As befitting the trickster god, his temperament is indecipherable. Does the smile mean he's in a good mood? Or does it mean something ominous? Judging from the sour taste flooding my mouth, my gut thinks it's the latter.

This is the class I've been dreading. This is channeling.

Holding a small leatherbound book, with hulking shoulders and no visible neck, the man is as massive as a bear. Chills shoot down my spine as I remember for the hundredth time that he argued in favor of my murder.

How am I supposed to learn anything from him?

Coyote is perfectly content to draw out the uncomfortable silence. The enigmatic grin disappears, replaced by an expression of boredom. He saunters over to the only chair in the room at the front of the class, swings it around, straddles it, and says, "Begin with your penultimate life."

Immediately, all the Agelings sit on the floor in the lotus position on pre-arranged yoga mats and begin channeling their past lives.

I stay standing, confused. I glance at Jessie, but she, like the rest of my shut-eyed classmates, knows exactly what he's talking about. I, on the other hand, have no idea what to do or how to do it.

So I do what any student would do if they were confused about an assignment. I raise my hand.

Coyote either doesn't see me or chooses not to react as he thumbs the pages of the book.

After a few seconds, I clear my throat. "Excuse me."

His dispassionate eyes rise. "Yes?" he replies professorially.

"Sorry, what—what is my penultimate life?"

Coyote stares at me with blossoming incredulity; then he slams the book closed and leaps to his feet. His chair flips over and hits the ground. "Stop!" he shouts.

The hairs on my neck stand up, and cold sweat trickles down my back.

"We have a question, a basic question, from our most ancient goddess. Gaia, what is your question?"

I feel the eyes of all my classmates turn onto me. Coyote's voice sends my stomach rolling, but I grit my teeth, and repeat, "What is my penultimate life?"

"Your penultimate life?" He paces the room while rubbing his chin in faux concentration. "Hmm, that's a hard one. Anyone care to explain?"

"The penultimate is an Ascended god's most recent past life," Daichsun replies.

"Correct. Why do we begin each class with the penultimate life?"

"Based on Athena's teachings, there is a proportional relation between the ease of channeling and the age of the past life."

"Whoa!" Coyote exclaims, blowing out a breath that rattles his lips. "That's way too complicated for our simple goddess." He narrows his dark eyes at me. "Let's dumb it down for her."

"Older past lives are harder to channel than younger ones," Daichsun explains. "Therefore, the penultimate is the easiest to channel."

"You would think that a goddess, one of the oldest among us, would remember one of the central principles of channeling," Coyote says to himself.

I feel my cheeks burn red. "But I don't know how to do this. That's why I'm here."

His eyes narrow. "It pains me to have to explain one of the simplest exercises, but I will do my best. You will begin by calling to your past lives, beckoning them. Naturally, your penultimate life will be the first to emerge. When it does, you will entreat them to form a union with you. If your request is accepted, you will naturally channel them."

"What if it's not accepted?"

Coyote snorts dismissively. "Penultimate lives never reject a channeling. It's unheard of." He picks up the chair, sits down, and reopens the book. "Stop wasting our time and channel your past life."

I hold my trembling hands still as the rest of the class resumes the exercise. A silence so thick it could be touched falls over the room. Am I the only one who doesn't know how to do this?

Steadying my pounding pulse, I breathe in and out. I sit down on the floor and cross my legs. I've never before channeled my penultimate life. I close my eyes and tell myself I can do this.

You can't, says another part of my brain.

There are two possibilities. Either nothing will happen and the past life will refuse me or I'll succeed, in which case I'll have no control.

I prefer the nothing scenario.

Going to the wall in my mind, I imagine reaching toward it. Surprisingly, as soon as I think about my intention to channel, a bright light appears in my mind's eye. It's a sparkling jewel of a life. I have only one shot to get this right, so I grab at the light and pull it into an embrace.

Despite Coyote's earlier statement, the past life fights my assault, but I am stronger. Overpowering its opposition, I channel it, and my vision explodes with haunting reds and foreboding browns.

The U-boat's hull juts out from the seafloor like a fossil. Despite the respirator and the steady flow of oxygen to my lungs, I'm almost breathless. I've been waiting my whole life for this moment.

"Hans, can you believe this?"

"You finally found it," he says, sounding surprised.

I check the amount of air I have left. I'm still well in the black. Plenty of time for an initial inspection. A school of grouper glides out of an open, inviting hatch. What mysteries await inside this untouched forty-year-old tomb? More importantly, is the artifact inside? "Let's take a closer look."

After several minutes of kicking my flippers, I'm hovering above the empty deck. Anemones cover the metal like a fluffy white-and-pink blanket. The waters off Africa's east coast are warm, but a shiver of cool excitement runs across my skin. It feels as if I've been searching for this wreck my entire life, though it's been only five years.

A bright light reflects off my visor. Hans floating above me like a jellyfish, points at the open hatch. "After you, Amahle. This is your find."

I hesitate. "Maybe it's best if we head back up," I reply, swimming until I'm a mere two feet away from the dark hatch. "I would rather come down more prepared."

"Look at your gauge. You have plenty of air."

A quick glance at my gauge shows that I have over three quarters left in my tank. "We don't know how long we'll be in there"

"When have you ever been this cautious? I've seen you free dive to one hundred meters and hold your breath for over ten minutes."

"Rather be cautious than dead."

"Fine, you head up, and I'll explore it for now."

What secrets lie buried in its dark depths? "Don't think you'll steal my glory."

He floats beside the rusted gun turrets. "After you, love."

"Well, one of us has to stay out here."

"It will be my pleasure."

"Thanks, Hans."

Turning to the derelict wreck's open hatch, I can't suppress a smile. Down here exploring, I'm free. I descend into this lost underworld, this haunted piece of history. My flashlight illuminates the murky abyss, showing me that the U-boat's interior is frozen in time: pots hanging from hooks in the kitchen, the Enigma machine open and unprotected, a chipped teacup, barnacle-covered torpedoes. At any moment, I expect the captain to enter with his starched shirt and shined shoes. It's for moments like these that I dive. To be an explorer.

I find the captain's quarters. The Germans were, if anything, precise. Every U-boat class has the same design. Every room is always where it should be.

Inside the dark room, I can't believe it—the U-boat's safe is open.

Likely, as the U-boat sank, the captain tried to rescue its precious treasure. A corroded metal cash box lies at the bottom of the safe, as if it were a gift from the heavens. The lock on the box dissolves to pieces when I lift the lid. A dagger rests inside, its sharp blade made from a strange red stone. A green emerald is embedded in its hilt. My flashlight's beam reveals the blade, inscribed with the same strange, foreign language that took me years to decipher.

Diamant's Dagger. The God Killer. I found it.

I'm lightheaded with joy, and my mind flips ecstatically.

"I'm sorry, Amahle," Hans says over the radio.

"What are you sorry for? We finally found what we've been searching for."

"No, I'm sorry you won't be alive to enjoy it."

I shake my head. What does he mean? I glance down at my gauge, and my breath catches. The tank is nearly empty.

A pit opens in my stomach. The lightheadedness is not from joy. It's because my oxygen is almost out.

"Hans! What did you do?"

I turn around and swim, but I appear to have gotten turned around. I was in the captain's quarters, but now I'm back in the torpedo bay. I have to concentrate. I can't get lost.

"The price they offered was too good to turn down."

My muscles cramp, and pure dread overwhelms my mind. Every breath I take means I have one less to get me back to the surface.

"What are you talking about?"

By the time I get my bearings and find my way back to the hatch, I'm on the dregs of my tank. My head swims, and each breath takes more and more effort. When I get to where the open hatch once was, a foul taste floods my mouth.

The hatch is closed and locked.

"Hans, open the hatch."

"I'm sorry," he replies, without a hint of remorse in his voice.

I push on the hatch, but it's stuck in place.

"Open the hatch!"

I can do this, I tell myself. I can control my breathing.

But my vision clouds and my limbs grow heavy.

A long sleep calls, and I close my eyes for a second. My thoughts blur into an unrecognizable mess. I don't have control; I never had control.

Amahle flees and seeks refuge behind the wall.

Gasping for breath, I stumble forward and slam into something hard. The collision sends me flying, and I land face-first on the ground. My body spasms uncontrollably. Am I having a seizure? I'm going to be sick to my stomach. I huff and pant as the realization crystallizes: I just experienced Amahle's death.

The excruciating last moments, the panic, the giving up.

The shock numbs my nerves.

Amahle . . .

"Do you know what I call that?" a deep voice asks, interrupting my grief.

No one responds.

After a long pause, Coyote answers himself. "Pitiful." His glare freezes my blood, and then his temper explodes like a geyser. "Pathetic! Why am I wasting time on you?"

I breathe hard, pushing down vertigo. "It was my first time," I reply, picking myself up from the ground. "I'd never channeled her before."

His nose wrinkles as if smelling something rotten. "Even a Youngling, without any training, can channel their penultimate life with ease. You are incapable of doing the simplest task." He plants his legs wide and points a thick, accusing finger at me. "As far as I'm concerned, you're not worth training."

My pulse hammers. My knees quake. "I can do better. Just give me another chance."

"I've seen enough. You don't want your gift."

The truth in the statement presses tears out of my eyes, but I refuse to back down. "I do," I lie. "Let me try again."

Coyote spins away. "We're done."

"What do you mean?"

"Leave," he says, pointing to the door.

I don't move. "No, I'm staying."

His eyes bulge with fury. "Get out!"

I jump to my feet. Is this a test? But the terrible silence doesn't end. More tears streak down my cheeks. "I'm not leaving."

"The Great Goddess Gaia," Daichsun says under his breath. "Our savior."

His comment is like a cut in my side, but I hold my ground.

"I have real gods to train!" Coyote roars. "Leave!"

The threat is all too real, and I break. Running from the classroom, I don't look back. I sprint down the hallway and get lost in the Lyceum's corridors. Somehow I emerge outside, where the afternoon's fading heat hits my skin. I climb a path up the canyon's walls, not knowing where it will lead. Sweat and tears stinging my eyes, I run to forget.

But the burn of the exertion doesn't dissolve the memory of Amahle's last moments, nor the terrible situation I'm in. I have no chance of surviving the Lyceum. I'm a dead woman running.

Cacti and brambles tear at my clothes and skin, but I keep going until I reach the summit. My heart slams against my chest; there is nowhere else to go. I turn slowly, hands on top of my head, breathing hard.

Across the valley, the Lyceum hangs from the cliff like a mirage, filling me with dread.

I collapse, sobbing. I dream of escaping, of running away and disappearing. I yearn for a new life—like the one I had in Hawaii. I never should have come here.

Is it possible to escape? To be free again?

The scratch of the tracking bracelet against my skin dispels the idea. No matter how far I ran, no matter how many miles I traveled, they'd hunt me down—not just the Mother Goddesses, but the Father Gods as well. They would both kill me in the end.

The realization opens a deep hole inside of me. Why was I cursed to be who I am?

The weight of history seems to be slung over my shoulders alone. Every one of my past lives carries a legacy, like a stone. One or two of these I could bear easily. Maybe I could even endure ten. But my thousands of past lives are like an uncontrollable hurricane inside of me. Even channeling Amahle was like walking a tightrope. One slip and fall could mean losing my sanity.

I drop my head into my hands. Some part of me hoped to find friends, maybe a family, at the Lyceum, but the opposite is true. Instead of support, there is a viciousness that mirrors the larger world. The hate I feel from Coyote, Daichsun, and the Elders makes my skin cold. Don't they realize that I'm not Gaia from Rome? Why do they expect me to be her? To have all her memories and powers?

To make things worse, it feels as if I have no allies in this world. Jared has left me, and ever since her Ascension, Jessie has been rightfully preoccupied with her own self-discovery.

The loneliness scrapes at my insides. Didn't I beat this old part of me? Wasn't I a new person? One who didn't need to feel depressed, sad, or alone? In truth, I know it's always been there, waiting to reemerge and remind me that there's no hope.

I stare over the ledge of the steep cliff. A fall from this height would be certain death.

An old, familiar voice asks a question: What if I just stepped off?

Everything would be over. I wouldn't be hunted by the Fathers Gods, or have to endure the Mother Goddesses' maliciousness, or suffer the burden of my past lives, or worry about a prophecy involving the death of the man I love.

I wouldn't have to be concerned about anything ever again. No more problems. No more pressures. Silence.

But invisible strings seize me in place as I realize that this is what Coyote wants; he wants me dead. That way, he can Ascend me into a new vessel, a child.

I double over, clutching my shoulders, shivering. For me, death is no escape. I am a prisoner of eternity.

I inhale sharply, filling my lungs with air, and roar. The sound echoes off the walls of the valley, ricocheting and reverberating in all directions.

When I'm depleted, I find the sun setting over the desert, the horizon an explosion of reds, oranges, purples, and blues. Small stars peek out from this primeval tapestry. The stillness of the air cools my fevered mind, calms my racing thoughts.

I am but one life among many, yet each life has the power and the capacity to create change.

I do have a choice.

I could revert to the scared, timid girl I once was. I could be unsure of myself, unsure of my life. I could be a glass bottle tossing in a sea of uncertainty.

Or I could be someone different.

When I ran away to Hawaii, I became someone different. I still wasn't the person I wanted to be. I was still afraid of myself, my powers, the prophecy, and the gods who wanted to be my friends and enemies. But I *was* a different person.

If I could choose to be that person, why couldn't I choose to be the person I want to be?

I rise from the ground, brush away the dirt, and plant my feet wide. I want to be strong and fearless. I will not be afraid anymore.

I spin around and race back down the canyon walls to the Lyceum.

In the hallways, I rush past Agelings, who stare at me curiously, until I arrive at his room. I knock on the door.

I hear a rustle of movement, and Enki asks, "Who's there?"

"It's me," I say. "Mattie. I mean Gaia."

The door opens, and he flashes a smile. "I was wondering where you went."

"I needed a moment."

He leans against the doorframe, his arms crossed. "So what are you doing here?"

"I need your help."

"Why should I help you?"

I step back, surprised, but then realize that just because I've had a personal revelation doesn't mean anyone else has. "At first, I thought I shouldn't be here. I thought it was a mistake, and I'd signed up for my own execution."

"OK."

"But I now understand that this is where I should be, and I need to get control if I'm going to keep living."

"And how do I fit into this?"

"You've been at the Lyceum for years. You have the experience I need to learn from. If I'm going to live through this week, I need your help."

He pauses. "Honestly, I don't know if I can help you."

My mouth falls open. "What do you mean?"

"You clearly don't believe in yourself. I don't know how I can change that."

"Why do you think I'm here now, asking for your help? I refuse to be beaten down by Coyote and the others."

"But I'm not certain you can do it," he says. "Coyote has a point. You can't even channel your penultimate life."

"That's not true," I reply. "I channeled her earlier. I just wasn't able to control her."

He sighs and shakes his head, disappointment evident on his face. "See, that's the problem. You *can't* control your past lives, just as you can't control another person. Channeling is a partnership."

I throw up my hands. "This is why I need someone, like you, to tell me these things and help me."

"Listen," he replies, his voice hardening. "I don't think that I can help you in a week. Maybe you should find someone else," he says, pointing down the hallway. "What about your friend Pele?"

"For one reason or another, she can naturally channel. She doesn't understand what I'm going through. But you do. You've been here for years learning."

He sighs and avoids my eyes. "That's true, but honestly, I still have a lot to learn. I'm supposedly some really old god, but I can't remember all my past lives. I can barely channel lives from a few hundred years ago. I don't want to let you down. I'm afraid that you'll blame me if you suddenly don't get it. I don't want to be held accountable if you fail."

"Let me down? I'm not looking for you to save me. I'm looking to save myself, but I need someone to show me the right direction. I want to live, and I mean living without feeling that being Ascended is a curse or a disease. I don't want to reject this life. I want to accept it fully."

Enki falls silent. He stares at his hands. Then he says, "You know, I was like you. When I came here, I didn't think I'd make it. I didn't believe in myself either."

"So what changed?"

"It took me a while to realize what defines Mother Goddesses. It's not the Lyceum. Sometimes we forget about our true purpose. We forget about the reason why we're fighting against the Father Gods. If we just remember, it puts everything into perspective."

"What is it that defines a Mother Goddess?"

"It's the most powerful force in the world. It's a weapon that can bend the will of man." I wait. "It's love. The most powerful weapon we have is love. I do believe you have a great capacity to love, but you need to temper your fears."

"So are you going to show me the ropes and help me out?"

"I haven't exactly been the most stellar guide so far."

"Hey, I'll give you a break. Besides, sometimes it's less about teaching and more about being there."

He laughs sharply. "That's rich."

"What's so funny?"

He pauses and shoots me a sideways glance. "When I came to the Lyceum, someone offered to help me. Although they didn't necessarily teach me a step-by-step channeling process, their presence really assisted me."

"Wait, so you're telling me that someone helped you when you arrived? You can't possibly reject me."

"No, you're right," he acknowledges. "It wouldn't be fair. I guess I never thought I'd be in a position to be mentoring."

"So, that means you will help me?"

"We start tomorrow. Sleep well, Gaia," he replies, closing the door.

I turn away and walk back to my room, relishing the first sliver of hope I've had in a long time. I finally feel as if I have a plan, a way to succeed. I know it's not going to be easy, but at least I've made a decision.

CHAPTER FOURTEEN

HISTORY LESSON

Č hápa is the largest rodent I've ever seen. There's very little that's odd about his human form, with its wizened, pointed chin, manicured goatee, and dogwood blossom of white hair. But his deistic form is a whole different ball game. Gigantic orange incisors descending below a bulbous black nose complement his dirty gray fur. Oh, yeah, there's also his paddleboard tail, which drags behind him as he walks.

History class at the Lyceum is taught by a pompous beaver in a three-piece suit.

When Čhápa speaks, his whiskers quiver as if they're alive. "In the beginning, there was blackness. For millennia, the human race floundered. There was little hope for a species so disconnected, so primitive." He pauses for effect. "From this blackness emerged a spark of light—the Ascended."

As he talks, I scribble down notes in a journal, dutifully committed to my newfound mission of learning to be Ascended. Pressing into the paper too hard, my pencil tip breaks, leaving me to frantically search for a replacement.

"Hey, here," says a voice in a whisper. Seuku, the girl I saved during the obstacle course, offers me a pen.

"Thanks," I reply softly.

She smiles and turns back to her notes.

Čhápa wobbles around the class, perched on a cane whose handle has been carved to resemble a medicine wheel as he lectures in a long-winded dull voice. "The Ascended have always been the torchbearers for civilization, and without them, mankind would still be living in caves." He fixes his bow tie while looking out the window of the classroom. "My Agelings, never take lightly the noble duty that you have been appointed."

My pen halts over the page as I process what he just said. In my experience, the Ascended have not been torchbearers—they've been the ones lighting infernos. Almost echoing my thoughts, Jessie mutters "Bullshit" under her breath.

I barely heard Jessie, so I'm surprised when Čhápa turns on her. "Pele, do you have something to add?"

She stares at him for a few seconds, maybe considering whether a confrontation is worth the consequence, but ever since her Ascension, Jessie has gained enviable confidence. Then she rolls her eyes, and her expression screams *Screw it!* "OK, I'll buy your argument that the Ascended have had influence, but give humans some credit. They aren't all idiots. Their progression through history—their evolution—is not all thanks to the Ascended."

I hide my grin as Čhápa recoils, seemingly unaccustomed to students challenging him. He recovers quickly. With an upraised nose and condescending glare, he fires back. "Can you answer me this? Who developed hieroglyphics, which evolved into alphabets? Who domesticated the wolf, which evolved to become the dog? Who remembered which plants were delicious and which were poisonous?"

Jessie's eyes narrow. "Knowledge can be passed from one generation to the next."

"It doesn't end with knowledge," Čhápa replies, wagging a finger. "No, no. The Ascended were the leaders in the community. They knew when to act and how. They were the prophets and kings and queens. Mortals are too often crushed by their insecurities to make choices in critical times." He pauses, eyes fluttering. "If mortals were in control, they would likely still be practicing child sacrifice."

I raise my hand to rebut his comments, but Jessie beats me to the punch. "Assuming the Ascended are behind religions and governments, let's remember some of the amazing things they've created." She counts on her fingers. "Dictatorships, royal families, fundamentalist religions, bad pop music—not exactly a sterling record. These institutions don't set humans free. They enslave them."

"Yet, what of democracy, Ageling? You conveniently exclude one of the Mother Goddesses' greatest gifts to mankind."

"Democracy today is hardly a shining example."

"Its failing as a system is a result of the limitations of the humans it serves. Now tell me this—what is the alternative?"

Jessie opens her mouth, but this time, she's slow to reply.

Čhápa sensing weakness, presses forward. "Search your past lives, Pele. Find a moment when your precious humans possessed that freedom and independence that you say we've stolen from them. What will you discover? In every case, I guarantee, there will be anarchy. Freedom is a myth. Freedom equals destruction. Have you seen how humans act without systems of control? They devolve into anarchy, death and destruction. They act no better than wild animals."

Jessie reclines in her seat, glum and silent. A part of me burns hot. I feel for her. There's something glaringly wrong with Čhápa's descriptions of the Ascended.

Čhápa continues, a satisfied grin on his lips. "Part of understanding ourselves is understanding what has already happened. Because it will happen again. I guarantee it. Life is cyclical—especially for the Ascended. We're born, we live, and we die. Then we do it all over again. Having this perspective, this understanding of existence, will give each of you a bearing when you channel. Yet, Pele has unintentionally brought up an excellent point and a question. What is the role of the Ascended?"

Čhápa answers his own question as he marches around the perimeter of the class. "Our role as Mother Goddesses is primarily one of shepherds to the flock of mankind. They are beasts that do not know their full capabilities. We are gentle guides who are always conscious of the impact we have."

Besides being demeaning to people who aren't Ascended, this type of high-minded talk sounds totally disconnected from my reality. I glance to my left at Enki who shakes his head imperceptibly, as if reading my thoughts

Despite Enki's warning, I slam down my pen in frustration. "How are we supposed to beat the Father Gods?" I ask. "They're willing to do anything to get more power. I've been hunted by them. They don't abide by tenets or laws. They kill first. How can we be gentle guides and shepherds when faced with such an enemy? What chance do we have against them?"

Chápa swings his attention to me, his face inquisitive, almost pleased. A part of me suspects that he enjoys the debate. "You're correct, Gaia. However, their devotion to violence is also their greatest weakness."

"I don't understand."

"The Father Gods are slaves to one past life—usually an ancient one. This past life has corrupted all subsequent incarnations of the god, enslaving all other past lives. Because of this, Father Gods lack the ability to form partnerships with their past lives."

"So they can't channel?"

"Correct. Mother Goddesses draw their power from channeling. We believe that every past life has something of value and that all are equally important. This union, this democracy of past lives, has incredible power when wielded by a master."

At that moment, I remember Patrick and the look of terror in his eyes before he was murdered. "But how does this power compare to violence?"

"Consider this. If you were playing chess with an opponent, would you rather be by yourself or have a team of experts to help you? I truly believe that love, respect, and hope will win against tyranny, evil and hate in the long run. Each of you is imbued with special abilities. Each of your past lives has shaped who you are in this moment. You must learn the powers that are inside of you." Čhápa points at me with his cane. "Gaia, you have not realized your true potential. If you do, you will learn that the Father Gods are actually quite weak. Violence is the weapon of the fearful and ignorant. You know only the most basic elements of your own Ascended powers."

"You mean channeling?" I ask.

Confusion falls across Čhápa's face, and then a widening grin emerges. "No, ah, I see. I had assumed you knew about the other powers of the Ascended. Some Ascended gods have specific powers. For example, you have the power to Ascend or Descend other gods."

I hadn't considered that this ability was special, but he's right. Within the realm of the Ascended, it is a unique gift.

"Some Ascended can change their deistic form or even conceal the fact that they are Ascended," he continues.

I remember how Coyote hid his deistic form when we first met him to trick us into following him. "Are there others?"

Čhápa nods eagerly, clearly enjoying the opportunity to share his knowledge. "Indeed, many. Perhaps my favorite legend is that some gods can transfer their souls between living bodies just by touch. They can switch among bodies as if they were driving different automobiles. They can even inhabit and take control of the bodies and souls of other gods."

"That's messed up," Jessie says.

"And every Mother Goddess has special powers?" I ask, trying to wrap my mind around this.

"They have the potential to learn these powers, but for most, it takes centuries, maybe millennia, of being Ascended to discover and master them. The majority of the Agelings, and even many of the Elder Gods, are not aware of their powers. Within our mythology, there are stories that say you, Gaia, were the first Ascended goddess to master these powers. You were the one who opened Pandora's box and let the Ascended flourish. Of course, this was before you were known as Gaia."

My mind spins. "What do you mean?"

"Gaia is just your most recent incarnation. Further back in your timeline, you were once known as Inanna in Mesopotamia. Many of your names have been completely forgotten by humans. Only the Ascended remember them now. Among us, we say that the legends about Gaia are more numerous than the stars."

This thought makes me feel incredibly small. It's hard to imagine that there were other Gaias, other Ascended versions of me, each with its own unique stories. "I guess I never realized that the Ascended, who are gods, would have their own mythology."

"Is it so surprising?" Čhápa asks, his tone surprisingly pleasant. "Go back and channel one of your earliest Ascended lives. You'll find that it's almost impossible. The memories of past lives fade and grow distant over time." He wipes his brow with a folded handkerchief. "When you have lived thousands of past lives, you have many secrets buried in your history. There's a reason why older lives are harder to channel than more recent ones. They lack familiarity. You could spend a whole existence channeling past lives and still not even scratch the surface of their collective histories." Čhápa turns back to the chalkboard. "But this is off topic. Let us return to the subject of the day. I believe we were discussing the transition from the nomadic lifestyle to one of agriculture. Pacha, give us your thoughts, and I hope you've done the required reading this time."

That evening, the moon shoots shards of blue light through the stained-glass windows. This particular grotto in the Lyceum resembles a primitive church, with its low ceilings of hand-chiseled stone. Judging by the closets filled with equipment, tools, and toilet paper, the room's chief purpose is storage. Despite the room's calming nature and cool air, hot sweat coats my skin and my heart pounds furiously.

A battle of wills rages inside my mind—a sort of tug-of-war between my penultimate life, Amahle Smith, and me.

With all my mental strength, I pull Amahle closer. I'm forcing myself to channel her by dragging the past life toward me. The amazing thing is, it's working.

Snippets of Amahle's past flash in my mind: a PhD student cramming for a final at Oxford, a merry-go-round spinning in Jozi's Brightwater Commons, a springbok staring across an open plain, a dense jungle, and the African sun blazing down.

Despite Amahle's resistance, she edges closer to me. Little by little, our union will be finalized. This time, I will actually do it. I'm going to channel her. Her soul—radiating heat and pulsing with energy—is about to merge with mine.

Just as I think I have control over Amahle, it's as if a bungee cord snaps. I'm flung backward, and Amahle rips free from my grasp and retreats behind the wall. After she's gone, I feel as though someone Velcro-ripped every neuron from my brain. I'm left with the painful aftermath—a headache so severe that I collapse to the ground.

There's a long pause, and then Enki says cheerily, "Try one more time, but maybe relax a little."

On my hands and knees, depleted of energy, the world spinning in front of me, I stare up at him as if he's asked me to go skinny dipping in Maine in February. "This is the fourth time I've tried to channel her tonight. Why can't we admit it?" I say, rolling onto my back and taking deep, calming breaths. "I can't do it."

"You can," he replies. "You almost did it that time. Have more faith in yourself."

"I knew this would be hard, but I didn't expect it to be this hard." I turn on him, fists clenched. "I wish you could tell me more than to 'have faith in myself' because it's honestly not helping." I didn't intend for my tone to be so harsh, and I feel bad when Enki spins around to hide the hurt on his face. He crosses the room to grab a water bottle, and I get up and follow him. "Listen, I'm sorry. I didn't mean to snap. I'm frustrated with myself. I suck at this, and I'm afraid."

When he turns around, there's a mix of tenderness and pain in his expression. "I'm trying to help you," he says, taking a drink of water.

"Listen," I say, clutching my shoulders, "the Lyceum isn't what I expected. I thought I'd find a place that was loving, kind, and accepting, not a situation where I'd be put to death if I didn't succeed. It feels like there's a mountain of stress on my chest."

He avoids my eyes. "I agree. The Lyceum is a messed-up place. Somewhere along the line, the Elder Gods decided that the ethos of the Mother Goddesses just didn't cut it against the sheer brutality of the Father Gods. But you shouldn't blame me. My life is as much on the line as yours."

My heart sinks. I really didn't mean to hurt him. "Why don't we take a break?" I say, walking to one of the closets and scanning the shelves. Lightbulbs, batteries, some weird goggles. "Where are you?" I say to myself.

"What are you looking for?"

"Tylenol," I reply, rubbing my temples.

"Top shelf."

"Bingo." I take down a box. "You know," I say, struggling with the lid. "It's a little weird calling you Enki since it's probably not your real name—unless your parents were some serious nonconformists."

He leans against the wall, eyeing me with a hesitant grin. "Chris Lonegon is my birth name."

"I never pegged you as a Christopher."

"That's because it was always Chris."

"Gotcha," I say, finally popping open the bottle. I dump a few pills into my hand. "What a humble name for someone who would become a god."

"Ha! Says the Great Gaia."

I roll my eyes. "Eh, don't get me started. Do you mind?" I ask, pointing at his water bottle.

"Sure," he says, tossing it to me.

"Where did you grow up, Chris Lonegon?"

"Long Island."

I gag on the water in my mouth. "No!" I say, coughing. "Really."

"Hey, step off your pedestal, princess," he replies proudly. "Long Island has great diners, awesome beaches, and Billy Joel. What else do you need?"

"Lesson learned," I reply, holding up my hands in mock surrender. "Long Island is a cool place."

"*Cool* doesn't even begin to describe it."

"I can't tell if you're being sarcastic."

"Maybe a smidge. Come on, it's Long Island, after all."

There's something refreshing about Enki. He doesn't have that arrogance and superiority complex that I've encountered in other Ascended gods. As I sit down on the floor, back against the cool stone, Enki stands across from me, arms crossed, wearing a sly grin—much better than the sad-puppy-dog expression he had before. "Do you have a family?" I ask.

"Yeah, of course I have a family. What do you think? I popped out of a vending machine?"

"Excuse me for not making an assumption. I can never tell with Ascended gods. Having a 'normal' upbringing is rare."

"Well, if you're looking for normal, I'm as close as you'll get," he replies, pointing his thumbs at his chest. "Married parents, older sister, house in the burbs, middle class through and through. I'm practically a statistic."

"What does your all-American family think about you changing your name to Enki and moving to the desert?"

"Ha! I told them that I'm at graduate school." He pauses and his eyes shift, exposing a crack in the joker facade. "I actually haven't told them the truth."

"Oh, what a surprise!"

He paces the room, smiling nervously. "They wouldn't believe it. Here's the thing. I fell into this world. I mean, for years, I knew there was something different about me. About two years ago, my ex-girlfriend got me a psychic reading as a gag birthday gift, but the psychic turned out to be a Mother Goddess priestess. That's when my entire world changed. She told me I was special—that I was a god. Isn't that what every twenty-two-year-old wants to hear? One thing led to another and I arrived here."

"What a wild trip," I say, feeling a strange jealousy.

"I told my family that I got a scholarship to go to graduate school. Now I'm supposedly getting my PhD, but I feel bad because I haven't visited them in years."

"Do you miss them?"

"Yeah, at times I do, but my perspective has shifted so much since I Ascended. Knowing that I've lived so many past lives and have had so many families has changed my view of relationships. Do you get what I'm saying?"

"Kind of," I reply, refusing to admit that for the past two years, I've worked hard not to acknowledge that change. Enki's story has parallels to my own. We're the same age, and we Ascended at the same time, but I also feel as if I could have known him growing up. He reminds me of people I knew in college. However, at a certain point, our lives diverged and he lived the life I should have had. He was never hunted by the Father Gods, he never felt the pressure of a prophecy from thousands of years ago, he never felt all alone. I wish I could have had what he experienced.

"What about you?" he asks, shaking me out of my head. "Do you have family?"

"No, not anymore. My mom passed away a year ago from cancer."

"I'm sorry to hear that."

"It's OK." A gash in my heart reopens, but I push back the raw feelings that threaten to overwhelm me. "I still miss her."

He stares into my eyes. "I used to be like you."

"How so?"

"When I first arrived at the Lyceum, I couldn't channel. I couldn't do things they wanted. My life was on the line, and I was scared."

I'm taken aback. "What changed?"

"Someone reminded me that true power comes from within." He sits down across from me, legs crossed. "You're having a crisis of confidence. You think that because you couldn't do it in the past, you can't do it now."

"Yeah, that more or less sums it up," I reply, finally feeling the pain-killers sooth the rager in my head.

"Maybe we're approaching this the wrong way," he says, face earnest.

"Oh yeah?" I shoot back. "What's the right way?"

He shrugs. "I don't know, but me and the other teachers telling you what to do doesn't seem to be working."

An idea pops into my head. "You know what, you're right. I've always hated people telling me what I can and can't do, so I'm going to try something different. I'm going to close my eyes and open my mind. I'm not going to channel any past life. I'm going to open my mind up to the possibility of channeling. Let whatever happens happen. If I channel, great. If I don't, that's fine."

"I like it," he says encouragingly. "Go for it."

"But do you think this will help me to master channeling?"

"This isn't about mastering anything," he reminds me. "You want to get a feel for it, and that means quieting your mind and opening yourself up to new possibilities. It can't hurt."

"Well, it could. What if all my past lives rush into me and my mind spirals out of control?" I ask, remembering the time on the in Hawaii.

"I'll be here," he says, taking my hand. If you look like you're losing control, I'll try to wake you from channeling. Does that sound good?"

I nod and close my eyes and breathe. I wait for a long time, imagining the brick wall in my mind that holds back my past lives. Nothing happens. But instead of giving into the impulse to stop, I continue to wait, keeping my eyes shut and forcing myself to quiet erratic thoughts.

In an instant, a past life escapes from behind the brick wall and rushes into me, and my body jolts with surprise. The channeling occurs naturally, and I'm filled with a deep sense of comfort.

Mattie. It's been too long...

My breath catches as I recognize the voice in my mind. She might be speaking sixteenth-century Castilian, but I'll never forget that voice. It was two years ago that I last channeled Maria Luisa. She was the only past life I could channel. At the time, I didn't have any control, and I was still Descended. After I Ascended, fearing for my sanity, I put up the brick wall in my mind, blocking off her and the rest of my past lives. When I constructed that wall, I lost my ability to channel her.

In truth, I've missed her. She's like an old friend I haven't talked to in ages.

"Maria Luisa. How are you?" I ask in Castilian but without speaking, immediately realizing how ridiculous this question is. Maria Luisa has been dead for almost four hundred years.

I have been as I always have been. I've missed our chats...

"Me too." For a while, she was the only one I talked with. It's weird to think that I had these conversations that took place all inside my head.

You've been having troubles...

"I can't channel."

You still fear us, don't you?

Maria Luisa has always been better at knowing the truth about me than I. "I do."

We are not here to harm you...

"I'm not sure about that. Every time I channel, it's like my mind is being invaded. I'm so scared of what I'll do. I don't want to hurt someone."

It is not our intention to cause pain . . .

"I don't like the idea of someone else controlling me."

Sometimes, in a relationship, giving up control is a good thing, like allowing someone to help you, or . . . to love you . . .

A painful spike of memory drives through me. It wasn't right to give Jared all those mixed messages. I should have told him about the prophecy earlier instead of running away and trying to protect him. Maybe if I had been honest with him in the beginning, he wouldn't have left me.

When you give yourself up, you can also set yourself free. Do you remember when you channeled me? We merged. We became one . . .

"But Maria Luisa, you're different."

Yes, Mattie, we are all different yet we are all the same . . .

"I don't need more riddles. I need answers. My life is on the line."

Mattie, if you were in a relationship with someone, would you force them to do anything?

"No."

Treat your past lives not as tools but as you treat me. If you show respect, they will respect you . . .

"It's not that simple."

I believe in you, and remember, I'll always be here . . .

She slips away, and I'm by myself again. When I open my eyes, Enki is staring at me with a fat grin. "Did you do it?"

"Yeah," I reply, a little pleased with myself.

He walks over to me. "You totally just channeled a past life—and you're still alive."

"I had a chat with an old friend, but it still wasn't my penultimate life."

"It doesn't matter. Take your successes when you get them. Good job, tiger." He throws an arm around my shoulder.

"Stop making me feel so good," I say with a smile. I avoid his eyes and brush my hair out of my face.

"You deserve it."

Our eyes meet, and a pleasant chill cascades across my skin. His lips seem redder than usual. My heartbeats pound loudly. Although I don't want to acknowledge it, I like the way his skin feels against mine. Enki makes me feel valued and important, the same way that Jared makes me feel, but the thought of Jared sends my mind tumbling into confusion.

Suddenly a bright light illuminates the room. I step back as one of the Lyceum's Protectors shines a flashlight at us. "Have you received permission to train after hours?"

Enki drops his arm from my shoulders. "Well, not exactly."

"Then return to your quarters," the Protector replies tersely, not leaving the room.

"I need to sleep," I blurt out to Enki, then hastily add, "I'll see you tomorrow." I rush out of the room.

When I'm outside the grotto, emotions bombard me like meteors. Was I just flirting with Enki? This thought fills me with unexpected excitement tempered by a shadow of dread. What about Jared?

CHAPTER FIFTEEN

CLOUD FEATHER

The tension in the bow is ready to explode. As I hold the nocked arrow, the string digs into my fingers. Ten meters down the field stands a withered, dead tree, with a target taped to it—a paper-cut-out figure with a red bull's-eye over its heart.

We're supposed to channel our past lives to practice with weapons. The reasoning is that our past lives may have mastered these tools, but our current bodies have not. Muscle memory is lost, and part of our training includes giving past lives the opportunity to practice. But since I'm still afraid of channeling, I've found that the archery classes I took at summer camp when I was thirteen have finally become useful.

I push the air from my lungs until I can hear my heartbeat and then let the arrow fly. It soars down the field and slams into the target, missing the bull's-eye by a few inches.

"Ugh." My shoulders slump.

"Nice shot," says Seuku. Unlike most of the Agelings, who so far have either ignored or showed disdain toward me, Seuku has been incredibly helpful. Whenever I've had questions I've been afraid to ask, she's explained things after class. Maybe she feels she owes me or maybe it's pity. Either way, I've been more than grateful for her help and kindness. Also, her Orca deistic form is still one of the coolest ones I've ever seen.

"I missed," I reply.

"But not by a lot."

"A miss is still a miss."

She studies the comfortable way I hold the bow. "What past life are you channeling?"

"One of the old ones," I say quickly.

"Hmm, maybe try holding it like this," she suggests, and then proceeds to give me a few helpful pointers.

"You're getting the hang of it," Seuku says, after observing a few more of my shots. "Let me know if you want to practice with the short spear."

"Sure. I'll do that," I say, as she turns away to pick up her own bow.

So far, I've been able to avoid many of the more dangerous implements of death. I'm praying that I won't spar with another Ageling. If so, I'll be as good as ground beef.

I reach for another arrow and see Coyote critiquing an Ageling who's tossing throwing knives. As if sensing my attention, he turns his stern, uncompromising gaze on me, making the hairs on my arms rise. I turn away quickly. Although I may have convinced Seuku that I'm channeling, I suspect that Coyote knows the truth.

Close by, Jessie walks toward a rack lined with rifles, while Enki and another Ageling spar with swords and shields. Gunshots ring out like Fourth of July fireworks. Although I theoretically understand why it's important to know how to use these weapons, in my core, this training bothers me. Yes, the Mother Goddesses are always being hunted, and they need to be able to defend themselves against the Father Gods, but doesn't the practice of warfare and violence go against the very nature of the Mother Goddesses? Are we any better than the Father Gods?

I nock the arrow, but as I pull it back and aim it at the target, I hear a dull thud. Something rolls up to my foot. I glance down.

A live grenade. Some reptilian survival instinct must kick in because before I have time to think, I'm diving for cover behind a barrier of sandbags.

There's a deafening explosion as soon as I hit the ground. Pieces of shrapnel whizz overhead. Pulse pounding, adrenaline surging, and ears ringing, I can't process what just happened.

If it weren't for the sandbags, I would have been ripped to pieces.

Enki discovers me huddled on the ground, desperate concern crawling at the corners of his eyes. Crouching in front of me, he asks, "Are you hurt? Are you OK?"

A loud ringing drowns out his words and makes him sound as if he's miles away. I shake my head.

"You aren't OK?" he asks, his brow wrinkling.

"No, I mean yes!" I shout over the ringing in my ears.

"You are hurt?"

"No, I'm not hurt, and yes, I'm OK!"

He lets out a huge breath as he reaches toward me with trembling hands. He pulls me to my feet, his expression slack-jawed with disbelief.

"Who threw that?" I ask, no longer shouting. The ringing has diminished to a dull buzz.

Someone screams.

I look to see the other Agelings huddled around something. I push my way to the center of the group and find a guy, maybe seventeen years old, lying flat on the ground. An ugly red bruise throbs on his face. Coyote towers over him, chest heaving and face afire.

"What the hell was that, Pacha?"

The kid whimpers, and his eyes are saucers. He grips a necklace with a small pendant in the shape of a pregnant woman, a symbol of the Mother Goddesses, as if it's a protective talisman. I doubt any object can protect him from Coyote's rage.

"Answer me!" our teacher roars. "Why did you throw a live grenade at another Ageling?"

"I—I—I—"

"Speak!"

Both relief and fear freeze me in place, as I rub my sore elbows. Coyote is defending me, which should make me feel good, yet, having been the target of his anger in the past, I know that his fury isn't fair. He's the very opposite of what makes a good teacher.

"I didn't know it was live," he replies, cupping his hands around the necklace. "I thought it was a dummy. I swear."

"Why would you throw a grenade—dummy or live—at another Ageling?"

Tears stream from Pacha's eyes. He scans the group until he finds Daichsun. Is he looking for help? Daichsun stares back with an unnerving blank expression. Next to him is Jessie, who looks as if she's watching a fight on reality television.

"I didn't mean to hurt her," Pacha replies, turning back to Coyote. "I thought it would be a joke. You know, to scare her."

A shudder runs through me.

"To scare her?" Coyote asks, shaking his head. There's a moment when it appears he's accepted this response.

But then, to my horror, he grabs the boy and lifts him off the ground. Pacha's feet dangle helplessly. "You idiot!" Coyote flings him to the side, and he crashes into the dust. "Let me give you a lesson about jokes." Coyote's fists rain down on Pacha, who curls into a ball.

I crumple forward, my stomach cramping. For some reason, it feels as if I'm the one receiving the beating. This level of violence makes me sick.

After delivering several vicious strikes, Coyote drives the toe of his boot into the boy's back. "Do you find this funny?"

Pacha spits up blood. The beating doesn't cease. Instead, it intensifies. The situation is quickly spinning out of control, and someone needs to stop it. Coyote can't get away with this. He's our teacher, yet at this moment, he might as well be a thug.

I glance around and spot Enki, staring on like a statue with the other Agelings. His expression is painted with fear. His eyes meet mine. Silently they scream a warning against an impulse building inside me.

"You're a waste of a life!" Coyote yells. "You waste my time and the Lyceum's."

Pacha wraps his arms over his head, trying to protect himself from the brutal attack, but Coyote's assault doesn't abate. "You'll take this lesson to the grave."

The threat rings like a siren as I remember Coyote's threat against my own life. He has no issue killing Agelings so they can Ascend into younger vessels.

Coyote crouches beside the semiconscious-kid and yanks him up by the hair, exposing the white line of his neck. Then he retrieves a short, glistening-sharp knife from his belt and places the blade against Pacha's skin. "In your next life, you'll not forget this failure."

That's when it hits me. He'll kill Pacha, and none of the Agelings will stop him.

In less than a week's time, I could have a knife at my own throat. At that moment, wouldn't I want someone to stand up for me?

I can't allow this. Coyote has no right to decide who lives and who dies.

Rushing forward, I tackle him. I must have caught him off-balance because despite his tank-like build, he goes tumbling to the ground, the knife slipping out of his hand.

For a moment he just stares at me stunned, but his mad-dog rage quickly replaces the surprise. What the hell did I do?

"How dare you!" Coyote says, rising and dusting off his pants.

My hands shake, but I meet his eyes. "You were going to murder him."

"What's it to you?" Coyote asks, lips curling back. "You could have died because of his actions."

My heart pounds. I feel my hands start to go numb. While I acknowledge that I could have died, I'm willing to forgive Pacha if it means saving his life. "He said it was a mistake."

"Would you feel the same way if the grenade had torn you apart?"

"I'm here now and that's all that matters. He doesn't deserve to die for a mistake."

"I'm teaching him not to make mistakes and prevent future ones."

"You shouldn't be threatening him—and certainly not beating him," I retort. "You're supposed to be our teacher, not our enemy."

Coyote's mouth falls open. I wonder if any student has ever challenged him. "I won't rationalize my methods to you. You're an Ageling who has no mastery of her skills."

"Fine, I'm helpless, but the teacher is as much to blame as the student. Fear only teaches us to be afraid."

"I instill fear because I know the dangers that you'll face when you leave the Lyceum. The only way for you to be prepared for those dangers is to confront them now."

"And you know what? That makes you no better than the Father Gods."

There are several gasps in the tight circle that has formed around us. I glance to the side at Enki, who is shaking his head and mouthing no. Nearby, Jessie wears an equally apprehensive look.

When I look back at Coyote, his face has lost its color. "Mind your tongue or I'll cut it out. You have no right to disrespect me when your own position is so fragile."

"Mother Goddesses are supposed to be the torchbearers for love, respect and kindness," I say, my hands clenched into fists. "Yet you fail to demonstrate any of these qualities."

"You test my patience," he warns. "Be wary, or I'll make you pay a far steeper price."

I know I should shut up but I can't. The dam is overflowing and there's no stopping my anger and frustration. With everything that's happened over the last few days—the threats against my life, my fear of channeling, Jared leaving—it feels as if I have nothing else to lose. "What price? You were planning to kill me in the end no matter what." I raise my chin, challenging him. "You're a coward and you're weak. You use fear as a substitute for courage. You're a role model for what we shouldn't become. You disgust me. I'm at least attempting to be a good person. You pawned off your soul for greater evils long ago. You're a wretched excuse for a god."

He moves faster than I thought possible; I don't have time to react. He sweeps me off my feet, and I crash into the ground. His body pins my arms, and I can't move. The knife that was on Pacha now presses against my throat.

A vein pulses madly on his flushed forehead. I gulp dry air. I pushed him too far. I backed him into a corner, and now, in order to not lose face, he has to retaliate. He has to prove that he's in charge.

In other words, I screwed myself.

"Gaia," he says, voice calm and friendly. The knife digs into my skin. Wrath billows in his eyes like smoke from a forest fire. "You're right."

I let out a ragged breath. "What do you mean?"

"I've treated you disrespectfully," he continues, his tone humble. "As a way to atone for my errors, I'll give you the opportunity you desire."

The sudden change in his voice, the swing from anger to joviality, does little to dispel the butterflies flocking in my stomach. But then he removes the knife from my neck and climbs off me. To my shock, he offers me his hand.

Despite my trembling arms, I grab it, and he pulls me up. In response to my confused expression, he smiles—a mean, canine smile—and walks over to Pacha, whose eyes stare out from a bruised and swollen face.

Coyote pulls the boy from the ground and drags him to the shooting range. "Go Ageling!" he says, giving him a rough push. "Keep walking until I tell you to stop."

Pacha doesn't move. His knees quake. His eyes are wide.

I clasp my hands in front of me to stop them from shaking. Blood pounds in my head as an overwhelming sense of foreboding freezes me in place as well. What is Coyote planning?

Coyote raises his knife as if to throw it. "Go now, or I'll put you down like the dog you are."

More tears fall from Pacha's eyes. With hesitant, herky-jerky movements, he turns and limps down the field, his body convulsing with sobs. He's walked fifty yards when Coyote shouts, "Stop! Stand in front of the target."

Shaking. Pacha obeys and places himself in front of the cut-out target.

My heart thumps like bass notes; I don't like where this is headed.

Silence stretches out like the moment before a classroom fight.

"Take off your necklace," Coyote shouts, "and hold it directly above your head."

A sick feeling oozes through my body. I know what will happen next.

Pacha does as he's told.

Coyote turns and walks to a table lined with rifles. His fingers dance along the stocks of the guns. Finally, his face flashing cruelty, he grasps one of the rifles and removes the scope. He returns to me and commands, "Stick out your hands."

My mouth is as dry as sand as the heavy rifle falls into my sweating palms.

"The challenge is simple," Coyote explains. "You must channel a past life and shoot the pendant. If you succeed, you will stay at the Lyceum and continue under my tutelage. However, if you shoot Pacha in the head, I will petition the Elder Gods to pardon you, and you may leave the Lyceum without consequence. You will get the freedom you desire." He smiles. "The choice is yours."

"Wh-wh-why are you doing this to me?" I ask.

"If you shoot the pendant, I'll know you can overcome your fear of channeling. However, if you kill Pacha, I'll know that you fear your past lives more than you care about saving the life of another."

Biting my lip, I flit my gaze from the rifle to Pacha. I've never channeled a past life that can shoot a gun before. He's pitting my fears against each other. What do I fear more—channeling a past life or the guilt that will come with murdering Pacha?

"What happens if I miss the pendant or hit Pacha anywhere but the head?" I ask, my voice trembling.

Coyote unholsters the revolver at his hip, thumbs back the hammer, and aims the barrel at my head. "I'll blow out your brains and Pacha's," he replies with unnerving determination. "If you miss both, I'll know you can not make a choice. I'll know that your greatest fear and weakness is yourself. In which case, it will be time to Ascend you into a vessel who will be able to master their fears."

My stomach churns. "This isn't fair."

"No, it is fair. Now you'll learn why I teach you to be afraid. Fear is important because it forces you to make choices. Some people try to live their whole lives without being afraid, and these people achieve nothing. You are a god. Every choice you make has a consequence, which carries its own fears. By finally confronting your fears, you'll master them instead of them mastering you."

I gulp, forcing down the lump in my throat. He knows that I can't shoot a rifle to save my life. Literally. I'll have to channel a past life to shoot the pendent.

But I have to try. My hands shake as I clench the gun. As I raise it to my shoulder, the weapon bounces with my nervous energy.

I'm way too scared to do this. How will I live with myself knowing that I murdered him?

I stare down the barrel of the gun. Nothing but a glittering spot, the pendant dangles on a thin gold chain, a mere inch above Pacha's head.

How am I supposed to shoot it? All I can focus on is Pacha's terror-filled face.

I take a deep breath but nothing can stop the shakes racking my body. To my distress, the barrel swivels and jumps. The barrel of Coyote's gun quivers next to my head. His finger is tight on the trigger—waiting for the opportunity to end me.

"Pacha's a dead man," says one of the Agelings.

"No, Gaia's going to her grave," says a voice I recognize as Daichsun.

"You can do it, Mattie," I hear Jessie say. Her voice provides a touch of comfort.

What's my best option? Shoot the pendant and I'm still a prisoner at the Lyceum. Kill Pacha and live with his death on my conscience. Miss both and we're both dead.

There's only one option.

Shoot the pendant.

After what feels like several minutes, I finally steady the gun. I think I've lined up the pendant in my sight, but I really can't be sure. I briefly consider channeling a past life, but quickly dismiss the idea, fearing that it would only make the situation worse.

I squeeze the trigger, knowing full well that I'll miss, but right when I steady myself for the kick of the gun, someone yells, "Wait!"

I startle and release a shaky breath. I turn to the source of the voice, lower the gun, and mouth, "What are you doing?"

Enki just nods at me then turns toward Coyote. "I'll take Pacha's place."

My jaw drops. "No," I say under my breath. This can't be happening.

Coyote raises an eyebrow and shakes his head. "You will do no such thing. You are one of my most promising Agelings. I'll not lose you so easily."

"Master Coyote, I insist," Enki says, standing taller, with a confident glimmer in his eyes. "I believe in Gaia and her powers. I'm willing to risk my life for her."

Coyote crosses his arms, but his eyes spark with curiosity. "Do you have a death wish?"

"No, sir. I insist that I'll be fine."

Coyote studies him for a few seconds. "It's your life," he says with a dismissive nod. "You may take Pacha's place. Although you are promising, I always prefer to mold Younglings. They're faster learners. Go and prepare yourself to be reborn."

I grab Enki by the arm and pull him back. "Don't be an idiot."

He doesn't waver. "Calm your breathing and concentrate. Channel one of your past lives. You'll do fine."

"I'll kill you. Don't do this. I might die, but you can still live."

"I trust you. Now it's time you trust yourself." He's about to turn away but adds, "Remember to breathe."

Enki jogs down the field, and after the two exchange a few words, Pacha comes limping back to us. Enki raises the necklace over his head.

"Get this over with. I've wasted enough time," Coyote says, aiming his gun at my head once again. "Shoot the pendant, kill Enki, or miss and die. It's your choice."

Jessie comes up to me and whispers in my ear. "You can do this. Just concentrate."

I beg to differ, but nonetheless, I raise the gun again, my hands shaking. The barrel of the gun jumps around, and my pulse pounds like the pistons of an engine. My body is soaked in sweat.

I can't mess up. I have only one chance. If I screw up, there will be death. I close my eyes and take a deep breath. Clear your mind, I tell myself. I focus on nothing. The moment when my mind becomes completely blank, the world freezes. Time slows and stops. Something warm and glowing slides into me. My vision clouds, brightens and in an instant, I'm transported to somewhere familiar—somewhere that I miss.

Sky the color of water floats above a sweeping plain of golden grass that stretches out flat and endless. Close by, I hear the laughter of my tribe. They're celebrating the success of a good hunt. Prairie Flower's newborn cries for her mother's milk. The smells of boiling meat make my stomach rumble. We will eat well after today's lesson.

"This is how you hold it," I show him, placing my hands along the barrel. "Now you try." Underneath the burning sun, I offer my rifle to Cloud Feather.

He eagerly reaches out to take it but stops short. He shakes his head. "Father, this is not how you shoot your rifle," he replies, as if he is as knowledgeable as one who has gone on his vision quest. "I must practice shooting on top of Brown Butterfly."

Pride blossoms in me, and I ruffle his hair. "Do you remember when I taught you to ride? I didn't put you on a stallion your first time. You started on a pony. It is the same for shooting. You must learn to shoot like this before riding."

"But when I'm a warrior, I will never leave my mount."

"When you are a warrior?" I ask, surprised by the confidence in his voice. "You haven't even hunted your first buffalo." This fact does little to dissipate the all-knowing stare in his eyes. "Tell me this, my great warrior son—what happens if you should fall from Brown Butterfly in battle? What would you do then?"

He scoffs. "I would never fall."

I let out a sharp laugh. "Yes, I suppose you wouldn't, but in case you do, pick up the rifle and practice as I tell you."

He lifts the rifle, which is wrapped in buffalo hide and studded with beads. How many times have I carried this weapon into battle, into hunts? Cloud Feather smiles. "It's heavier than I thought."

"Yes, it's not like a bow," I explain, remembering the first time my father handed me his musket and taught me how to shoot. It's been five winters since he fell to the taibo's disease. I shake away the memory. It will only bring sadness. "Over time, the rifle will become like a piece of your body, but for now, feel its weight. Get accustomed to its energy. If you trust it, it will trust you."

"Is this how you shoot it?" he asks, raising the gun to his shoulder, finger on the trigger, too ready to fire.

"No, not so fast. First lie on your belly like a snake."

He looks confused but does so nonetheless.

I join him on the dry ground and stare at the fallen tree at the edge of the muddy stream.

"You see the hollow in the tree? Aim at that using the dovetails at the end of the barrel."

He glances at me. "Red Elk says his father doesn't need the dovetails. He filed them off."

"And Red Elk's father can't hit the broadside of a buffalo from an arm's length away," I reply. "The taibo, despite their tyranny, are clever. They use the dovetails to find their targets. We should always learn from our enemies."

Cloud Feather nods and aims the gun, staring down the barrel.

"Now take a deep breath."

My son breathes in deeply, the way I remembered doing when I was his age, the same way my father did, and my grandfather before him.

"Gently exhale."

He lets out a long breath.

"When your chest is empty, pause, then press the trigger softly." I hear the slow hiss of air, the quiet before a dust storm, the moment right before the herd stampedes.

The gun's blast jolts me to the present.

My eyes open. I'm no longer on the Great Plains. I'm back at the Lyceum.

A horrible fear rattles through me as I stare down the shooting field. The eggy stink of discharged powder chokes my breathing. Ears ringing, I steel myself for the worst.

But then I see Enki walking toward me smiling and holding the necklace, the pendent broken apart.

I cry out with joy.

"Well done, Gaia," Coyote says, voice low and threatening. "I expect you to no longer fear your past lives."

Jessie wraps her arms around me, kissing my cheek. It feels like a boulder has been lifted off me.

But my celebratory mood dampens when I remember that before the grenade fell, Pacha was practicing with his partner, Daichsun. First there was the cut rope during the obstacle course, now the grenade. There is only one conclusion. Daichsun wants me dead.

CHAPTER SIXTEEN

REVELATIONS

*C*olumns of white marble rise over me like mighty trees. Down long, straight corridors, tall wooden shelves branch out in all directions. On each shelf lie thousands of yellowing rolled parchments representing the sum of human knowledge. I am but an insect, small and insignificant, crawling along a forest floor when compared to their majesty.

As I circle, gazing in awe, I'm met by head librarian Petronius Tulius's disapproving glare. He stares at me from the balcony, reminding me of my task and my tenuous nature at the library. Women are held under greater scrutiny than men here, especially those not of Roman blood.

"The library is not a place for idleness" he would have no doubt reminded me if he were closer.

Quickly locating the correct shelf, I reach out for Poetics, noting the ink smudges on my hand. I will have to allow extra time for washing before dinner, if I even make it in time, but I suspect my excitement for Aristotle will overshadow my hunger.

I take out the scroll, handling it as if it were a newborn. I fear the remote possibility of tearing the paper on an errant nail not flush with the wood.

With the scroll clutched to my chest, I rush back to my desk, passing old men, their voices rising with the intensity of debate. Behind them are row upon row of young men and women stooped forward, eyes dancing along the words of prophets, poets, and playwrights.

As I proceed down the row, soft skin briefly caresses my own. I stop, surprised, and find Fausta's secret smile. My breath catches and my cheeks flush as I smell the faint aroma of bath oils wafting off her skin. Lips parted, she leaves no doubt in my mind what she desires.

But this is not the time nor place for flirtation. Turning away, I walk past her, hoping that none saw our exchange. I don't need any more rumors against my character.

Yet . . .

Just maybe, if I do not stay up too late with Aristotle, I will visit her room tonight.

The thought burns its way through me.

I get to my desk, lay the scroll of Aristotle across it, and force myself to read the words, but my mind is running with the possibility of meeting Fausta. In my distraction, I look out a nearby window and marvel at white stone buildings sprawling far into the distance, where the blue sea demarcates the city's edge. The magnificent lighthouse soars one hundred feet over the ocean. High on its peak, a reflective mirror beams over the horizon.

I have work to do, but what about Fausta? No, now is the time for scholarship. I must continue my studies, I think, as my eyes return to the scroll.

The brightness dims. I'm sitting cross-legged in the grotto. I feel sweat drip off my brow as the past life slips beyond the wall in my mind. Through my bleary vision, I see Enki smile. "You did it again," he exclaims. "You're killing it tonight."

"Call it luck," I reply, though I can't deny that I'm doing better than I expected. This is the third time I channeled a past life tonight. I still haven't successfully channeled Amahle Smith, my penultimate life, but I've channeled snippets of other past lives including a French woman from the eighteenth century and the meditations of a sixteenth century Shaolin monk. The vision of the young woman in Alexandria was the oldest life besides Gaia I've channeled.

"Luck has nothing to do with it," Enki says, as he stands up to stretch, "You're getting the hang of it."

I unfurl myself from the lotus position and take his proffered hand. "It's been a lot easier." Something is different tonight. After the incident on the shooting range earlier today, I'm more confident. "But I still can't control which past life to channel. That's a problem."

Enki shakes his head. "Don't worry. You'll learn in time."

"But I don't have time. I only have two more days," I reply, old fears re-emerging. "Also, I can't channel for any significant amount of time. I remember a memory or two, and then they're gone."

"Hmm," he muses, retrieving a water bottle from his duffel bag. "Maybe you're having trouble concentrating. Is there anything on your mind?"

I stare at him. "Yes, there is something," I say, turning away.

"Well, what is it?" he asks, oblivious.

"You shouldn't have done that to me."

"I'm confused."

"Earlier today, you took Pacha's place. I nearly killed you."

"But you didn't," he replies with a pleased grin. "I knew you wouldn't."

Pangs of frustration reverberate through me. "You might have complete faith in my abilities, but I don't. Do you know how scared I was?"

He waves as if it weren't a big deal that I could have blown a hole right through him. "Fear is part of the learning process—or have you already forgotten Coyote's little speech?"

"Don't joke. I'm serious."

"You channeled a past life, didn't you?" he asks. "That's proof enough that you're improving. Pretty soon you'll be a master."

"Yeah, right."

"Don't roll your eyes at me."

"I'll roll my eyes at whoever I want, thank you very much," I say, smiling.

"You're finally learning."

"No thanks to Coyote. The man is horrible."

I watch as Enki's grin fades to a grimace. He turns away.

"What?" I press. "You don't agree that a man who treats us like disposable garbage bags, is a jerk?"

Enki's eyes dance around the room, avoiding mine. "I agree he isn't a nice person, but that doesn't mean that he isn't well-intentioned."

"No one has a right to be as cruel as he is."

"Listen, all I'm saying is that Coyote has his reasons for acting the way he does."

"He has reasons?" I raise an eyebrow. "Plenty of people in the world have reasons to be assholes but aren't. Ultimately, an individual gets to decide how they act. It's ironic that we're supposed to represent love and compassion and our teacher can't even display these qualities himself."

Enki crosses the room to the window, which looks down on the valley. "Well, considering what happened to him, I don't blame him for the way he acts."

I wait a few seconds, but he doesn't explain. "OK, now you have to tell me. What happened to him?" I join him at the window. Outside, I see the desert shimmering under the moon's blue light.

"You don't know?" he asks, surprised. "I thought you knew. You're Gaia."

"What part of 'I don't know how to channel' do you not understand? Of course I don't know anything about him."

"I'm sorry. Coyote's past is common knowledge, and I assumed you knew as well."

"So what happened to him?"

Enki exhales through his nose loudly, as if expelling some cancerous thought. His eyes survey the desert before he says, "In short, really horrible things. Coyote has probably suffered more than any of the Ascended."

"That doesn't actually make me feel bad for him. In fact, it gives me a bit of comfort."

He ignores my schadenfreude. "It began with the Purging over two thousand years ago."

I remember the flashbacks I've been having of Gaia in ancient Rome.

"You remember when Professor Čhápa told us that certain gods, especially the older ones, have special powers related to being Ascended?" he asks.

"Yeah, like my power to Ascend other gods."

"Exactly. Coyote has some of these powers. Rumors say he can awaken gods stuck in the limbo state, and —"

"He can hide his deistic form."

"Yes, and he mastered that power as well. But other powers we're born with. Much like your power to Ascend other gods, Coyote has something similar. When he dies, Coyote Ascends into the person physically nearest to him. Not only that, but Coyote doesn't need an Ascension ceremony or priests or priestesses. He instantly becomes aware of all his past lives."

I stop and pause to consider this. "That doesn't sound bad. It's better than what happens to other gods. If I were to die, I could end up anywhere on earth, but if I had Coyote's power, I wouldn't have been 'lost' for two thousand years."

"But don't you see?" Enki asks. "It could be a curse."

"Why?"

"Think about it. The Father Gods never had to hunt for him. When they found him during the last Purging, they captured him. After that, they always knew where he'd be."

"I don't get it."

"For hundreds of years, he's been a prisoner and slave to the Father Gods."

"Oh, OK. So when he died—"

"He'd still be a prisoner because he'd Ascend into a nearby person. At least when we die, we can end up anywhere. This is a good thing, especially if you've been imprisoned. Death can be an escape, but Coyote never had that."

"OK," I reply, "that is bad."

Enki shakes his head. "It gets worse. What does it mean to Ascend into the person nearest to you?"

"Well, I guess . . ." A chill goes down my spine as I make the connection. "Family and friends."

"Coyote has Ascended into his friends and family throughout history. It was once normal—part of the way he kept power. But when he was a prisoner, the Father Gods would twist this into torture. They would kill him to watch him Ascend into another family member. Then they'd kill him again. And again. If he ever made friends with cellmates, the same thing would happen. The Father Gods wiped out anyone connected to him many times in history. Think about how twisted that must be for him."

"No wonder he's filled with so much anger." I shake my head, now understanding the true nature of the curse. Always fearing for the ones closest to you. Knowing that one day you could be responsible for their deaths. "He's afraid of getting close to anyone, because if he cares for them—"

"Then there's a chance he may Ascend into them and risk their lives," Enki explains, completing my thought.

"How did he end up at the Lyceum? How did he break the cycle?"

"Up until five hundred years ago, he was a prisoner of the Kings of Spain, a lineage of Father Gods. They kept him as a prisoner, but they weren't careful. The story goes that when he escaped his cell, he used his curse to his advantage. Instead of leaving the prison, he ran to the gunpowder room. He blew up the prison, killing himself and all his captors. When he Ascended again, he was free, and he took passage on a conquistador's expedition to the Americas. There he connected with the Mother Goddesses and took refuge at the Lyceum."

I can't believe I feel sympathy for Coyote, but no one deserves two millennia of fear, pain and torture. His view of the world has been shaped by misery.

"It's getting late," Enki says. "We should call it a night."

"OK." The quiet, unbroken desert landscape—eternal in its presence—gives me some comfort. Hopefully, I'll be able to sleep tonight.

I turn away, but as I do, a flash of light catches my eye.

My gaze returns to the desert. What was that? I strain my eyes, but the scene is bathed in shadows. I'm about to chalk it up to exhaustion when the light flashes again.

All is still. Then, for a brief second, moonlight illuminates a lone figure walking into the canyon, and the light flashes again. The only thing I can imagine flashing like that is the metallic tracking bracelet that every Ageling wears.

The person wears dark clothes and stays close to the shadows. I wouldn't have noticed them at all if it weren't for the angle of the room and the half moon.

"Enki, who is that?" I ask.

"What?" he asks, peering out the window. "I don't see anyone."

"There," I say, pointing as the person treks down the trail, away from the Lyceum.

"No, I still don't—oh wait, what was that flash?"

"I think it's a tracking bracelet."

"Yeah."

"Can you see who it is?"

"No, but I can find out." Enki crosses the room, opens a cabinet, and removes a pair of night-vision binoculars. He aims them at the figure. After a few seconds, he says, "It's Daichsun."

A ball of shock rolls inside my stomach. I take the binoculars and confirm it's him. "What's he doing?"

"He's following a path down to the canyon, but other than that I have no idea."

"It's against the rules to be outside the Lyceum at night, right?"

"Yes. Unless you have permission from the Elder Gods."

"What's down there?"

"The canyon follows the course of a dry stream bed for miles. There's nothing down there."

"So there are no towns that way?"

He thinks for a moment. "There are some Neolithic caves from a thousand years ago."

In another thirty feet, Daichsun will disappear from sight. This is my chance. I loop the binoculars around my neck and head for the door. "I'm following him."

"What? Why?"

I pause at the door. "Daichsun has been trying to kill me."

Enki's eyes bulge, and he shakes his head. "No he hasn't."

"Yes, he has. First, there was the rope snapping during the obstacle course. Today, it was the grenade incident. Pacha's partner was Daichsun. I think he convinced Pacha to throw the grenade."

"I know for a fact Daichsun wouldn't do that."

"The man hates me because of something I did to him in a past life. He has all the motivation in the world to get rid of me."

Seemingly at a loss for words, he shakes his head again. "You're acting crazy."

"No, I'm protecting myself, as well as the other students."

"What are you talking about?"

"I think Daichsun is working with the Father Gods. Who better? He is a war god."

"I can't believe you're saying this. I know Daichsun. He was my mentor. He's definitely not working with the Father Gods."

His revelation sends a ripple of surprise through me, but does little to dissuade me from my intention. "OK, fine, prove me wrong—but the only way to do that is to follow him and see why he's leaving the Lyceum at night. Aren't you a little curious to find out what he's up to?"

"I don't know," he says hesitantly.

"OK, stay here, but I'm going," I say, heading out the door of the room. Daichsun is planning something, and I'm determined to discover the truth.

Enki follows me out. "We're not supposed to leave. You'll get into trouble."

I shot the pendent. I chose to do something, to not be afraid of my past lives. Now I see that I can continue to be afraid of what will happen to me in two days or I can save myself. "I'd rather take my fate into my own hands instead of waiting for someone else to decide it."

Leaving the stone grotto, I walk down a hallway and find a stone stairwell, which eventually leads to an exit. The cool air makes goose bumps arise on my skin. A minute later, I'm relieved to hear footsteps behind me.

"Don't worry," I say to Enki, as he comes up beside me. "We'll be back before anyone knows we're gone."

Enki gives me a look that says he doesn't believe me. "I'm here to keep you out of trouble."

It doesn't take long to find the trail Daichsun was following. It slopes down along a rocky path. When we've been walking for about ten minutes, the lights of the Lyceum dim behind us.

If it weren't for the half moon, a few faint stars, and the night-vision binoculars, we wouldn't be able to see a thing.

We hike for several hours in silence, except for the occasional curse when I walk into thorn bushes. There's a chilling stillness in the air; a rustle of movement makes me jump.

"Don't worry," says Enki. "It's just the scorpions."

"Great, I feel a lot better now."

Finally, the canyon walls shoot up hundreds of feet on each side of us. I feel small and insignificant.

"This is the cave settlement," Enki says, as we walk under an overhang of rock.

Through the binoculars I spot faint handprints and crude animal paintings on the cave's walls. Incredibly, humans used this place as a home for hundreds of years.

I gaze into the dark, deserted cave, which extends deep into the cliff. Daichsun is not here.

A creeping sensation of failure is running along my skin when a flash of light, farther down the valley catches my eye. It's as if someone turned on a flashlight. "What's that over there?"

Enki frowns. "I don't know. I've never been that far."

Trusting my gut, I continue down the path, leaving the cave settlement behind us.

Thirty minutes later, we come upon a half dozen run-down clapboard buildings. I'm surprised that any of the structures are still standing. They look a hundred years old. We keep to the edge of the settlement, crouching low. "What's this place?"

Enki takes the binoculars. "Looks like an abandoned mining town."

There's a flash of light in one of the buildings. "There," I say, pointing to a small shack one hundred feet away. "That's where he is."

We creep along behind one of the buildings. An eerie energy pervades the space, and my eyes play tricks on me, creating phantom movements among the shadows.

"We can't go in there," Enki says. "He'll see us."

"OK, follow me." We scurry to the side of the building that Daischun is in, and crouch below a window missing its pane. A plank has fallen off the wall, and we peer through the gap.

I exhale as if I've been punched in the stomach. Inside, Daichsun sits at a dusty table across from another person. As my eyes grow accustomed to the low light, my heart stampedes.

The strange man has a dark red aura surrounding him. He's a god. I don't know which one, but it's clear he's no Mother Goddess with his spiked horns, violent-orange skin and a long goat-like beard. A shiver of fear shoots through me.

It's a Father God.

We must have arrived at the end of their talk because less than a minute later Daichsun and the Father God abruptly stand and head for the exit. Enki and I fall flat on our stomachs, hoping that the detritus on the ground will hide our presence. The Father God disappears into the night.

But when Daichsun exits, I accidentally kick a small mound of pebbles, and they cascade across the ground.

Daichsun pauses and turns.

Did he hear us? He takes a step in our direction. I hold my breath; I can't make a sound. His gaze scans over the shadows. In the moonlight, he's terrifying.

He takes another step in our direction.

He's found us.

But right at that moment, a bunch of small shadows scurry from our hiding place toward Daichsun's feet. He jumps back and curses, stamping at the scorpions, and then retreats in the direction of the Lyceum.

I wipe cold sweat away from my eyes. We remain on our stomachs for a few more minutes, silent, waiting. Finally, we both rise.

"That son of a bitch," Enki says, under his breath.

"I told you so."

"That was a Father God," Enki says, disbelief and shock in his voice. "I recognized him."

"Really?"

"Yeah, from Čhápa's class. His name is Whiro—a lord of darkness in Māori mythology. He's rumored to sit on the Ancient Council of Father Gods."

My pulse pounds louder in my head. "Daichsun is the spy. We have to tell the Elders." I turn to walk back up to the Lyceum.

Enki grabs my hand. "What will we say to them?"

"What do you mean?"

"They won't believe there's a spy without proof."

"Proof? Did you not see what happened? Daichsun is a traitor. Meeting with a Father God after curfew should suffice as proof."

"I know, but will this convince the Elders? Daichsun will deny it if we expose him. It'll be our word against his. We need hard proof and catch him in the act."

"What do you suggest we do?"

"We keep an eye on Daichsun and wait."

"No, Enki!" I cry, louder than I intended. I lower my voice. "I don't have time to wait. Now is the moment. The Elders won't dare kill Jessie or me once I expose a traitor."

Enki appears to contemplate that for a moment. "It won't work, but something tells me that I won't convince you otherwise."

"No, because we're in different situations. I need leverage and this is all I have."

"Shh!" Enki says, grabbing my arm and pulling me down. "I hear something."

We crouch motionless. As we stare out at the shadows, Enki's breath on my neck sends chills across my skin. My heart pounds, but it's not from adrenaline or fear. My eyes meet Enki's, and my pulse runs faster. His presence fills me with a strange stew of excitement and fear.

"I don't hear anything," I say, shivering, "and I'm cold."

In the darkness, he wraps an arm around me and pulls me into a warm embrace. More pleasant shivers run across my body as his skin presses against mine.

After a pause, he says, "Mattie, you're not alone. I'm here for you. I will always be here for you, and I'll never give up on you. Whenever you think you're alone, remember that you have me."

To my surprise, he leans toward me, and I find myself mirroring his action. Our lips meet. A jolt of energy flows from my head to the tips of my toes. My skin feels as if it's on fire. His hands run across my back, and my fingers caress the light stubble on his face. The smell of his body only fuels the sudden flame burning hot inside my chest. For the briefest of moments, I think about Jared, but then I push the thought away.

CHAPTER SEVENTEEN

SPECIAL ANNOUNCEMENTS

It's pitch black as we climb the path back to the Lyceum. I can't form any rational thoughts. My mind, giddy and jumpy, repeats over and over the kiss Enki and I shared, trying to decipher its meaning.

At the Lyceum's towering cliffs, we're greeted by a long silence, as if the night has frozen time in place. The back of my neck breaks out into a sweat. "Do you notice anything strange?"

Enki stops and raises a hand. "There's no one around," he replies, gazing up at the empty balconies.

He's right. Even in the nighttime, Protectors are usually posted throughout the Lyceum. My head swivels from shadow to shadow. "Did something happen?"

"Follow me."

Minutes after entering the school, we still don't find anyone. My pulse slams. This can't be good. "Where is everyone?"

We creep down the deserted hallways, and my fear grows with every footstep. Was there an attack? Has Daichsun already betrayed the Lyceum's location to the Father Gods? Is Jessie OK? More and more questions pile up as my anxieties mount.

It's only when we hear the murmuring of voices that my fear deflates.

"Something is happening in the Ascension room," says Enki.

As we get closer to the room where I conducted Jessie's Ascension, the volume of the voices grows louder. Inside, I'm stunned to find every member of the Lyceum—Younglings, Agelings, Elders, Protectors, and priestesses.

"What's happening?"

"Mattie!" I turn and see Jessie waving me over to the far back wall. I rush over, Enki following. "Where have you been?" she asks. "They called an assembly an hour ago. I went to your room, but you weren't there."

Just as I'm about to reply, a gong rings out. The sound reverberates through my body. What is it with these people and gongs? A simple switching on and off of the lights would suffice.

The room falls silent. My stomach feels as if it's filled with snakes, as fear rears its head again.

A few seconds later, Coyote enters the room and stands on a raised platform. He looms over the assembled crowd, his cold eyes scanning us. Then he waves someone forward.

When they join him on the platform, it's as if I'm falling down an empty elevator shaft. Shoulder to shoulder with Coyote stands Jared.

My mind spins, and I'm filled with guilt. Just a little while ago, I was kissing Enki. But a part of my brain reminds me that Jared was the one who chose to leave, after I told him about the prophecy. He had every right to do so, but the pain of that abandonment still stings.

Before I can fully recover from my shock, Coyote says, "Members of the Lyceum. We live in dark times. We have received new reports that the Father Gods are escalating their efforts to eradicate Mother Goddesses." He places his hand on Jared's arm, who stares out, his face a blank slate. "Around the world, Father Gods are hunting us. They are murdering the Mother Goddesses as well as their followers. We cannot stand idle while these killings take place."

The silence in the room is so thick I could swallow it whole.

"Because of this, the Elders have decided to dispatch a portion of the Lyceum's teachers and Protectors to lead a task force that will seek to prevent future killings. Fortunately, because the Younglings do not require as many teachers, their studies will not be impacted. In fact, we have capacity for additional students. However, the unfortunate consequence is that we will no longer have the ability to teach all the Agelings."

He pauses, letting the new reality sink in. Sweat breaks across my skin.

"Therefore, you realize our problem: we have too many Agelings but not enough Younglings. There is only one solution. We must thin the ranks of the Agelings. We must separate the wheat from the chaff."

My stomach roils, and I have an urge to scream.

"At daybreak, we will begin a Pruning. This ancient ritual has not been exercised for almost four millennia. However, there is precedent for its usage in times of great need."

The *Pruning*? He's got to be kidding.

"The Pruning is a series of challenges that will test all the skills we have sought to impart here at the Lyceum ranging from the physical, mental, emotional, and spiritual. The Agelings will be divided into small groups to face the challenges together. The Agelings who pass the Pruning will live, while those who fail will be Ascended into new Younglings."

As in, murdered.

"I am so screwed," I say quietly to myself.

"The Pruning will quicken the process of finding the best, brightest, and most worthy among you," Coyote continues. "Let me emphasize one thing: have no fear. If you are not among the chosen, then your sacrifice will be far greater than any of the rest of us can provide." That self-righteous asshole wouldn't be saying that if it were his life on the line. "If you trust in your past lives, you will know no failure." Coyote bows his head and leaves the stage. The silence remains for a few moments after his departure. Finally, the crowd disperses.

I grab hold onto Jessie's shoulder, a dizzy spell overtaking me. It feels as if my face has turned green; I'm going to be sick.

"This is unexpected," Jessie declares.

"Are you OK?" Enki asks me, concern lacing his voice.

"They were never planning to teach me," I say, realizing why the Elders gave me one week to master my skills. "Their plan was to kill me off the entire time."

"You've come so far over the past few days. You'll survive the Pruning," says Enki.

"I'm not spiritually enlightened enough to believe that. I don't want to die."

"You won't die. You can channel. I've seen it. You're no longer afraid of your past lives."

I close my eyes to steady my breathing. "There's an alternative to the Pruning. The Elders wouldn't dare hurt us if we expose Daichsun as a spy."

"What are you talking about?" Jessie asks.

"We saw him meeting with a Father God."

"Really?"

"Yes, we have to tell the Elder Gods," I say, looking at Enki.

"How will you do it?" Jessie asks.

I pause. "I'll just tell them."

"Do you have evidence of their meeting?"

I shake my head.

"You need proof," she says. "Otherwise, he'll deny it. It'll be your word against his. Also, given that Daichsun is Coyote's prized student, I don't think Coyote will be convinced. In fact, it may leave you in a worse condition."

"This is what I was telling you before," Enki says. "We have to be one-hundred-percent certain about the accusation."

I sigh. "Why is it that only I can see this train wreck? There's a whole lot of evil happening at this school. This isn't what the Mother Goddesses are supposed to represent."

Enki places his hand on my shoulder. "The most important thing is to prepare for tomorrow. Let's get some sleep."

"Hi, Mattie." The voice is like a lightning bolt running through me. I rock on my heels, barely able to stay on my feet. A sharp stab of guilt cuts me again, yet why should I feel bad? He was the one who left me. I turn to face Jared. "How are you?" he asks.

My breath escapes, and apparently, I've lost the ability to speak. It's hard to say whether the strong feelings I have for him deep inside equate to love. But I do know that a few days can't erase all the things, memories, and experiences that we've shared.

Fortunately, Jessie comes to my rescue. "Enki and I are going to sleep," she says. "We'll see you soon." She wraps her arm through Enki's and pulls him away. He reluctantly follows. He looks back, confused, as she guides him out the room.

At first glance, Jared looks the same. But on closer inspection, I notice subtle differences. He's exhausted, judging by the big dark bags under his eyes and crow's feet spreading out along the sides of his face. He wears his usual beat-up jeans and leather jacket, but there are rips in his clothing. There's even a brown bloodstain smirching his shirt. Is that *his* blood?

"You're back," I say, regaining my voice.

"I am."

"I thought I scared you off."

"You did," he confesses. "When you told me about the prophecy, it honestly scared me. You'd never fully expressed how you felt toward me before, and while I was overjoyed that the feeling was mutual, I was shocked to learn that the price of my love would be my life."

His honesty leaves me stunned. Finally, no more games. All the cards have been thrown onto the table. "Yet you still left me," I reply, crossing my arms.

"I know, and I regret that I did."

"What changed?"

His eyes find mine. "The Elders sent me on a mission to prevent an attack on priestesses. Unfortunately, I was too late." He closes his eyes, and pain spreads across his face. "They were murdered."

"Oh Jared." I reach out and take his hand. "I'm sorry to hear that."

"Wh-when I saw them, it reminded me of my mother and what the Father Gods did to her." Gertrude, his mother, was one of the priestesses who found and recognized me before I Ascended. She paid with her life for helping me. "And I realized that my life was a small price to pay for being with you." He squeezes my hand and pulls me toward him. "I came back because I'm fully committed to you. I accept the prophecy. It doesn't change a thing. If I die, so be it. I want to be in your life, and I don't want to ever leave you, and I promise to always be honest with you. That's why I want to tell you something. Something you should have known since the beginning." He pauses, closes his eyes, takes a deep breath, and opens them. "I l— "

"Wait," I say, interrupting him. "I have something to tell you first." His confession has sent shock waves through me. I try to collect my thoughts and pull myself together, but I'm feeling a crashing sea of conflicting feelings. His words should make me feel happy, but instead, I feel only sadness. That's when I realize the truth. Something has changed. "I want you to know that I never considered your life a small price. It was a huge burden on my conscience." I turn away, avoiding his eyes, and add, "When you left me, it felt like you abandoned me at the time I needed you the most. I know you didn't think you were leaving for good, but for me, because of the challenges I was facing, it felt like you did. You have to understand that the threats against my life haven't decreased over the past few days—they've multiplied. I couldn't stay preoccupied with you. I had to focus on myself and overcoming my issues. Because of this, even though it's only been a few days, I don't know if I still feel the same way I did about you."

His hopeful expression withers to a frown. "What?" he asks flatly.

"Jared, I'm sorry. I appreciate your honesty, but right now, I'm too confused about how I should feel. I can't fully accept you. I can't reciprocate the feelings you have for me. The most important thing, the thing I need to concentrate on right now, is the next challenge ahead of me because it's life or death. Your feelings toward me and mine toward you mean nothing if I'm dead by tomorrow." I drop his hand and turn to leave. "If I survive the Pruning, then we can figure out our relationship."

"Mattie, wait," he says, voice on edge. "Don't leave me in limbo like this."

I pause, forcing myself to acknowledge the sadness in his eyes. "I have to go, Jared. I need rest if I'm going to live another day." I spin around, ready to run from the room and the discord sowed deep within me.

But he grabs my hand and yanks me back. "Wait!" he shouts desperately.

At that moment, Enki appears and shoves Jared, who stumbles backward looking stunned.

"Let go of her!" Enki warns, standing tall, his muscles tensed. "She doesn't want to talk to you."

I cringe. It looks like Jessie wasn't able to keep him away.

Recovering, Jared bunches hands into fists. "Who are you?"

This feels like my worst nightmare. It's as if the rift inside of me has been exposed to full light.

"I could ask the same of you," Enki shoots back.

This is getting out of control fast. One thing is certain: nothing will be gained by their attacking each other. I place myself between them. "Everyone chill out. Jared, this is Enki. Enki meet Jared. Please be nice." Neither one appears in any way ready to be buddy-buddy. "Jared, is there something more you'd like to say to me?"

"Yes," he says, his voice coming out tight from between his bared teeth.

"OK. What?"

Jared stays silent, his eyes shooting death beams at Enki.

"Come on," I push, growing impatient.

He turns to me reluctantly. "The information is sensitive."

I exhale, trying to calm my thumping heart. "Enki, will you give us some privacy?"

"First, tell me who he is."

"He was my Protector."

"Still am your Protector," Jared interjects.

They stare at each other for several awkward seconds—two peacocks fluffing their feathers.

A grimace of anger crosses Enki's face, but he acquiesces. "I'll be training in the practice room."

When Enki is gone, Jared says, "Your friend has attitude problems."

"Speak for yourself." I'm so confused. I wish I knew how to handle this situation. I would love to fully accept Jared into my life, and a few days ago, I would have done so without hesitation. But I can't deny my ambivalence. "What do you have to say?"

He leans close. "I—I—I—" A shimmer of uncertainty flashes across his face, and the words fail to come.

"What is it?" I ask, trying to coax the truth out of him.

His expression hardens. "You have to be very careful."

"What do you mean?"

"I caught one of the Father Gods' men. He took a cyanide pill before I was able to extract much information, but he told me that there's something major at play. The Shadow is planning something. Something involving you."

"OK," I reply, shaking my head, frustration mounting. "What am I supposed to do about that? How does that change the situation I'm in?"

"It doesn't. I just . . . want you to be prepared."

"Jared,"—I pinch my lips and clench my jaw—"you telling me this, right before the Pruning, just adds another fear to all the others I have. It doesn't help knowing I need to worry about the Shadow having some plan for me."

"Mattie, I'm trying to protect you," he replies defensively.

"Protect me?" I ask, feeling my anger bubble over. "You were the one who brought me here. You put me into harm. Maybe it would be best if you took a break from protecting me? Maybe I'd finally be safe?"

Jared flinches. "If that's what you want, then fine."

"I'm sorry. This is what I tried to tell you before. I don't know what I want. But I do know that I need to focus on surviving tomorrow."

There's a long pause. Finally, he says, "I understand." He peeks down at his watch. "I gotta go. Maybe, I'll see you before I leave the Lyceum, but maybe not." He spins around and leaves.

"Wait, Jared," I say, but he doesn't. He's already gone.

CHAPTER EIGHTEEN

PROPHECIES

*C*amilla plunges a spear into the pirate's chest. The man staggers backward, hands gripping the shaft, eyes wide with shock, and tumbles into the bloody waters.

"Child, it's time to leave," I say.

She looks up, surprised, a faint smile lingering on her lips. To my alarm, I suspect that she might be enjoying this bloodbath. "Why? We've almost defeated all the scum."

I point to the flames engulfing the sail and mast of our trireme as well as that of the pirate's boat. "And your reward for victory will be a charred corpse."

Dropping my sword and shield, I rush to the stern.

"Where will we go?" she asks, following me.

I unstrap my sandals and kick them aside before stepping onto the edge of the boat. "There is a reason why the priestesses threw you into the Tiber's waters as a child. Sink or swim. Now come."

Not waiting for a reply, I dive into the swirling sea, and the cold water blasts away any other thoughts. Camilla comes splashing up beside me a few seconds later with inelegant and awkward strokes. Growing up in Rome, she had little need nor opportunity to swim as if her life depended on it.

The pirates attacked our trireme right before sunrise, when the fog was so thick I could taste it. They invaded our boat like ants escaping a flood, murdering our crew and other passengers, but they clearly underestimated us.

In silence, Camilla and I swim for hours, the dense fog obscuring our vision. The sound of our trireme alighting like kindling is a distant memory. The ocean surrounds us. All I can hear are the cresting waves and Camilla's breathing, which has become labored. I have to slow down for her, as her strokes weaken.

For help, I've channeled a Mycenaean ship captain who spent more time in the water than on land; however, being much younger, Camilla does not have the experience or past lives to assist her.

Her arms strain with each stroke, while her face blooms a deep crimson. "How long are we expected to swim?" she asks, between heavy breaths. She must be nearing the end of her strength, for her pride would never usually allow such an admission of weakness.

"Not much longer," I say, remaining hopeful. "Before the attack, the captain said we were near the island."

"But we can barely see a few feet in front of us. We could be swimming in circles or further out to sea."

"We swim with the waves, which will eventually take us there," I reply, silently damning the horrible fog. If it weren't for the knowledge from my past life, I too would be filled with doubts. I can not let Camilla falter; she's too young to pass on.

"Damn pirate scum," she says through gritted teeth.

"They weren't pirates."

"What?"

While swimming, I've had time to give the matter some thought. "Pirates are neither so well armed nor well trained."

"Who were they?"

"I fear that the Father Gods know of our departure," I explain.

She is silent. Then, with a new tightness in her voice, she says, "Goddess, if I slow you down, feel no hesitation to leave me. Our mission is more important than my life."

I tread water, waiting for her to catch up. My Mycenaean past life assures me land can not be too far off, but Camilla's face is as ashen as the fog around us. She's weaker than I've ever seen her.

"Camilla, you annoy me too much to allow you to drown. I will swim with you on my back if need be."

Her smile is forced yet relieved. "I can manage a bit longer."

"Stay strong. We can't be that far away."

A few minutes later, I hear waves breaking in the distance. The sound is sweet music to my ears.

Land arises suddenly, as if it were always waiting for us. The curling waves break and crash on a sandy beach. The sight fills me with overwhelming relief—mostly for Camilla's sake. I release the ship captain from my channeling and silently thank him as he rejoins the collective.

After we crawl out of the sea, we sprawl on the sand, our soaked robes cold against our skin. The midmorning sun burns away some of the fog, revealing jagged cliffs crawling high above us. Tendrils of mist still waver over the sea's tumultuous green waters.

"This land is different from Rome," Camilla remarks, sitting up and wringing out her robe. She appears rejuvenated. It's amazing how fast the young can recover. Yet, when this ordeal is over, I must remember to include more swimming in her training.

"The Greeks are an old people," I say. "It's fitting that their land is ancient as well." I scan the beach for threats, but our only enemies appear to be the screeching gulls above us.

"How will we be received by the Oracle?"

"There is one way to find out. Come, if my memory serves me correctly, there is a path to his temple farther down the beach."

We follow the thin dirt path upwards, past scraggly olive trees and gray boulders. As we hike, the heat of the day settles over the land like a quilt.

"Goddess," Camilla says as we climb, "if those men who attacked us were sent by the Father Gods, could we be walking into a trap?"

I shake my head. "The Oracle takes no side in our feud. He is a rare god—neither Father nor Mother. His skills and abilities have marked him as something different. He is simply concerned about the future"—I pause—"and his earthly delights."

"What prophecy does the Oracle have for you?"

I let out a sharp laugh and continue up the trail. "Young one, if I had any inkling of this, we would certainly not have traveled all the way from Rome."

"Caishen could have lied."

"No, not if he values his future lives. I would never forget nor forgive such treachery." I pause to catch my breath and stare up at the steep cliff. "I do believe that the Oracle has information for us."

"I never imagined that I would meet him. I always thought he was a rumor." She hesitates. "Would he predict my future?"

I turn to look at Camilla. "Is this something you truly want?"

She shrugs, avoiding my probing stare. "Maybe it would be of some interest."

"It is my belief that ignorance is bliss concerning one's future, especially for the young. It's a burden enough to remember my past. To know my future will be a heavy weight to carry, though it may be a necessary one."

Her silence reveals that she isn't convinced. "Can the Oracle really see into the future? Is such a thing possible?"

A shiver of anxiety runs across my skin. "On occasion, he has been correct. But his prophecies are exceedingly rare and are often so cryptic that it's hard to find the seed of truth within the words. It was almost a thousand years ago when he last predicted the future."

"What was the prophecy?"

"The last Purging," I reply, turning away to hide the pain in my expression. "When the Mother Goddesses turned against the Father Gods."

Camilla must sense the tightness and heartbreak in my voice, as she falls silent. We continue walking, focusing on the rugged path that rises ever higher.

But after a few minutes, she asks, "If the Oracle made a prophecy about you, why weren't you included in its disclosure?"

"We will soon be finding out," I say, pointing to our destination.

It's a cave cleaved out of the side of a mountain. A red light beckons from inside, and the well-trod path goes deep into the cavern. The language of the Ascended, Littian, the first language ever created and the foundation of all other languages—is inscribed along the edge of the entrance. I personally believe it to be too esoteric as a medium for communication.

As we enter the cave, clouds of smoke whirl across my vision. The heavy aromas of incense and fragrant oils fill the steamy room. Through the haze, figures materialize into people. A half dozen couples embrace in all manner of positions. A woman caresses the skin of a fair-haired girl. Next to them, a man mounts a woman as if she is an eager mare. Others writhe and moan, their bare skin illuminated in the light of the flaming torches.

"What is this place?" Camilla asks.

I hold back a scoff. "You're no virgin, Camilla, so don't feign innocence." I signal one of the Oracle's attendants—a girl who is much too young to be here. I am not surprised; the Oracle has always been tempted by younger flesh.

"Take us to him," I say.

The girl hesitates but then notices the jagged-crescent-moon birthmark on my face. Her eyes grow large. She nods and rushes into an adjoining room. We follow her, passing through the feast of flesh.

Camilla stares wide-eyed and maybe a bit curious. "I never knew that bodies could make such combinations."

I repress a smirk. "Supposedly, Ganesha knows of sixty-four such positions."

"Incredible," she replies, her face burning red.

She begrudgingly follows me into the next room, which is filled with smoke. Several young girls, wearing the flimsiest of robes, lounge on pillows, their eyes rolled up in their heads. The Oracle likes to say that the gases seeping from the ground help his attendants to see the future. In reality, he likes that it subdues them and makes them more willing partners for his own desires.

We enter the inner temple, sumptuously decorated with thick rugs, bright pillows, and heavy blankets. Janus reclines, surrounded by his attendants, smoking from a pipe. His deistic form—two heads looking in opposite directions—fades away, revealing a handsome young man with blond hair, blue eyes, and rippling muscles. A thin, unnerving smile breaks on his face. "My, my, Gaia. It has been too long. When was the last time you were here?"

"I believe it was a hundred and fifty years ago."

"That's right." *He sucks on his pipe and then releases a plume of yellow smoke.* "Remind me of what you wanted to know."

My gaze does not waver. "I came to see if the truce would hold between the Father Gods and Mother Goddess."

"Ah, yes. I remember."

"You said peace would reign for thousands of years. Your skills as a future-teller have grown dull. A new Purging sweeps across the land."

He jolts to his feet, eyes flaring. "You simple goddess. I never said such things. My exact words were 'Peace will reign for thousands of years as long as your love stays true.' If you fail to interpret the true meaning of my words, it is your fault and not mine. You are a simpleton for not understanding such truths."

"Hold your tongue!" *Camilla barks, her hand gliding to her side, where her sword would have been.* "Do not dare talk to the goddess in such a way."

"Your Protector needs training like a new pup," *Janus says, his eyes sliding over to Camilla.* "Perhaps you could give her to me. She would make a wonderful addition to my family."

"Be careful, Janus. She is her own woman—a dangerous thing."

He glares at me. "How dare you? You come to my temple to insult and threaten me. I know the fate of the universe." *He snaps his fingers and guards appear from the shadows of the room. They wear heavy armor and carry swords with gleaming edges. Neither Camilla nor I have any weapons, and Janus's guards will not be as easily defeated as pirates and legionaries.*

I pause and don my most obsequious smile. "We began poorly, Janus. Let me beg your pardon. I have come to seek your wisdom."

Camilla's muscles are a bundled mass of energy, and it takes some obvious eye signals on my part to make her bow her head.

The display of fealty has a calming effect on Janus. Nothing gives him greater pleasure than knowing he is superior to others. He settles back onto his pillow throne. "For what reason do you come here?"

"I have been told that a prophecy was given concerning me."

"It is true. I had a vision—a vision of blood. I've seen the future."

My temper explodes. "How dare you reveal a prophecy to others that is intended for me!"

His smile twists into a sneer. "Oh, not just you, Goddess." He runs his fingers along the bare shoulder of one of his attendants. "It was intended for your husband as well. You are a pair, and as your counterpart was included in the prophecy, I was in my full right to inform him."

"Semantics will not work on me. Tell me the prophecy. My patience is short, and no doubt my enemies are near."

"As you wish, Goddess." He closes his eyes halfway, and they roll up inside his head until they're two white orbs. When he speaks, his voice is deeper. "You will die and be reborn in the City of Peace when the dead arise. You will bring the Father Gods into submission. You will master them and restore balance back to the world. And lastly, you will kill the person you love most."

The prophecy hits like a hammer blow to my chest. I stagger backward, Camilla catches me.

It can't be true. This is a burden far too great for me to carry. I am the reason for a war. How can I be the center of all of this? "You lie, Janus!"

"You dare doubt my gifts of prophecy? I've always spoken the truth."

"You realize the repercussions? The world will fall into war and destruction. If the Father Gods rule supreme, their tyranny will sweep across the world like a fire. If the Mother Goddesses disturb

the balance—well, we remember what happened during the last Purging."

"I am not the one who decides the future; I am only the one who sees it." Janus takes a long sip from a goblet filled with purple wine, clearly uninterested in the implications of his dire prediction.

"You make me the reason for both the fall of humanity as well as its redemption." I fall silent despite my anger. Now it all makes sense. "This is why the Father Gods launched a Purging? They think that if they can destroy all of us, then they will be able to save themselves?"

"If that is what you assume, so be it."

"The Mother Goddesses already bring balance to the world. If they extinguish that light, all will be dark," I say, speaking to myself.

"They don't care, Gaia," Camilla says. "They care only for their own survival, so there can be only one solution."

The realization sends goose bumps across my skin. I search my mind for any other possibility, but there is nothing else.

"Your young protégé is astute," says Janus, focusing on Camilla. "You know, I've seen her future as well." Camilla's eyes widen. He continues. "You are a complicated one, but your fate is clear. No matter what, you will always stay true and devoted to your master," he says, playfully flicking his eyes to me.

"She does not need you to tell her such an obvious truth," I reply, brushing aside his comment.

The next moment, we hear the distant clang of metal armor. I rush to a window chiseled out of the rock. A line of Roman soldiers marches toward Janus's temple.

"They come for you, and I doubt they will respect the sanctity of this place," says Janus. "I suggest you leave."

"But where?" Camilla asks.

I pull Camilla close, bringing her head near my lips, away from Janus's ears. "There is only one place we can go, and one thing we must do," I reply, my chest aching under the building pressure. "We must fulfill the prophecy before more blood is spilled."

"But that means—"

"I must kill my husband."

Cold sweat drenches my body, making me feel as if I were outside during an ice storm. The dream is like a clanging pipe in my head. The vision shimmers too close to my reality. Gaia, my past life, is telling me something.

But what is the message?

The clock on my bedside table reads 4:00 a.m. The Lyceum will wake up soon. Today is the Pruning. I know I won't go back to sleep, though I need the rest. I get out of bed and stare at the desert through my window. The dream's implications pinballing through my mind.

Who was my husband? And did I kill him?

CHAPTER NINETEEN

THE PRUNING

L ate in the morning, a knock at my door wakes me from a brief
sleep. "It's time," I hear Enki say.

I find him nervously pacing outside my door. He's holding two
headlamps and breakfast. Despite having no appetite, I force-feed
myself the toast he offers me.

Enki leads me to a part of the Lyceum I've never been to before,
where we follow a stone stairwell down into the earth.

"Where's Jessie?" I ask, as we descend.

Enki flashes an uneasy grimace. "She was paired with Daichsun.
They left an hour ago." I squeeze my cold fingers into my palms
to stop them from trembling. For some reason, I'd assumed that
Jessie would be with me for the Pruning; instead, she's paired with
the traitor. The thing that kills me is that there's nothing I can do
to help her.

For the next hour, we walk in silence. All the while my worries
build up. When we arrive at a door that reminds me of a yawning
mouth, I can't help but feel that whatever is behind the door will
swallow me whole.

"What's in there?" I ask.

Enki inspects the faded carvings etched onto the splintery door.
"Cibola," he finally says. When I don't respond, he adds, "You
know, one of the lost cities?"

"I have no idea what you're talking about."

"It's where all Ageling go to get tested after their training," he explains.

"Oh, like the final exam?"

"Yeah, except for the part that if you fail you die."

"Super-duper. Can't wait."

"Don't worry," he says, taking my hand and flashing a confident smile. "I'll keep you safe." The comic-book-hero way in which he says this is corny but makes me feel better.

He pushes open the door and warm air—odorless and crisp—whips up, making the hair on my arms stand on end. We follow a spiral staircase of rough stone even further into the black depths. Our headlamps create a bubble of light, but we can't see even ten feet in front of or behind us.

The air turns hot and stale. Vertigo, a sensation I never knew I could have, ripples through me. My hand shoots out for balance and touches walls laden with moisture. The rocks press the air out of me the deeper we go.

We emerge into a gigantic open cavern and I gasp, grabbing Enki's arm. "What is this place?"

It's a massive underground city frozen in time. Three-story buildings, glinting in our light, rise along streets laid out in a grid. My breath catches; the houses are made of gold.

"Cibola," Enki explains, spreading his arms wide as if to encompass the massive space. "When the Father Gods invaded from Europe, they brought war, disease, and destruction. The Mother Goddesses of the so-called 'new world' didn't have the technology nor the means to protect against the invasion. Instead of fighting, they hid their followers. They created seven golden cities, hidden from the Father Gods. For decades, the Mother Goddesses survived and thrived."

We reach ground level and walk among the buildings. It looks as if hundreds of people once lived here. The architecture is beautiful—flowing lines and adobe-style buildings. It's incredible to imagine what life might have been like at the height of the city's occupancy.

"Why was it abandoned?"

"The Mother Goddesses learned how to infiltrate the Father Gods' society. They learned how to subvert it and use it to their advantage." He pauses then adds, "They learned they didn't need to hide."

When we turn down the main avenue, we find a lifeless young man pinned to one of the buildings, a rusted metal spear protruding from his neck. A puddle of fresh blood pools at his feet, while his face is locked in eternal agony. I freeze as my stomach sinks. I touch my throat, wanting to turn away. I can't. It's Pacha.

"What happened to him?"

Enki carefully edges closer to investigate. "It looks like he was checking out the building. Maybe searching for a tool or a weapon. We should be careful. This whole place is booby-trapped."

I move toward the corpse, wanting to lay Pacha to rest, but Enki pulls me back. "Don't," he says. "There could be more traps."

It pains me to do so, but we leave him. I fight the urge to glance back. Despite remembering Coyote's reasons for the Pruning and this killing, I struggle to understand how it reconciles with the Mother Goddesses' mission.

We cross through a main square, and it doesn't take me long to figure out where we're headed. A tall arching wall filled with Littian inscriptions stands at the far end of the cavern. There's a dark tunnel at its center.

After we enter, we stop at a fork, where the path branches off into two smaller tunnels. Enki approaches a placard between the two paths.

"Which way do we go?" I ask, walking off to inspect the tunnel on the right.

Enki spins, eyes wide. "Wait! Don't!" he yells, but it's too late. As I take a step, the stone floor sinks slightly, and I hear a lever click.

On instinct, I dive away just as a solid sheet of gold comes crashing down from the ceiling. It slams into the floor where I once stood.

"That was close," I say. "Are you OK?"

I hear no reply.

Terror dawns on me. Enki is nowhere to be found; he's on the other side of the gold wall.

"Enki!" I scream, pounding my fists on the wall.

Although I suspect he's screaming his lungs out, I can't hear him. The wall must be at least six inches thick.

My knees buckle. I attempt to dry my clammy hands on my tracksuit but give up.

There's no going back out the way I came. I'm trapped, which means I have to do this alone.

CHAPTER TWENTY

TRIALS AND TRIBULATIONS

I spend five minutes freaking out and brainstorming ways to get back to Enki. My schemes range from improvising an explosive device from a headlamp to digging a tunnel through solid rock with my bare hands. And I come to the disheartening conclusion that there's only one direction to go.

I follow the tunnel, and after about thirty feet, it widens out to a cavern. The far wall bears the outlines of six closed stone doors. On each door is a single word written in Littian.

It's obvious what I must do: choose the correct door.

I stare at the flowing, curved script, willing my mind to comprehend, but all I come away with is a headache.

Out of six choices, how bad could one be? I wonder, tapping a finger against my chin. I tell myself not to think about it and approach the door on the far left. But as I'm about to push it inward, I remember Pacha's dead white eyes and Enki's warning about booby traps.

I back away slowly. Bad could be worse than I can imagine.

"Shoot," I whisper, pinching the bridge of my nose and exhaling my frustration. The only way I'll get out of here is to channel a past life. "It will be OK," I say, comforting myself. "Do what you practiced with Enki. You can do this." I don't fully believe the words, but a part of me likes how they sound. Heck, sometimes the lies we tell ourselves are our best truths.

I sit down on the stone floor, legs crossed, eyes closed, and imagine the barrier in my mind. It looms high and ominous. I know all too well the dangers lurking behind it.

In the past, I would have forced a hole through the barrier and wrenched a life toward me. Violent and ineffective. At least I know what I shouldn't do. That's a piece of reassuring knowledge.

Trying Enki's method, I calm my thoughts and call out to my past lives. I beckon to them, like a girl asking a boy to a dance.

And . . .

Just as I was at my middle-school prom, I'm rejected. Nothing happens. None of my past lives come to my rescue. I bite the inside of my cheek. I can't do this. I'm a failure, and I'm going to die.

I tell myself not to slide into self-doubt. Once again, I muster up my false bravery. I *can* do this. A part of me feels that this self-motivation mantra is bullshit and a waste of time. It's like screaming at a hurricane to stop being windy, but another part of me feels good, proud, and strong when I boost myself up.

Please, help me, I think again, coaxing my past lives.

I wait.

And wait.

And wait.

Again, no answer.

My eyes spring open; I'm doing something wrong. I glance back at the six doors, focusing on the elegant script. I realize I don't need any old past life—I need one that can read Littian.

Huh, well isn't that a pickle? There are only two past lives I know who have this ability. One is Gaia, but I've never come close to channeling her. She only shows me what she wants me to see.

The other is Amahle, who's more stubborn than a cat. She understood the Littian written on the dagger in the U-boat, but I wouldn't call my channeling of her a success by any means, and I don't see why my attempt this time will be any different.

Yet, I have no other option. She's the only one who can help.

"I can do this," I say, getting used to these little lies that make me feel good. "I'm in control. I'm strong. I can channel her."

I silence my thoughts, close my eyes, and return to the wall in my mind. I pretend I'm with Enki. I don't force myself through the wall; instead, I let my fears melt away. I smother my anger and frustration as if they're a smoldering fire. When my ego flashes, I silence its screams.

It's at the moment when my thoughts are as quiet as ice that I call out to Amahle.

A golden light appears between the cracks in my mind's wall. It dances through the air like a firefly. The next moment, it glides inside me, and sauna-steam-like warmth envelops my thoughts. In an instant, Amahle's memories flood my mind.

Life is hard in Joburg, and even harder for a colored. Though my father's white skin would have granted me a free pass into society, my mother's blackness marks me as null and void. But a hard life builds strong character. The attacks of bullies teach me how to fight. I learn that not all confrontations have to be physical, and that outsmarting my enemies can be as effective as force. A childhood marked by constant strife does not bode well for a happy future, though. If it isn't for the kindness of a distant uncle in London, who gets me into Oxford, I would have never escaped the hate of Joburg.

At college, no longer needing to fight to survive, I apply all my energies to my studies. Archeology attracts me. There is something comforting in the abstractness of long-dead people. They are simpler to figure out than the complicated nature of living humans. But after graduation, reality comes crashing down. Few professors want a colored as their assistant. Finding no opportunities, I return to South Africa and work as a nurse in the countryside.

Life may have continued on a simple trajectory, except I find something that changes everything. One night there is a storm with torrential rain and howling winds. The next day, as I go to check on a patient living in the hills, I come upon a cave, newly revealed by the storm. My curiosity overcomes me. Inside, I find a stela inscribed with a language that I have never seen before. This mystery will consume the rest of my life. It takes years for me to decipher the language. The stela describes a group of immortal gods hiding among humans. They are the masters of the world—the kings and queens. The Fathers and the Mothers. The stela mentions a dagger with the power to kill these gods. Diamant's Dagger.

I open my eyes transformed. Amahle's passions, fears, and loves linger like a mother's embrace. I am myself, yet I am also Amahle. We are one and the same.

I continue to view the world through Amahle's eyes, which are filled with curiosity, wonder, and excitement. A woman with a fighter's heart, she loved the search for truth and the thrill of discovery and adventure. Perhaps this is why it has been so difficult for me to channel her. Amahle and I are completely different types of people. Amahle was confident, brave and fearless. While I always steer away from risk, Amahle ran straight toward it. Could it be that until this moment, I wasn't ready to channel her?

Muscles trembling, I fall to my knees as the epiphany hits me. I finally understand my trouble with channeling. Up until this point, I've been too self-absorbed and selfish. This prevented me from empathizing with and understanding a past life that would allow me to become a vessel for it. By relinquishing my own ego, I allowed space for another soul to channel me. I gave them permission to love and embrace me.

I'm humbled by this realization. Several minutes pass before I focus on the doors aligned against me. I now understand the meanings of the previously incomprehensible words.

Suffering, Despair, Loss, Fear, Anger.

And on the second door to the right, the word *Life* is chiseled.

Without hesitation, as Amahle would do, I walk up and press on the door of life. There is a rumbling beneath my feet, and the door swings open to reveal a path. I pass inward, expecting more traps and danger. Instead, I find a small room with a still pool of water, dark and deep.

After a minute of investigation, neither Amahle nor I can find a hidden door or alternative route. There is only the pool of water. My stomach sinks.

But lucky for me, I'm still channeling Amahle. Her presence tugs at my subconscious.

Time to swim, Mattie. Too bad you didn't bring a cozzie . . .

Staring down into the bottomless pool, her voice reassures me because behind it there's a confidence that I lack. Amahle was a freediver who could hold her breath for over ten minutes. I wonder why she's not afraid of this challenge, given that she died a slow death in the bowels of a U-bat. But then it makes sense—she already died. There's no need to fear that which has already happened.

Get kaalgat, bokkie . . .

Translation from Afrikaans: "Get naked, honey."

I strip down to my underwear, lay my clothes aside, and dip my big toe in the icy water. Coldness runs up my leg. This will not be fun.

No, no, this will be super fun . . .

Sure, I believe that. I scan for an easy place to wade in but come up empty. So I take a deep breath and jump in. My subsequent scream suggests that I'm being tortured.

Oh, it's not that bad . . .

Yes, it is that bad, Amahle, or did you just not hear me?

While treading water, I rub my shoulders to raise my body temperature. I tighten my head lamp, and whisper a silent thanks that it's waterproof. Then I take a breath and stick my head under the water.

Ten feet down, there's a horizontal tunnel. A quick dive reveals that the tunnel disappears beyond the bubble of light from my headlamp. I return to the surface, doubt rising in me.

Have faith. It will lead somewhere . . .

Faith?

Trust me. I've done this before. First step is to breathe deeply . . .

Following her directions, I concentrate on filling my lungs with air. I will need every molecule of oxygen. After a few minutes, I'm lightheaded from the effort.

Now that your body is filled with air and your head is light, take one last big breath and dive . . .

I do as she says, not knowing whether I'll ever take another breath.

Swim hard and don't breathe . . .

With strong and purposeful strokes, I enter the submerged tunnel. I can't hesitate. One stroke after another, I surge farther into the abyss and away from my only air source.

At about a minute, the pressure on my lungs is excruciating.

Ignore the pain and keep pushing . . .

Depressingly, the tunnel doesn't have an end. After another minute, I wonder if I should turn back. What should I do?

Amahle makes the decision for me. *Keep going . . . There is no turning back . . .*

But a half minute later, my headlamp illuminates a sight that breaks my concentration and seizes my heart. I wish I'd turned back.

It's a bleached skeleton. Someone left to decompose in the darkness alone. The thing that really sends shivers across my skin is that there's a thin gold necklace looping around their vertebrae. This detail makes the skeleton a real person. A person who had an agonizing death; I must turn back.

Calm yourself . . .

Easier said than done. Through sheer force of will, I calm my stampeding heart.

I swim past the skeleton without peeking down at it. The pressure on my lungs makes them feel as if they'll explode. I can't go any farther.

But I push myself onward because I have no choice.

As if answering my prayers, a wall appears. Through the hazy water, I see the tunnel's end, and not a moment too soon. I'm dying to breathe.

When I reach the wall, my hopes plummet. It's a dead end. There's nowhere else to go, and I'm almost out of air.

Panic ensues.

I will myself to control my beating heart.

Relax, Mattie, you missed something . . .

My trembling hands run along the smooth wall searching for anything that will help me escape—all the while, air escapes my lungs in small bubbles.

I must have taken the wrong tunnel. I screwed up. I'm going to die. My desire to breathe is overpowering, and I'm tempted to open my mouth.

Concentrate . . . control your fear . . .

Out of frustration, I claw at the wall. As my nails scratch the surface, a piece of clay becomes dislodged. With frantic movements, I pick away at the spot until it enlarges like an open wound.

With my fingers, I feel inside.

A keyhole.

My desperation returns with full force. I don't have a key. I'm out of air, and soon I'll be another skeleton left to rot in this watery tomb.

That's when I remember the skeleton and the gold chain around its neck. Could it be?

Quickly . . .

With my last bit of strength, I swim back to the skeleton. When I arrive, my body convulses. Somehow I prevent myself from inhaling water.

I grab at the gold chain, and as I do, the skeleton's skull topples to the tunnel's floor. I fight the fear filling me. The light of my headlamp fades. Turns out it was only somewhat waterproof. I can't see the chain, but my fingers wrap around the shape of a hard object.

A key.

Everything goes black out as my headlamp dies.

My strength continues to falter, but somehow I swim back to the tunnel's end.

My fingers weakly fumbling along the wall, I can't find the key hole. Simultaneously, my will to continue disappears. I finally admit the truth.

I've failed.

I have to breathe. I open my mouth. Water gushes into my lungs. Painful yet sweet. Soon I'll be asleep and none of this will matter.

I'm out of time, but a part of me, the part that is Amahle, refuses to give up. She forces her way into my consciousness. Taking control, she lifts my hand, finds the hole, slams the key in, and turns it. Then she propels me through the opening that emerges over my head.

I break through the surface, spew out a gallon of water, cough violently, and breathe in stale yet sweet air. No breath has ever been as delicious. Somehow, I pull myself out of the water onto a cold stone floor, where I curl up, close my eyes, cough, and breathe.

CHAPTER TWENTY-ONE

WHEEL OF FORTUNE

I don't know how long I slept. Maybe ten minutes, maybe an hour, maybe five hours. But when I finally uncurl myself, I'm in a room much like the one that I entered on the other side of the tunnel. For some reason, this depresses the heck out of me. It's as though I swam all that way to end up where I started. The difference is that there's a dim, wavering light coming from an adjoining passageway.

I haul myself to my feet. As Amahle recedes behind my mind's wall, I silently thank her for helping me. I tread across the stone floor, cautiously, and the light grows brighter as I turn a corner.

Suddenly, I slam into a person coming from the opposite direction. The light snaps off, and we're plunged into darkness.

Surprise is quickly followed by alarm then fear. My adrenaline spikes. "Shit," the person mumbles.

My jaw drops. It can't be. "Jessie?" I ask. Her headlamp blinks on and I gasp.

"Mattie!" she cries. "What the hell? Where did you come from?"

My relief in finding her is tempered by her appearance. The mud and grime covering her face doesn't conceal the black-and-blue bruises on her cheeks. Her clothing is in tatters, and dried blood mats her hair. She looks as if she were kicked down a flight of stairs.

"What happened to you?"

"What happened to me?" she asks. "The better question is why are you only in your underwear?"

"Long story," I say, reaching toward a cut on her forehead. "You're bleeding."

She brushes my hand away. "Daichsun," she says, her voice hot with anger. "He tried to kill me."

"Are you OK?"

"More or less."

My stomach twists at the thought of the traitor. "I told you we couldn't trust him."

"I know, but I didn't have a choice." She attempts to push her disheveled hair out of her eyes while avoiding her head wound.

"We need to warn the Elders."

"Yeah, but first we have to get out of here." She turns her head, illuminating the passageway. We're at a T. There's a third passageway that branches off. "Don't go the way I came, trust me."

"My way was no better."

"How about we try door three?"

"Sounds good."

"Here take this." She unzips her sweatshirt and hands it to me. "I'm all for nakedness, but even I have limits."

I take it, grateful. Though it's toasty warm in the cave, the sweatshirt makes me feel less vulnerable. Also, because she's taller, it comes down to my thighs, so one could presumably say I'm now in a dress. Presumably.

We follow the passageway and after a few yards come to a door guarded by two stone gargoyles on each side.

Jessie reads the Littian written on the door. "It's a warning. *Dangerous prisoner inside.*"

We exchange a worried glance. "Prisoner?" I ask. "Down here?"

"From what I've seen so far, I'm not surprised. This place is a funhouse on meth. Come on," she says, pushing open the wooden door without hesitation.

The foul smell of a cesspool hits my nose, and the overwhelming stench forces me to breathe through my mouth. An eerie light, coming from flickering torches, filters through the dust-encrusted space. Tall rickety shelves crowd the interior, and on them sit hundreds of mason jars filled with spoiled and rancid liquids. Many contain fetuses of unidentifiable creatures at various stages of development.

Jessie picks up one of the jars. "*Fate*," she whispers, reading the faded word scrawled in Littian on old masking tape. I briefly channel Amahle again, who helps me read the words on several other peeling labels: *Love, Trust, Glory, Hate.*

Rank smoke drifts through the room, and the broiling temperature and smell makes me gag. There isn't enough room to breathe here.

The sound of a conversation freezes us in place. Unsure if this is a trap or a test, we listen. Through the shelves, we can discern two figures, one of whom I recognize. Seuku is listening to a man in a rocking chair, whose face is concealed under a ratty black shawl.

He rocks back and forth and says something we can't make out. We edge closer, still keeping our distance and staying hidden among the shelves.

That's when I notice that Seuku is holding one of the mason jars. She nods and says something. I can't hear her words, but I sense decisiveness in them.

The next moment, to my alarm, she raises the mason jar, filled with a putrescent purple liquid, to her lips.

My gut tells me that something is wrong. "No! Don't!" I scream.

Seuku turns to me, but my warning came a second too late. She's already taken a sip from the jar.

She cringes, as if expecting a blow.

A few seconds pass. Nothing happens. She smiles, relieved. She's about to say something to me when her body convulses. Her mouth opens like a chasm, as if to breathe, and a sickly choking sound emerges. Her skin shrivels around her face, and a skeletal, agonizing expression materializes. She collapses and hits the ground hard, body spasming.

My heart pounds as I rush toward her, ignoring any possible dangers. I cradle her head. Seuku scrambles to undo her sweatshirt as if it's suffocating her. The zipper jams. Her body convulses again, and blood hemorrhages from Seuku's nose and mouth and oozes down her chin onto my fingers, hot and sticky.

In less than a minute, Seuku's deadened eyes stare upward. Her blanched face appears wilted over a jutting, still jaw. Despite knowing the truth, I check her pulse.

Nothing.

I'm speechless. Yet again, an Ageling, an ally, a friend has died. The tears come fast, spilling onto Seuku's withered corpse. What was the point of this? She was just a girl. She deserved more than this. It's pointless that she died.

A chuckle punctuates my disgust. I glare at the man in the rocking chair, whose face is shadowed under the hood. His rocking has stopped. "Ah, more guests. Welcome," he says, his voice as pleasing as fingernails across a chalkboard.

He lifts his hood and I scramble away, back to Jessie, who remains frozen and motionless next to the shelves. Our reaction is a collective "Yuck."

He's a god the likes of which I've never seen before. His aura is a brownish black, almost unnoticeable in the dim light. His face looks like something a cat vomited up: twisted, mangled, rotted.

When his deistic form fades, we find an old man draped in layers of filthy blankets. His talon-like fingernails—curly and stained black—form a steeple in front of him. Thick, matted tangles of hair spill over his pruned face but don't hide his milky-white eyes, which follow our movements like a bird of prey. He's as shrunken and shriveled as the creatures in the jars. "I'm so pleased," he says. "I've had more visits today than I've had in a hundred years. Come and make yourselves at home."

This thing killed Seuku. I'd rather receive an enema than a chair offered by this monster.

"We're leaving," Jessie says, pointing to the door behind the man. Something tells me that we won't simply be able to waltz out of here. There will be a price for our freedom.

He chuckles again, the way I imagine vermin would. "Yes, yes. You will have your turn." He clucks, pleased. "It's been many years since I've witnessed a Pruning. Who among you will survive this ordeal? Who among you is worthy? Many have come to be tested and many have failed. They were all so sure of themselves." He notices me, and his pupil-less eyes widen. "It's been millennia since Gaia has graced my presence. Tell me, Goddess, have you come to beg for my forgiveness?"

My stomach hardens; I have done something bad to this guy. But then I remember Seuku and I don't feel so bad. "Whatever I did to you, you deserved."

He points a twisted, arthritic finger at me. "Don't insult me! I will never forget what you did to me. Never, never, you nasty woman."

"Shut it!" Jessie warns.

The old man eyes her hungrily. "Yes, yes. You too will be delicious."

"Who are you?" I ask.

His eyebrows, two dirty smudges, rise, and his colon-clenching smile reappears. "You don't recognize me?" The wheels circle in his head as he puts it together. "That means only one thing. You have not mastered your abilities." His fingers dance gleefully. "You will never answer my questions. On an ancient soul like yours, I won't go hungry for hundreds of years. Oh yes, yes, my luck has finally come."

"Hey!" Jessie yells, interrupting his ruminations. "We're not answering your questions. We're leaving, and we're taking the girl," she says, pointing to Seuku.

The man's sneer could skin an animal. "All who enter must answer my questions to pass. That is the bargain I made with you

Mother Goddesses, and it is the price you pay to become truly Ascended."

"Well, guess what? We don't care." Jessie heads for the exit, but from the folds of his blanket, the man produces a revolver, old but well oiled. He aims it right at her.

"Run, please. I've collected more than enough souls this day, and two more will only add to my feast."

His words strike like a punch to the gut. "You never answered my question," I say. "Who are you?"

He blows hot breath through his broken teeth, and his cracked lips turn up. "I am the Lord of Waste. The King of Bowels and the Eater of Excrement. I am Kawaya no-kami."

"You're shitting me," says Jessie, without a hint of sarcasm.

"Wait," I reply, "am I missing something? Who is this guy?"

"He's the toilet god."

"There's a god for the toilet? You're making this up."

Jessie covers her nose. "One of my past lives had heard stories about him but hadn't met him. Kawaya is a god of human waste. He's a Father God who's described as a parasite, a vampire, among the Ascended. The legends describe him as being able to suck out the souls of other gods, which he feeds on in order to extend his corporeal life. I assumed he was a myth—an urban legend to scare young gods."

"How do I compare to my legend?" Kawaya asks with a lurid sneer. "The Mother Goddesses were jealous of me. I discovered the secrets of true immortality! But my methods were distasteful to them." He spits on the ground. "As if they have the right—or moral high ground to judge me. They imprisoned me here and fed me the soul scraps of rats and the rare sip of an Ageling. But mark my words, one day I will break free. One day I will feast on the souls of you all."

"I now understand why it stinks in here," I say.

"Savor the stench of my temple because you will be mine for eternity," the god says with a satisfied grin that sends fear rocking through me.

"What do we have to do to pass?" Jessie asks.

Kawaya runs his black tongue over hungry lips. "Answer my questions by drinking from my jars. If you drink correctly, so shall you live and pass freely. If you drink incorrectly, so shall you die and your soul will be mine." He rises from the chair with more grace and speed than I would have imagined possible. When he walks, thick manacles around his ankles rattle with each step. He picks up Seuku's mason jar, half-spilled. He raises the jar, smiles, and takes a sip. On the outside is written *Wisdom*. He wipes his mouth with the back of his grizzled hand and says, "She will be spicy for my tastes, but I'll still savor her nonetheless. Pity she lacked that which she drank."

"What are in the jars?" I ask, stomach churning.

"The distillate of the bodies and souls of dead gods," Kawaya replies. He toasts us again and drinks its dregs.

"Disgusting."

He turns toward me, eyebrows lifting. "Disgusting? I've lived thousands of years feasting on the souls of gods. I haven't known a true death in six hundred years. You small gods cycle through different bodies, but I know only one form. Look upon true beauty." His lips part, revealing several rotting teeth.

"You killed Seuku. I'll make you pay for that."

"I can't wait to taste your soul, Gaia. I expect it to be like a fine wine, aged to perfection."

I turn away from him. "Why would the Elder Gods send us against him?" I ask Jessie. "He feeds on our souls."

"You want to make sense of madness," Kawaya replies. "This is the way the worthy succeed. You pass my test, and you have truly earned the mantle and crown of Mother Goddess. If you fail, perhaps you were never meant to be a god in the first place."

"Fine," I say. "Ask your questions."

The god clucks like a happy hen and clears his throat. "One guest, one question, one answer. If you succeed, you will pass. If not, you are mine. Who goes first?"

We exchange an uneasy glance. "I'll start," says Jessie.

Kawaya speaks immediately:

"One king dies, another arises.
Peace withers, chaos blossoms.
The just punished, the corrupted awarded.
Laws broken, manipulated and remolded.
Always hate the other, sacrifice one's brother.
Daughter's future is nightmares of Mother.
I am there."

"A riddle?" I say. "I hate riddles. We're supposed to risk our lives for that?"

"I didn't even hear half of it," Jessie adds.

"I remember it." I glance at Kawaya to see if he's opposed to my helping Jessie, but all I find in his eyes is a greedy, insatiable hunger. I suspect he thinks that since we've fallen into his spider web, we're as good as his and it doesn't matter if we help each other or not. I repeat the riddle, and add, "But I have no clue what the answer is." A nervous itch works its way up my arms.

We spend five minutes thinking it through, reciting parts of it. Something about the riddle is odd, but I can't place it. Jessie, whispering to herself, presses her temples and channels a past life. I'm amazed at the ease with which she can do so. After a minute, she repeats, "'Peace withers, chaos blossoms,'" and then her face brightens. "I know it."

I turn, surprised. "You do?"

"Fear, right?" she asks Kawaya.

His face is blank. "If you are certain of your answer, drink from the jar," he says, pointing toward the shelves.

Jessie runs her fingers along the mason jars until she finds the one marked *Fear*. It's filled with a radioactive yellow liquid and a floating animal fetus. She stares at it for a long time, uncertain. Finally, determination blazes in her expression. She raises the jar to her lips, but right as she's about to drink, I grab her hand and pull it down. "No!" I shout, realizing the trap. Wouldn't Kawaya want us to go with our first impulse? "It's not only fear. Fear is one part of it. He's referring to something deeper. Something more primal than fear." I stare into Kawaya's milky eyes, seeing the truth. "It's terror."

"If you're sure, then drink," Kawaya prods, his expression still blank. He gestures toward another shelf.

Jessie searches the shelves and finds the jar marked *Terror*. It's filled with something resembling dirty engine oil. Jessie pauses and narrows her eyes. "Are you sure about this? *Terror* and *fear* seem to mean the same thing."

I recall being hunted by the Father Gods, hiding in Hawaii. The terror of the unknown. It was beyond fear. "Yes. This is the one."

"OK. Bottoms up." She raises the jar and gulps back a mouthful, grimacing the next second. "Ugh, tastes like someone made a smoothie out of cockroaches."

I hold my breath, expecting the worst, praying she doesn't keel over. After a few minutes, she smiles, relief washes through me. At the very least, Jessie will walk away from this in one piece.

"Hmm, you have chosen correctly." Kawaya shakes his head as if her success means nothing. He sneers then taps his long fingernails excitedly and begins again.

"Can there be a crime when no victim is found?
Like a scream which has no sound.
Empty, open without matter.
Accusations were nothing but the latter.
Guilty as charged, claimed the lawyer, judge, executor.
All one person, the corruptor, the liar, the persecutor.

Lady truth should be blind
To the lies that they maligned.
Let the crime meet the punishment, they decreed.
To the dungeon, the victim will never be freed.
So I ask one last time
Who am I?"

This time we both remember the poem, but we stare blankly at Kawaya before looking at each other with baffled expressions.

"Do you have any idea?" I ask.

Jessie shakes her head. "Sorry, I'm stumped."

"My gut says that it's justice. 'Lady truth,' 'lawyer,' 'judge,' 'executor.' It's all related to judgment and justice. That's what it sounded like to me at least."

"If that's what your gut says, by all means go with it, but you should be damned certain. I don't want you to become an energy drink for this asshole."

She's right. I remember that my initial impulse could likely be the incorrect one. I need to be certain.

I'm sure that one of my past lives knows the answer, but my attempts to channel them are unsuccessful. I thought I had the hang of this. "It has to be justice," I say. "It's the only one that makes sense."

"If you're certain," Kawaya replies, his face as featureless as a tombstone without a name.

I search the shelves, and on the bottom shelf, covered in dust, I find the jar marked *justice*. The liquid is the color of Mountain Dew, and the jar is by far the most inviting because there's no floating creature inside.

When I glance at Jessie, seeking reassurance, she shrugs. I stand frozen in indecision for a minute. Will I end up like Seuku if I drink this? Racking my brain for another alternative, I come up short. This is my only option.

I raise the jar to my lips, and from the corner of my eye, I see a glimmer of eagerness in Kawaya's expression. Or did I imagine that?

Right as the liquid is about to hit my tongue, I pause. Something isn't right. I need more help, so despite past worries, I tear down the wall in my mind completely. I throw myself on the mercy of my past lives, which are aligned in front of me, a towering wall of bright lights. Yes, they could drown me, yes, they could make me go insane, but I now know they won't.

Help me, I say.

From the collective, a light shoots down and surges into me . . .

From the temple's raised platform, I can see Purattu lapping at the nearby sandy shore closeby. I stand while the manacled prisoner kneels below me. My eyes burn hate into him. There's a hot brand in my hand.

Šulak always prided himself on his beauty and youth. One might have called it vanity, but I discovered the truth. He consumes souls; they bring him new life, making him fair and handsome. He says it is a wonder, a joy, a triumph.

It is a disease.

He boasts that the souls are animals, but I suspect he is feeding on my children—both god and mortal alike.

His knowledge must never fall into the hands of the Father Gods. He cannot be allowed to live forever. It is unholy.

Death is the only true balancer.

There is only one thing to do.

We welcomed him as a guest, lured him here on the promise of tribute and respect and treasure. He had no idea what I placed in his drink. We betrayed him. This trial is a sham, but a necessary lie in a country like Bābilim.

He will be a prisoner of the Mother Goddesses. A liability and a weapon for eternity.

I am creating a monster.

The past life turns to the wall. Now I understand why I wasn't able to channel it. That was an ancient life, much older than even Gaia of Rome. The shock burns in my mind—I was the one who made Kawaya, or Šulak, as I knew him in Babylon. I created this monster now testing me.

As I glance at the liquid I'm about to drink, I see the truth.

Kawaya's riddle is a trick question.

It's not only justice. Justice is one part of it. From Kawaya's point of view, the answer is both justice and revenge.

Justice for the betrayal by the Mother Goddesses, and revenge against me for the crimes I committed against him.

Two jars, not one.

I lower the justice jar and search the shelves.

Revenge sits on the top shelf near the back of the cavern. It's a red, poisonous-looking liquid with an engorged shrimp inside. Under any other circumstances I wouldn't have touched it. I mix revenge into justice and justice back into revenge. The liquids mixes together to make a dirty brown soup.

I raise the jar to Kawaya and then sip from it.

His face boils over with anger. "You devil woman. How did you know the answer?"

Despite what he did to Seuku, I have sympathy for him. "I'm sorry for what we did to you. It was not right."

"Your apology means nothing. I'll not lose this opportunity for revenge." He raises the gun and aims it at me. "I will taste your soul one way or another."

Jessie and I dive behind one of the shelves right as he fires. Jars of souls explode above me, raining their liquid contents down.

Kawaya rises from his chair and stalks toward us, metal chains rattling. There's no cover, and we don't have any weapons. Kawaya looms over us, aiming the gun at my head. "Revenge will taste sweet."

Then there's a crash. We turn and see Enki standing at the entrance. I gasp, as relief floods through me. He shoves another one of the shelves. They fall into each other like dominoes, spilling hundreds of mason jars onto the floor. The shelf nearest to us crashes into Kawaya, throwing the gun from his hand and pinning him to the ground.

He screeches in agony.

"What did I miss?" Enki asks.

"Damn you, Gaia," Kawaya says weakly.

Enki picks me up from the ground. My knees nearly buckle on my wobbly legs. Seeing him brings a sudden lightness to my chest. "Where did you come from?" I ask.

He smiles. "You wouldn't believe me if I told you."

"Your timing was impeccable."

"Listen," says Jessie, "you guys are cute and all but let's get out of here. This place stinks."

"Agreed," says Enki.

We're about to leave Kawaya's prison when we hear a cackle. We freeze and look back. The god cradles one of the broken jars; the only thing he had was his stolen souls, and now we've taken even that from him. Despite the god's miserable state, his cackle morphs into a maniacal laugh. He reaches out to the wall of his prison and pulls a hidden lever.

I hear the twang of a trip wire snapping, and the floor disappears beneath us. The three of us tumble into the abyss and freefall for what feels like forever before plunging into turbulent, black waters, which sweep us away.

We're blind as the underground river carries us swiftly into a world of darkness.

"Hold on!" yells Enki, grabbing my shoulder. "Stay together!"

I grab Jessie's arm as the powerful, rushing river sends fresh terror through me. I fight to keep my head up as we're swept along. Adrenaline pounds through my veins. The river twists and turns.

I have no idea where it will lead us, and I have a sinking sensation that it might never reemerge outside.

The current picks up speed as we descend deeper underground. Muscles cramping, I kick to keep my head above the water. Once again, my lungs feel like bursting. The blackness is so complete it's as if I'm in my own grave.

"We have to get out of here!" I scream.

"Obviously!" Jessie yells back.

But the waters have no intention of letting us go. The current quickens.

Enki, still holding onto my shoulder, is now floating in front of me. "Grab something!" he yells. But the sides of the narrow tunnel are smooth and polished.

The water drops again.

We spin out of control in the darkness for what feels like an eternity.

How do we get out of here?

Suddenly, Enki cries out and falls silent, and we pile into him as if he's a dam. I stick out my hand and feel the stone wall that he smashed into. A moment later, the current sucks us beneath the wall. I barely have time to take a breath before we're underwater, and I do my best to hold onto Enki's limp body. We remerge a few seconds later.

"Is Enki OK?" Jessie asks.

"He's not moving."

I check his pulse, desperation rising like a sickness from my stomach. "He's barely breathing. We have to get him out of here."

"Look ahead!" Jessie shouts. A dim light has emerged in front of us. A pearl of hope. "Hold on to me."

I make out shadows in the darkness.

Right as we pass the light source, Jessie throws herself toward the side of the tunnel and amazingly finds a hand hold. I grab onto her, despite the strong current wanting to pull me back in. Jessie's grip remains firm, and she's able to pull herself out of the river. Then she hauls Enki and me out as well.

We collapse onto dry land, and I've never been so thankful for the feel of earth under my body. Jessie and I lie exhausted next to the river with Enki passed out beside us.

"Jessie, I don't ever want to go inside another tunnel for the rest of my life."

"Agreed."

After resting for several minutes, we follow the light source through another tunnel, carrying Enki. As we trudge toward the light, I can't help but think that this is a horrible way to train the Ascended. Why kill us off? This isn't right. Something about this process has been corrupted. Are Mother Goddesses not guided by love, compassion and harmony? How does the Pruning fit?

The light grows brighter. As we step into sunlight, tears of relief fill my eyes. I suddenly realize that we're in the Neolithic cave that Enki and I passed the night before, when we followed Daichsun.

We lay Enki on the ground; a black-and-blue bruise is stamped on his forehead.

"I'll get us help," Jessie says, pushing herself to her feet. "You stay here and watch Enki."

"I'll go with you. The Lyceum is a few miles up the valley."

"No. I'll be back soon. I'll bring back help." Jessie kisses my cheek and runs off.

When she's gone, exhaustion catches up with me. I want nothing more than to sleep, but I will myself to stay awake as the sun sets and the air gets cold. I lie back, place a hand on Enki's side, and pray he's OK.

CHAPTER TWENTY-TWO

CAMPING

O nce upon a time, my mom took me camping at a state park. There was nothing more thrilling than sleeping under the stars. I can still remember the crackling fire, the mouth-burning s'mores, and my snuggly warm Care Bears sleeping bag.

Who wouldn't I kill right now for that sleeping bag?

My body shudders. The desert air is freezing, and Jessie's thin sweatshirt is doing little to fight off the cold. Stripping down made perfect sense when I needed to swim through an underground tunnel, but now, as I freeze my butt off, I can't believe what an idiot I was.

I wrap my arms around myself, and my teeth chatter. I glance at Enki, passed out beside me, and I have a brilliant idea. Why should I be cold when there's a perfectly warm, fully-clothed body right beside me?

I proceed with the only logical course of action for fighting off hypothermia: I strip Enki down to his boxers, press my near-naked body against his so he's spooning me, and drape his clothes over us.

It isn't a Care Bears sleeping bag, but it does the trick; the heat of his body spreads into mine, and I stop shivering.

I sigh. "That's nice."

There's the briefest of silences. Then: "More like a dream come true."

I jolt. Then the thawed portion of my brain registers that the newfound heat source is a person who has regained consciousness. A surge of relief warms my chest. "Don't get too excited," I say over my shoulder, refusing to relinquish the perfect position I've found nestled in the curve of his body.

"How can I not be? You already took off my pants."

"I requisitioned them for our survival."

"I once used that as a pick-up line."

"Can't imagine it worked." I pull part of his shirt over my exposed shoulder. "How are you feeling?"

Enki groans. "I have a hell of a headache but otherwise I'm fine. Also, when you pulled the shirt, you exposed part of my butt."

"You should wear baggier clothes."

"I'll remember that." He wiggles a bit and then drapes his arm over me. "Hey, what happened to you after we were separated?"

I tell him about my misadventures in Cibola, and he's especially happy to hear that I channeled Amahle. "What about you?" I ask.

As he shifts, I feel every movement against my backside. A different kind of heat spreads through me. "More or less the same," he says. "A bunch of traps, obstacles, and puzzles. I thought I was doing well until I got knocked out."

"Yeah, it sounded painful."

"Given how I feel right now, we can assume it wasn't fun."

None of that experience was fun. Anger rises in me as I remember Seuku and Pacha. They died. We all could have died, and for what purpose? I hate that Coyote and the Elder Gods made us risk our lives. They might not care much for an individual life, but it's a life nonetheless. "It was all such a waste."

"It wasn't a waste. We survived, and that's something to be thankful for."

I face him, and my chest presses against his. "I'm not in the mood to celebrate."

"You should still be proud of yourself."

I'm reminded that I wouldn't even be here if it weren't for him. I never could have channeled Amahle if it weren't for Enki's training. I owe him my life. And what have I done for him? I've been worried only about Jessie and me. "I'm sorry I haven't said this before, but I'm incredibly appreciative of all your help. When I arrived at the Lyceum, I didn't have a chance. You believed in me when I didn't believe in myself. I wouldn't have gotten this far without you. I'm eternally thankful."

His fingers dance along my back. "You've already thanked me by taking off all my clothes."

I glance away, embarrassed by his response and my honesty, but Enki guides my chin up so he can stare into my eyes. "You are amazing. From the moment I saw you, I wanted to be part of your life. I needed it. You have so much love and kindness in you. I sensed it the moment we met. I fully believe you can heal this world, and if the least I could do was help you realize your true potential, then that's enough for me."

Our lips are only inches apart, and his rapid heartbeat matches my own. My throat is dry like kindling. I don't know what to say, but I do know what I want.

I kiss him.

He kisses me back, running his hand through my tangled hair and caressing my neck. As his fingers graze my shoulders, quivers of pleasure cascade across my skin.

Part of me whispers, "Push him away—there's someone else," but I silence it. I listen to the part that yearns for more of his touch.

His hands travel over my body, and I give them permission to wander where they wish. He pulls me closer to him, and I inhale his sweet, almost vanilla scent. It's as if our bodies are connected, and a fireball of heat builds inside me.

His breath against my neck makes my muscles clench. He touches my hips—testing the safety of some unnamed border. I lean toward him, allowing him to cross.

My breath falters. There isn't enough oxygen between us. How much I've wanted this. How much I've been waiting for this. How much I've yearned for this. I tilt my head back. His mouth finds the skin on my neck. My desire burns hotter. I feel as if I'm floating. My lips part, but no sound emerges. Each breath escapes without my control.

His kisses are like water, and it's as if I've been thirsty my entire life. I savor each one.

I throw the makeshift blanket off my shoulders, push him onto his back, straddle him. His hands linger on my stomach as I smile down at him.

His hands wander up my body. My face flushes, and I let out a long, heavy sigh. In the rush, we lose what little clothes we have on. Our bodies melt in a rising symphony of desire and passion. If there's one thing I know for sure, it's that I'm no longer cold.

CHAPTER TWENTY-THREE

Truth Hurts

The sound of footsteps wake me from a deep sleep.

"Woah!" someone says.

Bleary-eyed, I pull Enki's shirt off my eyes and blink in the bright light of morning. I'm still exhausted, and I wouldn't have woken up if it weren't for the person staring down at me. Jared's eyes are round, his face ashen. His jaw hangs open. Next to him, Jessie wears a huge grin.

A burst of shock reverberates through me. I freeze, not having a clue what to say or do. I feel like crawling back into the cave and never coming out, but there's nowhere to hide. I'm exposed, lying naked on the ground next to Enki, who shares my deficit of clothing. He snores, unaware of the horror that I'm experiencing.

"We have clothes for you," Jared says weakly, before spinning away.

"Thanks," I reply, but he's already left.

"I'll give you a minute," says Jessie, handing me a small bundle of clothes.

When they're out of sight, Enki stirs and yawns. "Good morning beautiful," he says with a smile.

I feel like throwing up as I remember how Jared basically professed his love for me. He was willing to accept that he might lose his life in order to be with me. Yes, my feelings toward him might have changed, but this wasn't how I wanted to tell him. "I messed up."

"What are you talking about?"

"Jared. He found us. He knows what we did."

"So what?"

"So, I—well." Where do I even begin? "I have to talk with him," I say, pulling on the blouse and jeans Jessie handed me. My mind swirls. Jared deserves to understand why I slept with Enki. Although it won't make him feel any better, he needs to know how I've changed, and why I'm not the same person he knew and loved.

I follow the path out of the cave to find Jessie leaning against a large rock. Off to the side, Jared paces, avoiding me, hands on his head. He looks as if he's having a panic attack.

Seeing him in such a state makes my entire body tenses. I need to take a moment and figure out what to say because I can't screw this up anymore. Jessie wags her finger at me as I approach. "You had fun last night."

"Let's table this discussion for later."

"Sure thing," she replies, still smiling.

"How did you find Jared?"

"I hiked up the valley and was almost at the Lyceum when he found me. He was looking for us and said that he had to talk to you right away, but he refused to tell me what's up."

I glance in Jared's direction, but threads of fear stop me from moving toward him. He radiates anger.

"You have to say something to him," Jessie says.

"I know."

At that moment, Jared turns toward me, his eyes filled with hurt. To make matters worse, Enki abruptly appears and gives my cheek a quick peck. Jared's face swells with fury.

I turn to Enki and just stare—unable to communicate how I feel.

"What?" he asks, smiling innocently.

"You guys had *a lot* of fun last night," Jessie says.

"This really is not the best time," I reply. I have to talk to Jared. Now.

As I approach, his back is turned, his body rigid. When I get closer, I notice his clenched fists. "Jared, I'm sorry you found me with him." After searching my mind for the right words, I add, "I know that it must have been very difficult for you to fully commit to me." I pause then take a step closer. "I did love you, Jared. I truly did. I would have sacrificed my own life for you."

He doesn't speak, doesn't move.

"I feel horrible. I didn't mean to . . . I mean, what I want to say is . . . I'm sorry that I hurt you, OK?"

His body shakes. With each passing second, I feel worse.

"Will you talk to me?"

Silence.

"Jared, I know that I gave you mixed messages from the beginning, and that wasn't fair. I didn't know how to reconcile my strong feelings for you with the knowledge that I might hurt you. And when you left, it felt like you made the decision. There was an emptiness inside me. How was I supposed to feel? I was alone, and Enki—" Jared's body jerks. "He was there for me. He helped me. You don't know how hard it was. I've been fighting to survive, and Enki believed in me." He still doesn't move. "Damn it, Jared. Will you say something to me?"

His head turns, revealing weary, red-ringed eyes. His whole body appears weighted down. With a seemingly herculean effort, he says, "Something is wrong."

"I know. I'm saying—that—well, I'm sorr—"

"No, I'm not talking about that," he replies, avoiding my gaze.

"I don't understand."

"All my sources. Mother Goddesses, allies, and spies among the Father Gods—everyone has gone cold since the Pruning began."

"So what?"

"It means something is wrong."

"Jared," I say, frowning with confusion. I'm trying to have an honest conversation about our relationship, and it feels as if he's trying to change the subject. "Maybe you're being paranoid."

He shakes his head. "You're in danger. We have to leave now."

"Back to the Lyceum?"

"No, go into hiding."

All of this is too familiar. It's as though we're back in Hawaii and he's telling me that I have to go to the Lyceum. But I've changed and he doesn't seem to realize this. "I'm not leaving. I've finally proven myself."

"I'm not giving you a choice in the matter." He grabs my arm.

A second later, Enki appears and shoves him hard. "Back off."

Jessie appears beside me. "Are you OK?" she asks me, glaring at Jared.

I nod, rubbing my wrist and also glaring at Jared. "Yeah, I'm fine."

"What's the problem?" Enki asks.

"He says we need to leave right away. Apparently, something is wrong."

Enki turns to Jared, arms crossed. "Care to explain?"

Jared releases a tense breath. I briefly wonder if he's about to slug Enki. "I have dozens of sources outside the Lyceum. They keep me informed about the Father Gods' activities, but ever since the Pruning began, all of them have gone silent. No one is communicating."

"They could be ignoring you," Enki replies with a smirk.

"Or they've all been compromised, or they've gone into hiding—or worse, they're all dead. In which case, we have to leave right away."

"Is he always this paranoid?" Enki asks.

Jared's face breaks into a snarl. "Paranoia is justified if an attack is imminent."

I finally have control. Although I might hate the brutality of the Lyceum, I can't deny that it's changed me. I'm proud of how far

I've come at the school. I can channel—something I never thought possible. I'm no longer filled with fear and uncertainty. To follow Jared, would be like going backward in my development. Also, it would mean leaving Enki. "I'm staying at the Lyceum to complete my training. I survived the Pruning, and I've earned my place at the school. I'm sorry, but I can't do what you want."

His face contorts with anguish. "I'm not doing this for myself," he says. "Everything I've ever done has been for you, Mattie. My job is to protect you, no matter what. And this is how you repay me?" He points at Enki. "How could you ever think that?"

My mouth drops open, and indignation flares in my chest. "And a fine job you've done protecting me!" I shout. "You brought me to a school where I have to fight to survive. Where failure means my death. You were never there. You never helped me. You never protected me. I had to fend for myself or get help from people who really cared for me," I say, placing a hand on Enki's shoulder.

Jared's face is as cool as granite. "Aren't you stronger?" he says, his voice stinging and venomous. "Wiser? Can't you channel your past lives? Wasn't that the goal? I'm sorry if it was hard. We knew that you'd have to fight to survive."

My body goes slack, as if it's a deflating balloon. This can't be. Was he really lying to me the entire time? "Did you know what they'd do to me at the Lyceum?"

His face remains hard and unyielding. "We thought it was the only way for you to master your abilities."

We. He keeps saying *we*, which can only mean that he's been collaborating with the Elder Gods the entire time. The cold truth sends shivers along my skin. He knew the struggles I'd face at the Lyceum. He knew how much suffering and pain I'd endure. He knew that my life would hang in the balance. He knew all of this before we even left Hawaii, yet he never told me. The betrayal hurts in my core.

Feeling that same emptiness I felt when he left me in the cafeteria, I stare into his eyes. "What was it that I told you?" I ask, not waiting for him to respond. "To be honest with me. That was one of the ground rules, Jared. From the very beginning, you lied to me. You manipulated me." I take a small breath and whisper, "I don't love you anymore." It hurts but it's true.

"I made you stronger," he says defensively. He crosses his arms, and the stern expression hurts me even more. "I was never meant to love you, Mattie. My job was to protect you."

"And now you know the price of your actions." I nod toward Enki, who looks unapologetic. "You have no right to judge me or the choices I make, and I don't need to feel guilty about any of my relationships. You were the one who set all this in motion, and now you can live with the consequences. I'm staying at the school, and you can leave."

The silence is so thick I could drown in it. I can't believe that our relationship has changed so much. I would have sacrificed my life for Jared. Now, seeing him is like drinking poison. He might think that what he did was for the greater good, but for me, it's the last straw. I'm done with him.

There's relief in knowing that I'm no longer shackled to him, that I can love whoever I want.

I can be free.

CHAPTER TWENTY-FOUR

RETURNING HEROES

As the four of us climb the path back to the Lyceum in tense silence, it's hard to believe what I've been through in the past week. I never could have imagined enduring all these challenges yet they're what shaped me. They molded me into a new person by pushing me beyond what I thought were my limits. I now understand that my fear of the Lyceum was paired with my fear of changing and becoming a different person.

And it's undeniable: I've changed. When I arrived, I couldn't channel a past life. I was afraid of ending up on the ground, my mind shattered into a thousand different voices. I was afraid of my power. That fear, though still present, no longer holds me back. I don't think I've completely mastered channeling; as is the case with any knowledge or skill, there's always more to learn. What I do have is a newfound curiosity and the tools needed to advance. I can calm the storm in my mind, focus, and accept the wisdom that has always been inside me.

Perhaps the greatest change has been my feelings toward the person walking ahead of me. When I arrived, I was in love with Jared. That love is no more, and strangely, I'm not sad about this. To a lesser degree, my heart has shifted toward Enki, and with him, I have faith that I'll continue moving forward with my abilities and goals.

But one thought haunts me. The Lyceum isn't a place that exemplifies the qualities of the Mother Goddesses. The Pruning best proved this. How many Agelings lost their lives? No one deserves to be pitted against another. Something is wrong with the world when violence is the only way to decide who moves forward.

Now that I've gained the right to stay at the Lyceum, I want to transform it. As I've been told over and over again, Gaia is one of the oldest and most powerful goddesses. So who better than I to change the Lyceum into a place that embodies love, tolerance, and acceptance? We don't need to use fear and brutality to train our own. No doubt, it will be a difficult task, but I can't think of a more important mission. If the Lyceum changed me, it can change others. Going forward, I want that change to be a positive, uplifting one.

Heart pounding and sweat dripping down my back, I'm both excited and anxious about this new chapter in my life.

My thoughts are interrupted as we arrive back at the school. A sudden coldness hits my heart as my jaw drops. None of us could have prepared ourselves.

Blood. So much blood. The Lyceum's courtyard is scattered with the dead bodies of priestesses and Protectors left to rot in the afternoon sun. The rancid smell makes me gag. Flies hover around the freshly killed. A battle took place here. The walls are pockmarked with bullet holes. Shattered glass litters the ground alongside the bodies. Furniture has been piled up in makeshift fortifications. Within the school a fire rages. Plumes of black smoke billow from the frames of broken windows. There's no sign of attackers—only the victims.

"What happened . . . ?" I ask, pushing down the nausea rising inside me.

"Look," says Enki, pointing across the courtyard. "Some are still alive." A Protector raises a hand, groaning in pain. Enki and Jessie rush over to him.

But as they leave, Jared turns in the opposite direction and rushes into the Lyceum. I know why. There are no gods among the slain here. If any are still alive, then they're inside—and maybe they need our help. I follow him, my feet splashing through puddles of blood.

As we sprint through the empty and ravaged hallways, searching for survivors, it feels as if we're running through an alien world. Death fills the classrooms where learning once occurred. To my horror, the victims are Agelings. My classmates. The young men and women I was supposedly in competition with. Now, they're all dead. All the pain I endured at the Lyceum—both physical and emotional—is small compared to this wanton destruction. Strangely, none of the victims are Younglings.

As I pass a classroom, a flash of movement makes me halt. Peeking my head inside the room, I see an upside-down trash can slide across the floor.

I approach slowly, unsure of what danger awaits underneath. As I reach toward it, the can skitters straight at me and knocks against my shins. I jump back and kick the can by mistake.

A blur of black and white rushes out and circles me, barking and nipping at my heels.

"Poppy!" I exclaim, bending down to pick up Coyote's frightened Boston terrier. She does a little shake and licks my hands. "Hey, girl! Are you OK?"

She isn't injured, and judging by her kisses, she's relieved to see me.

I put her back on the ground and continue following Jared. I find him in the room where the Elder Gods first declared that I'd have a week to prove myself. For a second I hold out hope that someone might have survived the massacre, but the battle appears to have been fiercest here, as evidenced by the charred walls and a smoldering fire in the middle of the room.

As I edge closer, fresh horror ricochets off the walls of my chest. The fire is a funeral pyre fueled by the burning bodies of the Elder Gods including Manat, Čhápa, and all the other teachers and masters of the Lyceum.

I gag but force myself not to run away; instead, I focus on their corpses, whispering a soundless prayer.

Yes, the Elders and teachers often pitted us against each other, and it's not how I wanted to be taught. But their intentions were good. They wanted to rebuild the ranks of the Mother Goddesses and bring balance and peace back to the world. They sought to stop the endless cycle of violence perpetuated throughout humanity's existence by defeating the Father Gods. They didn't deserve to die like this.

Jared leans against the wall—fists clenched, chest heaving, shoulders slumped. He shakes his head. The hissing orange flames are reflected in his eyes.

"Who did this?" I ask, not knowing what else to say.

But there's no need for an answer because we both know. The only beings capable of this much bloodshed are the Father Gods.

Looking as though he can't take anymore, Jared turns to leave. I follow, but when we reach the door, we hear a voice on the edge of death. "They took them."

We spin and rush toward the source. Hidden in the shadows, among debris and the bodies of several dead Protectors is Coyote. The god who didn't believe in me. The god who tried everything to get me to fail. The god who wanted me dead. Now, he's hanging by a thread—a shadow of his former self. His body is broken and his clothes are soaked with blood. Once, I might have felt a smidgen of satisfaction, but now all I feel is a deep sadness. Death and pain bring joy only to the petty and cruel.

Poppy is most concerned. She whimpers by his side.

"What can we do to help you?" I ask. Although I acknowledge his abuses of me, I forgive him. Past grievances don't matter anymore.

Coyote brushes me away with a weak wave. "I am too far gone to be helped. Don't waste your time." He's lying in a pool of his own blood. One hand holds onto his stomach, and I suspect that if his grip fails, all his insides will spill out.

"You'll die if we don't get help," I reply, kneeling beside him, refusing to be brushed away. The Mother Goddesses have already suffered too many casualties today, and I'll do everything in my ability to save one life, even if it's someone I might have hated.

His eyes close, as if he's meditating. "It doesn't matter. I'm cursed. Unfortunately, death is no obstacle for me."

That's right. When he dies, he'll Ascend into the nearest non-Ascended person. A worrying thought enters my mind. "Does this mean that when you die, you'll take over Jared?"

He eyes Jared and shakes his head. "Your oaths to the Mother Goddesses protect you from my curse." Coyote finally notices Poppy, and he smiles for the first time since we met him as Hank at the gas station in the desert.

"Can you tell us what happened?" I ask.

"We were attacked by the Father Gods. There were too many of them," Coyote explains, his voice trembling. "They overran our defenses and slaughtered everyone."

"But how did they find the Lyceum?" I ask. "Its location is a secret."

"Someone helped them." Coyote's body spasms, and he bares his teeth. The pain sends him into a coughing fit. When he recovers, he says, "I suspected that there was a traitor among us. I'd even setup preparations for the attack and an evacuation, but I underestimated the enemy's strength and speed." Coyote gazes at me. "Before I pass, there are two things I ask of you."

"What are they?"

"Take care of Poppy," he says, hugging the dog to his side. "She's a sweet soul who's always a joy in a cruel world."

"Of course. What's the second?"

"The Younglings." Coyote's face clenches. "The Father Gods kidnapped them."

I gasp. "Where were they taken?"

"I don't know."

"Why?"

"I don't know." Coyote reaches out and grabs my arm. "You must get them back, Gaia."

"What?" I try to yank my arm away. How can I possibly save anyone after so many Mother Goddesses died at the hands of the Father Gods? What can I possibly do? And why does Coyote suddenly have faith that I can do what he wants?

But his hold tightens and he pulls me close. "They are the future," he says, his eyes focusing on mine. "Without them, the Mother Goddesses will fail."

"But . . ." My voice shakes. "I don't know how."

"You will find a way," he says, his grip loosening. Blood dribbles out the side of his mouth as he grins. "You, Gaia, are stronger than I ever could have hoped. I never had a doubt that you'd rise to your former greatness. Now, it's time for you to assume your rightful place. You are our queen, our leader. You are also our last hope. You must be the goddess that you once were. Be the Gaia of the legends of old. I believe in you. I have always believed in you. When I return, I'll follow you wherever you lead us." A bout of coughing cuts him off.

The truth hits me like a meteor, and I stumble backward, tripping over debris, before finding my feet. He has to be lying; there's no other explanation. I recall all the abuse, fear, and loathing that was heaped upon me, often without reason. "You believed in me the entire time?"

"I did."

"Why did you treat me so horribly?"

A shred of regret flashes in his eyes. "We believed you needed to know true fear. If you were truly afraid, then you would push yourself harder to control your powers. I take all the blame. I thought that in order to beat the Father Gods, we had to be more like them. You showed me that I was wrong. But it is now too late to correct my mistakes. Nonetheless, thank you for reminding me of our true purpose."

The confession shakes my world. All Coyote's insults, threats, and pressure—he was pushing me to master my abilities. My entire time at the Lyceum was based on a lie. Jared knew the truth. Coyote knew. Even the Elder Gods.

And they succeeded in their mission.

Before, I might have been upset about the manipulation, but how can I be angry when so many were murdered? I feel grateful simply to be alive.

Coyote runs his fingers along Poppy's fur. "I'm weary of this life. I've lived too long. I used to think of memories, my past lives, as an anchor. Something to keep me grounded in place. A stable force to help me navigate the centuries." He pulls Poppy closer to him. She accepts his embrace and curls up in the crook of his arm, though his blood mats her fur. "I still consider my memories an anchor, but not a stable force. They are like an anchor dropped into the deep sea, destined to sink forever into a bottomless trench, and pull me along with them, drowning me in an abyss of darkness and cold." Coyote's head falls backward, and his eyes close.

"No! Stay awake."

"Find the Younglings," he whispers with his last bit of strength. Within a minute, his breath has stopped. My insides are hollow as I check for a pulse on his cold, lifeless skin.

"Mattie," says Jared, beside me. "We have to go. They might return."

Poppy whimpers, little moans. I gather her in my arms, and her body shivers against mine. As I stand, I sway on my feet. It's as if I'm sleepwalking through a nightmare. There's no logic. I have no control.

"Come on," he says, tugging my arm.

I shake off his hold. "We can't leave him like this." I feel empathy for Coyote; he's tired of life, but he has no escape from it. He's a prisoner to eternity, just as I am. Anger boils inside me. It's not fair. Why so much death and pain?

"He's passed. You're alive."

Jared's right, and it's because Coyote died that I'm able to forgive him. I cannot force myself to forgive Jared. "Why are you still here?" I ask, throwing all my spite into the question. "You knew all the horrible things they'd do to me, yet you still lied to me."

He turns away, hurt flashing in his expression. "I'm sorry, Mattie. I really am. I never meant to hurt you. I only wanted what was best for you."

"I wish I could accept your apology," I reply, fists clenched. "But I don't even know you anymore. I thought I could trust you. I don't think I can, which means that I can't have you around me."

"I don't have anything else in this world besides the Mother Goddesses and you. Please don't push me away."

His words strike like a dagger in my chest. "Jared, you wanted me to become this person. You wanted me to gain control. Well, you succeeded, and unfortunately, this means—" I'm cut off by a scream that cuts through the Lyceum's empty halls. A chill shoots up my spine, and my insides freeze into a solid, cold mass.

It's Jessie.

I rush back to the courtyard, still carrying Poppy. My thoughts race. Please, Jessie. Don't be hurt. I brought you into this. I can't lose you.

I'd never forgive myself.

Outside, we find Jessie frozen in place, her attention focused on the haggard figure holding a gun to Enki's head.

It takes me a second to recognize Daichsun. Clothing ripped and stained. Face covered in bruises. Blood seeping from a wound on his arm.

My heart hammers against my chest, and I freeze. Daichsun's eyes flicker like those of a rabid animal caught in a vehicle's headlights.

"He overpowered me," Enki says. "I'm sorry."

"Shut up!" Daichsun yells, pressing the barrel of the gun hard against his head.

Jessie points a finger at him. "He's the spy for the Father Gods."

"Liar!" Daichsun says. "I didn't do this." He looks right at me. "You're the true spy."

My jaw drops. "Me?"

"We were fine until you arrived," he says, tightening his grip on the gun. "The Lyceum didn't have problems. But strange things happened when you arrived. There's only one explanation. You betrayed us to the Father Gods."

"Why would I do that?"

A malicious scowl emerges on his face. "You don't even remember. This isn't the first time you've betrayed the Mother Goddesses. You betrayed us during the first Purging with the Father Gods, and then again during the second Purging, when you allowed the Father Gods to wipe us out. Your collusion has resulted in the deaths of innumerable lives. You've always been the Mother Goddess's greatest enemy."

His accusations leave me speechless.

"Daichsun, you know you won't hurt me," Enki says. "You're my mentor. You helped me learn to channel. Put down the gun and we can figure this all out."

He hesitates for a second, looking confused, and in that moment, a brick flies through the air and smashes into Daichsun's head. He stumbles, dazed. The gun falls from his hands, and when it hits the ground, it fires. Enki screams in pain.

I track the path of the brick and find Jared. He'd crept up and caught him off guard.

Daichsun freezes momentarily before sprinting into the Lyceum.

An intense dread fills my insides as I turn to Enki, but I exhale with relief to find he was lucky. The wound on his hand appears minor. "Go after Daichsun. I'll make sure he's OK," Jessie says to me, kneeling beside Enki. "I'll make sure he's OK."

Jared and I rush back into the burning building. We twist and turn down the empty, dark halls, passing dead bodies along the way, and finally corner him in one of the classrooms.

He pulls a knife from his belt and brandishes it. "Stay back," Daichsun warns. We keep our distance. There's nothing more dangerous than a cornered animal.

"How could you do this, Daichsun?" I ask. "How could you help the Father Gods?"

"I would never betray my people!" he shouts, and points the knife at me. "You've always been a trickster, Gaia. Why keep up the act? Just finish us off like you've always intended."

"Excuse me?" I reply, shocked. "You're the sole survivor. How did everyone else die while you lived? There's only one explanation. You were the spy."

He shakes his head. "I came back to look for survivors," he says, anguish filling his voice. "My friends, the other Agelings." He pauses and appears to be trying to compose himself. "I survived Cibola but was attacked on my way back to the Lyceum. I knew they must have attacked here first. I was able to break away and escape. But by the time I arrived, the damage had already been done. The Father Gods had massacred everyone."

Is this an act? Did he really care for the other Mother Goddesses? "I don't believe you," I say. "The entire time I've been here you've treated me like an enemy. You tried to kill me twice this past week."

His brow furrows. "No, I haven't."

"Yes, you have. During the race, you cut the rope Seuku was climbing."

He scowls. "I didn't do that, but I suspected you did."

"Stop lying!" I yell. "The second time, you made Pacha throw a grenade at me."

"I didn't do that. I thought you set that up to gain sympathy." A flicker of hesitation crosses his face. "You're accusing me of the things I thought you did."

I shake my head, not buying his words for a second. "Enki and I already knew you were the spy," I say. "We followed you last night, when you met with Whiro, a Father God. That's when we knew for sure."

Daichsun's mouth opens, and surprise flashes across his face, but he recovers quickly. "I was meeting Whiro because he's spying for us. Coyote suspected that there was a Father God agent at the Lyceum and sent me to gain information to confirm it. That's why the Pruning was announced. It was believed that the spy would never survive the challenges in Cibola."

"More lies. Why would a Father God ever agree to meet you?"

"He was afraid for his life. He wanted protection."

"Why?"

Daichsun narrows his eyes and he lowers the knife. "Something isn't right. Someone is confusing us."

Jared launches himself at Daichsun. Catching him unawares, he forces the knife from his hand and pins him to the ground.

"You'll pay for what you did."

"You're making a mistake," Daichsun says.

He doesn't struggle as we escort him back to the courtyard. And when we arrive, my blood freezes.

"I'm sorry, Mattie," Jessie says.

Dozens of soldiers wearing black combat gear and armed with swords and guns crowd the open space, where they hold Jessie and Enki hostage.

But then, Jessie walks toward me.

She isn't a prisoner. The revelation shocks me like a lightning bolt. Jessie is leading them. She holds a sword stained brown with blood. Her eyes refuse to meet mine. "I'm sorry," she says again, "but I didn't have a choice."

CHAPTER TWENTY-FIVE

WOLF IN SHEEP'S CLOTHING

The horizon has erupted in a patina of purples, yellows, and deep reds. The beauty of the desert sunset stands in contrast to the black masks of the armed invaders in the courtyard. Breathing unsteadily, I feel my back muscles clenching. Shock reverberates through me.

Jessie. My best friend. The person I trusted, loved and did everything to protect—she's leading these killers? I shake my head. No. It can't be. "Jessie, what are you doing?"

She finally looks at me, and there's a sad weariness in her eyes. "I'm doing what has to be done."

The words are like a gut punch. There's a fatalistic undertone to her declaration

"This can't be," I say, hoping to convince myself. "You're like a sister."

"He made me do it."

The hairs on my arms stand on end. "What are you talking about?"

"I had to do what he told me."

I can't believe what I'm hearing; this isn't the Jessie I know. "Look around you," I say, gesturing to the victims on the ground. "These people were innocents. You couldn't have helped murder them. You're a good person. You wouldn't have done this."

"I swear. I didn't have a choice," she repeats defiantly, yet a tear falls from one eye, a slight crack in the facade. "He took my parents and my sister. He held them hostage and promised to hurt them if I didn't do exactly what he said. Don't you see, Mattie. I really didn't have a choice."

That's when I realize that this was the bad thing that happened to her in Chicago. The thing she always refused to talk about. She's been living under the pressure of this threat the entire time I've known her. But that means . . . "Everything was planned," I say, the grand scale of the betrayal dawning on me. "Our meeting in Hawaii? Coming to the Lyceum? All the challenges . . ."

"I'm so sorry. I didn't know what I was. I was scared and didn't know what to do. I just . . ."

"Who's making you do this?"

"The Shadow, of course," she says, trembling.

The world spins, but my gut is frozen solid. I still can't believe it. "Our relationship is a lie. It was planned. You deceived me."

"I do think of you as a friend."

"Don't you dare say that!" I shout, anger replacing shock. "If you were my friend, you would have told me the truth. I could have helped you. We could have worked together to figure something out."

Her face blanches. "No one could know. He'd find out. Don't you realize that the Shadow knows all. Don't judge me too quickly." She stares into my eyes with an earnest, desperate need for validation. "What would you have done? This was the only way to get my family back. Wouldn't you do the same thing to save the people you love? You've sacrificed so much for love. Can't I do the same?"

Her words strike a chord. I do understand Jessie's situation, but her betrayal is still too fresh and hurts too much. I can't trust anyone. "You were my best friend . . . and now I don't know what you are. You were the traitor the entire time." As I say this, I let go of Daichsun. He was right. I did betray the Lyceum—by bringing Jessie here.

Her eyes narrow as she attempts to hide her pain. "It doesn't matter what you think. I must do as he commands." She wipes the last tear away.

"What does the Shadow want?" Daichsun asks, shaking off Jared's hands as well.

With that question, Jessie's weak facade cracks further. Her shoulders slouch and shake. One of the hooded soldiers steps forward and slaps Jessie hard across the face. She stumbles, shielding her face from more blows.

The soldier rips off their hood. Just when I think nothing else could shock me . . .

Tatiana flashes a cruel smile. "You're weak, just like her," she says to Jessie, pointing at me. "If you can not prove your usefulness, I don't see why my Lord will keep your family alive any longer."

Jessie's eyes go wide. "But he promised."

"Silence her," she says, as one of the soldiers grabs Jessie.

My skin prickles. I thought we'd seen the last of Tatiana in Hawaii. "What are you doing here?"

"I am here to ensure that my Lord's will be done."

"I don't understand you, Tatiana."

She appears taken aback. "What don't you understand, Goddess?" she says spitefully.

"Why do you serve the Shadow? He represents evil, yet you're perfectly content to follow his commands. You're like a child who doesn't question their parents' scolding."

Anger flares in her eyes, but she tempers her voice. "You still don't get it. Has it been that long, Goddess?" I have no idea what she's talking about, but she continues before I can reply. "I'm not here to explain the obvious to you, Gaia. I'm here to accept your unconditional surrender to my Lord. You must pledge to be his servant and do his bidding." She raises her chin in a show of arrogance. "You must agree to be his slave."

"What happens if I don't?" I ask.

She bares a mean smile, tilts her head, and snaps her fingers. Two of the soldiers drag Enki up to her. Despite his bullet wound and the dire circumstances, he radiates defiance. Tatiana places the edge of her sword against his neck. "We will kill this one, and then we'll kill the Younglings."

Time freezes as I consider my options. If I surrender, there's no guarantee the Shadow won't kill them all. I'm the only bargaining chip that matters to the Shadow. I'm the one who can make a change, and if I'm going to do anything, now is the moment.

"If they move an inch, kill them," Tatiana says. "I would rather bring back corpses than nothing to my master." Tatiana's men advance on us.

I glance at Jared, who looks as if he realizes the same thing. We have to do something, but what can we do that won't result in all of us being cut down? We're unarmed, beaten, bruised, exhausted, and surrounded, and I'm not expecting anyone to come to the rescue.

Our savior doesn't soar from the light. She leaps from the shadows.

A ball of fur flies across the ground and launches itself at Tatiana. She has no time to react before Poppy sinks her small jaws into her leg. Tatiana screams, taken by surprise by the ferocity of the little dog, whose teeth draw blood. They pair lurches in between the approaching men and us.

The scene devolves into chaos as Tatiana frantically tries to dislodge the Boston terrier from her calf. Taking advantage of the distraction, Daichsun leaps to a nearby wall and slams his fist against a protruding brick, which collapses inward.

A hidden door snaps open at our side. Daichsun disappears into the tunnel, and Jared grabs my arm and pulls me into the passage. Right as we disappear, gunfire roars behind us. We race down a short corridor and turn a corner. Daischun hits another brick, and I hear the door close. "That should buy us a minute or two," he says. "Let's go." He takes off down a stairwell.

"Enki!" I scream, anguish shivering through me. I left him behind. "We have to help him!" I rush to the door, but Jared pulls me back.

"You can't help him if you're dead," Jared says, and he's right, and I hate him for that. I follow them down the stone stairwell.

We reach a tunnel, and Daichsun opens another hidden door. But before we enter, the sound of frantic footsteps reaches us. Someone must have gotten through the door before it closed. We turn, ready to fight.

Jessie emerges a second later, her face drained of color. She's breathing heavily.

"Traitor!" cries Daichsun, rushing toward her, fists raised, but Jared and I yank him back. His eyes go wide. "She deserves to die."

The sight of her sickens me, but I keep my voice calm. "Why did you come after us?"

"I brought her," Jessie says. It's only then I notice she's carrying little Poppy, who yawns and licks her button nose.

"That dog has more courage than you do, but that doesn't answer my question."

"You heard Tatiana. The Shadow will kill my family no matter what."

"You already killed everyone at the Lyceum. Why should we trust you?"

"I know you'll never forgive me, but at least use me. I know where they'll take Enki and the Younglings."

"Tell us now!" Daichsun yells.

"No, you help me and I'll help you."

"I'll be damned if we help you," he says, struggling against our hold.

"No, she'll come with us," I reply, pointing at Jessie. "We can still use her."

"She can't come with us!"

"She can, and she will."

Daichsun stares with cold eyes at Jessie before spinning away. We follow him through a labyrinth of tunnels beneath the Lyceum. I hear people behind us, and the sound keeps me moving quickly. We run for half an hour in darkness punctuated with faint, flickering light bulbs. Eventually, we emerge into the cool nighttime air.

"This way."

We follow Daichsun across a flat stretch of earth to a large object covered by a camouflage netting, which he pulls off to reveal a single-engine airplane.

We pile into the vehicle, and Daichsun takes the pilot's seat. The engine starts, and we taxi across a long stretch of desert. An airstrip, I realize. Daichsun accelerates the craft. The engine roars as we race across the bumpy ground. Right as the plane lifts into the air, Tatiana and her soldiers emerge from the tunnel. Two men are dragging Enki along with them.

I wrap my arms around. It's going to be OK, I think, but I can't believe my lie. Enki was taken, and I couldn't save him. I couldn't save any of them.

CHAPTER TWENTY-SIX

REVELATIONS

O ut the window of the safe house, the volcano reaches high above Antigua, casting a long shadow over the cobblestone streets. The afternoon air is hot and humid. I hear a vendor down the road shouting out the prices of avocados. In one of the bedrooms, Poppy sits on my lap calmly licking my hand.

The safe house in which we've found refuge is one of hundreds that the Mother Goddesses have around the world.

The dog's ears perk up as a knock at the door interrupts my momentary peace. "Come in," I say.

Jared enters a second later. "Did you sleep?"

I point to my red-ringed eyes. It's been almost twenty-four hours since the fall of the Lyceum. "After what happened? No, I didn't sleep."

"The clock is ticking."

"I'm collecting my thoughts."

Jared grimaces. "The Shadow has the Younglings. He literally controls the future of the Mother Goddesses."

The mention of the children makes my throat go dry. "What will he do to them?"

"He won't keep them alive for long. He wants you. That's what Tatiana said. But what are his true plans?"

Jared conveniently forgets to mention that Enki is also a prisoner. My world darkens. I have to keep it together. "Has Jessie told you anything?" My skin crawls at the mention of her.

"No, she refuses to talk to Daichsun, and all she does with me is flirt."

"Classic Jessie. What should we do?"

"You need to talk to her."

I feel nauseated. "I might strangle her if we're in the same room."

"We're running out of time, and she'll only talk to you."

"I'm too angry."

"Mattie, you know her the best. You know how to get her to open up. Get over your anger and remember what's at stake. Will you please talk to her?"

I stare at the volcano for a long time, wondering why all the relationships I hold dear end up poisoned. "Fine."

As I rise, Jared leans in and touches my elbow. "There is one other thing." I turn toward him, and his eyes stare into mine. "I apologize for not being honest with you in the beginning. I've only ever cared for your well being. I never intended to hurt you."

"Jared, it's OK. You only know how to be one way. You can't change and that's all right."

"No, I can change," he insists. "I have. I hope one day you'll be able to see that. And you're the reason I changed."

"Sure," I say. "But our relationship doesn't matter in the grand scheme of things. What matters is saving these kids and getting Enki back. That's what matters to me."

I walk past him before he notices the tears in my eyes. How does he always know what to say to get under my skin?

I give Poppy one last kiss on her head, and then place her on the floor. Sadly, I'll likely never see her again. Whatever happens next won't be safe, but thankfully, one of the priestesses here has agreed to adopt her.

Jessie is in one of the spare rooms, handcuffed to a chair. Daichsun looks ready to bite her head off. "Where are they?" he shouts, making me grateful for the soundproof walls.

In response, Jessie rolls her eyes and yawns. She appears as tired as I am. Her clothes are ragged, and deep lines of worry crisscross her face.

Seeing her in such a state softens the wound of the betrayal. A knife was held to Jessie's throat. Like me, she didn't have a choice. It was forced onto her in the most vicious way possible. Although I shouldn't, I empathize with her. No one deserves the feeling of having to do something terrible to save the ones they love.

When she sees me, a smile shines on her face. "Hey, how're you?" she asks, the way she used to in Hawaii. She sounds like that fun, carefree, live-in-the-moment Jessie. The Jessie who was a lie.

"Cut the bullshit."

"We should kill her," Daichsun says, in the tone one would expect of someone discussing the weather. "She hasn't given us a single piece of information."

I nod and open the door for him. "Give us five minutes."

Mumbling a curse under his breath, he shakes his head and then leaves. I close the door behind him.

"A lot has happened in the last twenty-four hours," Jessie says.

"You're telling me. Don't you wish we were back in Hawaii?"

"Simpler times."

"I can't make you talk, but I'm hoping that you'll want to help us."

She glances away. "I'm scared. It feels like I've been scared my entire life, and I don't know how to stop being afraid."

"How about you start at the beginning? When was the first time the Shadow approached you?"

Her eyes dim. "It was about three years ago. I was in grad school."

"I didn't know you went to grad school."

"I studied social work. I'm afraid there's a lot you don't know about me."

"What happened?"

"During spring break, I went home to visit my parents and younger sister." She flinches, and her breath halts.

"And?"

"The place was completely wrecked. I thought it was a robbery, but then she appeared."

"Tatiana."

Jessie nods. "She told me that I had to do exactly what she said or my family would be killed. She showed me a video of them in captivity. After seeing that, I couldn't say no."

"What did she say?"

"She explained that I was a god." Her head drops into her hands. "Christ! I didn't believe her, of course. How could I? It sounded so impossible. But I had to do what she said because she was holding my family hostage. She told me that I had to go to Hawaii and befriend you."

"So they knew I was going there?"

"They had a lot of information about you, and they even trained me on the best way to make contact with you."

My head spins. It really was all planned. "If they were watching me the entire time, they knew we'd go to the Lyceum."

"Yes. That was the ultimate goal. They said that I had to get you to the Lyceum. They didn't know its location. But also, more importantly, they wanted you to learn to channel."

"Why?"

"They never said. Once we got to the Lyceum, my main mission was to make sure you succeeded. My secondary mission was to sow confusion. I was the one who cut the rope during the obstacle course, and the one who made Pacha throw the grenade."

I stare dumbfounded at this stranger. "Jessie, what are they planning?"

"I honestly don't know."

"Did you ever speak with the Shadow?"

"Never. It was always Tatiana."

"Come on, think. What's the Shadow planning?"

"I don't know," she says. "They never trusted me, so they never told me anything."

It's time to ask the most important question. "Where did they take the Younglings and Enki?"

"I'll tell you, but I want a promise."

"You're in no position to make demands."

"Then it's a request." She leans forward as much as she's able under the constraint of the handcuffs. Her lips quiver. "Please, help save my family. I only want them to be safe. I don't care what you do to me."

"How can we trust you?"

"What I did was horrible, and I deserve whatever punishment you think suits me. Do what Daichsun suggests—kill me. I'm fine with that as long as my family is saved."

I'm taken aback by her earnestness. True, she could be tricking me again, but the selfless nature of her request is at odds with possible betrayal. I rub my neck as I consider my options; I have few. "If your family is with the other hostages, then yes, I'll help you."

She sighs, and the skin around her eyes crinkles with relief. "Beijing. That's where they are."

"Beijing? Why there?"

She shakes her head. "Tatiana mentioned it at the Lyceum. She wants you to know."

"Do you know where in the city? It's a big place."

"No."

"This sounds like a trap."

"I completely agree."

I turn away, thinking for a moment. "I'll talk with the others." I rise to leave.

"Mattie, I never wanted any of this to happen. Will you forgive me?"

I stare into my former best friend's eyes. "I recognize that you were forced into a bad situation, and I can't say that I wouldn't have done the same thing. But I don't know if I'll ever be able to forgive you. You betrayed me. You should have told me the truth. I don't know what the solution is. There's no handbook for betrayal, but everything has to be set right—and that means saving the Younglings and Enki."

She leans forward, her cuffed hands clenched. "What will you do?"

"I'll figure it out." I leave before she can say anything else, locking the door behind me.

Jared and Daichsun are in the living room. There's a long silence after I explain everything to them. "We can't trust her," Daichsun finally says.

"I know we can't," I reply.

"In all likelihood," Jared says, "going to Beijing will be stepping into their trap."

"We must gather our remaining forces and fight them," Daichsun says. "This is the only way we have a chance of winning."

"Forces?" Jared shakes his head. "No, it will only be us."

"What about the Mother Goddesses, Protectors and priestesses around the world? They would come to help us."

"Yes," Jared agrees, "they would, but I won't pull them into this. In all likelihood, I bet that's what the Shadow would love—a final showdown to destroy the Mother Goddesses in one fell swoop. I refuse to be responsible for more deaths. We have to consider the survival of our entire cause."

I hadn't thought of it that way. He has a good point. "So if we do this, it'll be us fighting alone against the Shadow."

"Yes."

"This is madness," Daichsun says. "We don't stand a chance."

"Who says that you'll help us?" I ask Daichsun, my voice sharp. "You never cared about me."

"I still don't," Daichsun says. "But I care about the Mother Goddesses. I care about the Younglings, and the future of the world."

"You've hated me from the moment I arrived at the Lyceum. Why should we trust you?"

"Why should I trust *you*?" he asks, pointing an accusing finger at me. "You failed the Mother Goddesses in the last Purging. I was the one who stole back Diamant's Dagger, and hid it well, after you failed. Did you even know that?" His harsh expression morphs into a smirk, and he opens his palms. "Look. We're in the same boat. There are only two of you, and you're not even an Ascended god," he says, looking at Jared. "No offense." Jared shrugs. Daichsun focuses on me again. "We both have the same goal, and we need all the help we can get. You're hardly the best ally. I've seen how you fight, and truthfully, I'm not impressed. But I'm not too proud to reject help when I need it. Are you?"

His words silence me. He's been an asshole, but Daichsun was the most advanced student at the Lyceum. He was there for years, mastering channeling. His experience would be invaluable.

"Fine," I say with a sigh. "One last thing—what is it you want?"

He bristles. "Revenge against the Father Gods."

"But why?"

He looks down and is silent for a moment. "They killed my parents," he says, meeting my gaze. "I was sixteen when the priestesses found me. I had no idea why the killers came to our house, but it was because of me. I hadn't been there when it happened. The priestesses took me to the Lyceum. The school has been the only home I've known since my parents' deaths, and now, once again, the Father Gods have come and taken everything away. My sole goal is to destroy them."

Upon hearing this, I'm silent, feeling a lump arise in my throat. Daischun is as broken as any one of us. "Fine," I finally reply. "But we do this together. That means you have to show some respect to both of us. We're a team now."

He nods. "I'll do the best I can."

"Then it's decided," says Jared, "We're going to war against the Shadow. Three of us against an army."

"Four, actually," I add.

"What?" Daichsun asks. His eyes spark with suspicion. "You're letting Pele fight with us? We can't trust her."

"We can trust her to do anything to get her family back. We can use that to our advantage."

"I won't allow this!"

"Jared, what do you think?" I ask.

"We can't trust her, but we can use her. She should come along."

"Two against one, Daichsun. Are we still a team or are you already backing out?"

Daichsun opens his mouth to protest but then nods begrudgingly. "What's the plan?"

"I have no idea," I reply. "I don't even know where in Beijing we should go."

"Oh, that's easy," says Jared, surprising both Daichsun and me. "There's only one place where the Shadow would be."

"Where?"

"It's where the Shadow has ruled for centuries," he explains, his face paling. "The problem is, getting in will be suicide."

CHAPTER TWENTY-SEVEN

ALEXANDRIA

*W*e've come to Alexandria to kill, but death has beaten us here. Camilla and I stay close to the shadows of the city's buildings. Our long cloaks trail behind us as we navigate the back alleys. Fresh graffiti on the walls chills my skin and makes my insides twist: "Death to the False Goddess and her supporters."

The acrid smell of smoke assaults my nose. Large portions of the city are up in flames. As we were entering the harbor, we witnessed them burning women at the stake. Some of them were Mother Goddess priestesses, but many were not.

Nearby, mobs chant and cry as they kill and loot.

We turn a corner, and I pull Camilla back into the shadows as one of these angry mobs passes us.

Camilla turns to me, frustration flashing in her eyes. "Why hold me back, Gaia? Those ten fools deserve to feel the edge of my blade."

"In times like these, ten fools can multiply to a hundred with one scream."

She breaks away from my grasp. "But they are killing our people. Our sisters are dying, and we do nothing."

"No, child, our mission is much more important. Yes, our sisters die, but as long as we are successful, their deaths won't be in vain."

Her expression burns intensity. "I am tired of fleeing. It is time to stand and fight."

I understand her frustration. Roman sentinels harassed our trireme from Greece. They outnumbered us three to one, and fleeing *was wiser than fighting. If it had not been for a storm, which dispersed our pursuers but tossed and turned us in the open sea, we likely would not have arrived alive. However, I am certain our mission in Alexandria will ultimately save more lives if not win us the war.*

"Be calm," I say. "We are close to the temple."

She follows, her grip on her sword tightening.

The city rises from the sea. I peer back to see the lighthouse shining out over the black ocean. Besides the city's famous library, it's the grandest structure—both illuminate the ignorance of mankind. Despite the lighthouse and the library, I sense chaos encroaching on all that we gods have sought to build in the world. Dark times are coming, and I fear that there is only one way to stop this advance.

The street broadens into an open square, and at its center is a magnificent building. We have finally arrived, but my hopes plummet as I see a crowd of shadows camped in front.

"Is this the temple?" Camilla asks, and I nod. "That mob does not appear to be planning to move anytime soon."

There are about thirty of them armed with clubs, knives, and other weapons. Their loud, drunken, bawdy cries echo through the square.

"True, child. I only pray that our sisters were able to escape."

"We must enter the temple, correct?"

"Yes," I reply, racking my mind to come up with a way to do so that doesn't alert the mob.

"Is there another way besides the front gate?"

"No. There is only one entrance. It was never meant to be a military installation."

"Then let me help clear a path for you."

Before I can restrain her, Camilla leaps into the square and screams, "You small-dick bastards! Come and get me!"

Every head in the square turns to her, and every hand reaches for a weapon. "I'll meet you back at the trireme by first light," she says, sprinting away.

The men chase after her, their screams and yells reverberating down the streets.

I shake my head. That foolish girl. She better not get herself killed. Yet I can't restrain a smile. Camilla has cleared the entire square. Still keeping to the shadows of the surrounding buildings, I make my way to the temple's entrance.

It is worse than I feared.

The temple is in ruins. Across the floor lie dead Protectors and priestesses. There is blood everywhere. Black smoke stains the floor, and crude graffiti and pictures desecrate the walls. All the holy relics have been stolen and the treasury has been plundered.

My stomach churns, and the chaos makes me dizzy, but there is only one thing that I can do. I must focus on my mission. I move into the interior, heading toward the inner sanctum.

When I arrive, I quickly realize that I'm not alone. I see a shadow rummaging through the shelves. A looter searching for treasure.

No. Not a looter. A Roman soldier. He pushes aside shelves and is close to the secret compartment, which holds the artifact I am seeking.

I hate to kill, but my mission here must be a secret.

Creeping silently, I move behind the figure. I raise my sword and leap forward to deliver a fatal blow.

But to my amazement, the soldier swings around in time and blocks my blow. He parries my blade and swings his sword at my unprotected side. I leap away just as his blade slices the air where my flank would have been. The soldier takes advantage of my loss of balance and slams his foot into my side. I tumble to the ground, and my sword slips from my hand.

I'm stunned by the skill of this soldier.

He rushes at me, blade aiming for my throat. There is no way to stop this. I'm as good as dead, and I'm as surprised as a rabbit caught in a snare. The blade thrusts down, but the attacker freezes when the sword's edge is a hand's width from my neck. "Gaia?" the soldier whispers.

The blade lowers, and as my attacker removes their helmet, ribbons of luscious, red hair come cascading down. A wave of relief rushes through me. "By the Gods! Hathor, is that you?"

Hathor steps into the light of a burning torch, revealing her beautiful face. Her red hair, with stripes of blonde running through it, stretches down her back. Her deistic form scintillates and sparkles in the fire light.

"Gaia!" she says again, this time excitedly but voice still low. "You're alive!" She offers me her hand and hauls me up from the ground. "I almost killed you."

"I could say the same for you. It warms my heart to see you alive. I thought they killed all the priestesses and goddesses. How did you avoid the massacre?"

Hathor shoots me a mournful expression, and she slips her sword back into its sheath. "I was upriver, visiting the temple at Memphis. Thankfully, the locals warned us about the Father Gods. When they attacked, we experienced only light casualties. I was able to help most of the priestesses escape."

"Did you receive my notice? About hiding?"

She shakes her head. "We received no such notice."

My shoulders slump. "I fear that the Father God's intercepted my messenger."

"I came to Alexandria to warn our forces. But when I arrived, I found the mobs and killings had already occurred." She peeks out a small window. "Why do they murder us? What about the truce?"

I tell her about the prophecy and what I learned from Janus.

She stares in disbelief. "It can't be. Janus must be lying so that he can force us into war."

"Unfortunately, I believe him. There is only one way for us to avert this fate—fulfill the prophecy before it is too late."

"Kill your husband?"

The truce between the Mother Goddesses and the Father Gods has been maintained for hundreds of years because of our marriage. This marriage of equals sealed the truce, but the Purging has proven that peace cannot last. He seeks total power. That is why I must end him. If I kill him, balance can be maintained. "The last I heard, he was in Alexandria."

Hathor shakes her head. *"He left for Jerusalem a week ago."*

"Damn!"

"Gaia, you're only one goddess. You cannot possibly defeat him by yourself. He is the most powerful Father God. Let me come with you and help. Together, we have a better chance."

I briefly consider her offer but decide against it. "No, my friend. For this type of mission, fewer is better. Besides, this is my destiny, my fate. I must confront him alone. You must keep the Mother Goddesses alive."

She nods. "If that is the case, you will need this." From her tunic, she removes a dagger with a blood-red blade.

"Diamant's Dagger," I say, another wave of relief passing through me. I had feared that it had been looted. I take the weapon, holding it with care.

"Is it true what they say about it?" Hathor asks.

"Yes. I have used it before and know its power. I will be able to kill not only my husband's body but also his soul. Either by the touch of my hand or this blade, his death will be permanent, and he will never Ascend again."

"Let us hope that it will save us." She grabs my hand. "Be careful. The fate of the Mother Goddesses rests on your shoulders."

"I will not fail. I will destroy him and restore peace to our world. He will pay for the deaths he has caused." I slip the dagger into my belt. "Where will you go?"

"East. I will lead our sisters to Ganesha's dominion. He will give us sanctuary. We will keep alive the bright light of civilization and humanity."

"I fear that this war will spread across the world and no place will be safe, but Ganesha will hold up a wall against the evil that is spreading like a disease through humanity."

Our conversation is interrupted by the clang and clatter of armored guards. The servants of the Father Gods are close by. "May the winds of luck always be at your feet," she says, "and may you arrive at your destination without injury."

We embrace one last time and escape into the night. To Jerusalem I must travel. I pray that my efforts to bring peace back to this world will not be in vain.

The plane lands, and I jolt awake. Beijing's dull smog blankets the sky outside my window.

"Is everything OK?" I turn to Jared. His eyes are round with concern. "You were mumbling and acting strange in your sleep. What did you dream about?"

How can I begin to explain that the Shadow, the one behind the Purging, the one who has kidnapped my friends, who has committed all these murders, was my husband?

Once again, the fate of the Mother Goddesses rests in my hands. If I fail, all of humanity will fail, and the world will fall back into darkness and war.

CHAPTER TWENTY-EIGHT

FORBIDDEN CITIES

Bright yellow lights illuminate Tiananmen Square, and the pollution-filled nighttime air glows like a sick fog. As Jessie and I walk toward the Forbidden City's looming closed gates, the hairs on my arms stand on end. What did we get ourselves into?

I tell myself not to be afraid, but that reassurance does little to ease my bone-dry throat and fast-beating heart. Jessie's terrified expression also provides no comfort. She knows full well what the Shadow is capable of.

As our taxi drove toward Tiananmen Square, I thought it was strange that we didn't see a single person. In a city of millions, I'd expect to spot a passing car or bicyclist. This lack of people only confirms the disconcerting fact: they know we're here.

The Forbidden City's gates swing inward automatically, ominous and inviting. Cold sweat beads on my neck as we pause before entering. We really need a better plan.

I should feel glad that I don't have the hard job. That dubious honor belongs to Daichsun and Jared, who are performing a Mission: Impossible-esque exploit—complete with setting off explosives, eluding guards, climbing through water mains, dodging booby traps, and, of course, planting more explosives—to help us escape. It's a Hail Mary type of plan. A crazy, could-not-possibly-work type of plan. Everything has to come together perfectly for us all to escape in one piece. If they fail, we don't have a chance, and Enki and the Younglings are as good as dead.

Unfortunately, it's the only plan we've got.

"Are you sure you want to do this?" I ask Jessie, who's stooped over. "You don't have to come."

"This is the only way to save my family." She's different from the Jessie I once knew. The pressure and stress have taken a toll. It's as if she's carrying the weight of the world on her shoulders.

Jessie starts forward, but I pull her back. "If you betray us again, you won't leave here alive. You understand?"

She nods wearily.

We walk through the open gate, and the Forbidden City's pagodas tower over us. A chill wind sweeps through the empty cobblestone square, sending shivers through my body.

When we arrive at the center of the square, the gates close behind us. An air horn blasts, and hundreds of armed soldiers spill in from all directions, blocking all means of escape.

What follows are several seconds of tense silence. Hundreds of eyeballs watch us, waiting for our next move. Perhaps they think that we've come to fight?

Neither Jessie nor I have any weapons.

Tatiana emerges from a huddle of soldiers. She frowns and shakes her head. "You're surrendering? What a disappointment."

"Did you give us a choice?" I ask.

She smirks and twirls her finger through her hair, a gesture more appropriate for a girl half her age. "I had hoped you would attempt something clever."

"Apologies for not meeting your expectations."

"Where's your boyfriend?" she asks. "And the Mongolian war god?"

"I told them not to come."

Tatiana turns to Jessie. "Is she telling the truth?"

"No," she replies without hesitation. "They're in the city, and they'll attempt to rescue her."

It feels as if my heart has dropped into my stomach. I knew I couldn't trust Jessie, but her immediate betrayal is still a blow.

"Where are they?"

"We split from them an hour ago. They're west of the city."

I exhale quietly, holding onto an ember of hope. What Jessie said was a lie. And as long as Jared and Daichsun are alive, there's a chance.

Tatiana turns to a soldier. "Two are missing. Find them." Then she continues to press Jessie. "Why are you here?"

"Fulfilling my end of the bargain." Her face is expressionless. "I'm delivering Gaia, as you wished."

Tatiana rewards her with a lizard smile and a slow clap. "Well done. My Lord will be pleased."

"Do what you promised. Let my family go."

She raises a hand. "Aren't you curious as to why we want her?"

"Not really."

Tatiana laughs without humor. "Your impertinence is admirable if not foolhardy. My Lord still has plans for you."

"This was not part of the deal."

"You're not in a position to make demands. Take her away." Several guards grab Jessie, and pull her toward one of the buildings.

"Are the Younglings and Enki still alive?" I ask.

Tatiana flashes her teeth. "My Lord is waiting for you." She turns and I follow, silently praying that Daichsun and Jared will succeed.

As we enter one of the temples, the sharp smell of incense assaults my nose. Brass basins hold burning fires. Red banners adorned with a strange symbol decorate the pillars. The symbol reminds me of a mouth swallowing the world.

"I'm surprised you came to us without resisting," Tatiana says, as we walk.

"Just because I came doesn't mean I'm surrendering."

"You are nothing. Thank my Lord for your survival. He had demanded that no matter what challenges you were put through, you were to be kept alive."

"Why?"

"You haven't realized it?" She stops, surprised. "You had to master your abilities. The only way he could be certain was by testing you."

"So all the deaths and murders happened because he was testing me?"

"You do not control your fate," Tatiana says. "And what do a few deaths mean to an eternal god like my Lord? Nothing."

"You people are sick."

Anger ripples across her pretty features, and she bares her teeth. "You will bow to him in the end."

"I still don't understand why you're helping him. What is he offering you?"

She smirks. "You don't recognize me? When you do, you'll realize why he is the true Lord, and why you are but a shadow of his greatness."

Then it hits me. "Are you Ascended?"

She levels her cool gaze at me, and her hate-filled eyes make my skin crawl. "Follow me, Gaia."

At the far end of the temple, we enter an elevator. Tatiana presses the down button, and the doors open. Bland Muzak drifts from ceiling speakers.

The numbers blink as we sink.

Sublevel 1

Sublevel 2

Sublevel 3

"Where are we going?" I ask.

"During the Cold War, a Father God and servant to my Lord, built a city beneath Beijing as a last-stand retreat in the case of nuclear attack," she explains, "They called it the Underground City. After their fall, my Lord repurposed the city for his own uses."

Down we travel until we reach sublevel twelve. The elevator jolts to a stop, and the doors chime as they open to reveal a modern, sleek, corporate-like facility. Everything is sterile white. The polished floors shine, and a strong smell of antiseptic cleaner wafts in the air. The same symbol as the ones on the banners—a mouth swallowing the world—is painted on the wall in front of us.

I follow Tatiana down a hallway past glass windows that reveal rooms filled with humming computer servers. Despite the cold air pumping through the space, sweat prickles my skin.

We turn down another brightly lit passageway. This one is lined with laboratories. Along the back walls are shelves filled with petri dishes. Dozens of scientists in white coats and medical masks work in the closed-off rooms.

My attention is drawn to a huddle of scientists gathered around a dagger that stands upright in a glass sphere of bubbling liquid. I recognize it. It's Diamant's Dagger. The same one that Gaia had in Alexandria, and that Amahle died retrieving.

I gasp and inhale sharply as nausea ripples through me.

A corpse lies exposed on an examining table.

I recognize the Ageling. Her face is blue and lifeless, her chest opened up like a Thanksgiving turkey. A female Father God with the deistic form of a serpent peers into her innards, probing organs with scalpels and tiny mirrors. She places a piece of pale veined flesh onto a petri dish.

That's what's in all the petri dishes. Pieces of gods. Pieces of people.

I rush to the glass barrier and slam my fist against it. The god glances up, surprised. "Stop!" I shout at Tatiana. "What the hell are you doing to her? Why are you dissecting her like a lab rat?" I ask, my nausea replaced by rage.

"Because she is a lab rat," Tatiana replies. "My Lord, in his wisdom, has been studying the biological and physiological aspects of Ascended mortals' flesh. He is searching for the connection between the spirit and the corporeal. He has made great advances in the field." Her eyes shine with admiration as she looks at the dead girl.

My back muscles tighten. How can she be so insensitive?

We leave the laboratory hallway and arrive at a large steel door. Tatiana puts her face in front of a retinal scanner, which beeps a second later. The doors swing open to reveal another dark passageway.

Tatiana stands to the side and gestures for me to enter. "My Lord awaits you."

I enter but then halt. She still hasn't answered my questions. "Why do you serve him?"

She flashes her familiar mean smile and shoves me hard into the dark room.

I stumble backward into a thick black curtain, and when I emerge, I find myself in a huge spherical room that reminds me of a planetarium. Hundreds of televisions flash scenes from around the world. News channels in dozens of countries display a torrent of images and sounds. Streaming CCTV footage shows a riot in Europe; next to it, black hooded figures exercise at a training camp in a desert. A Go-Pro video shows soldiers exchanging gunfire with unknown assailants. There's even a live feed from what appears to be the International Space Station. The sound is deafening, and the speakers compete with one another. How can anyone garner anything from all the media, from all the noise?

"What the hell is this place?" I say to myself.

In the center of the room, on a raised podium, is a rocking chair. Its white paint is peeling and chipped. It takes me a second to see the shriveled, diminutive figure sitting. Shrouded in shadows, the person unfurls their arm like a praying mantis extending an appendage. A withered hand clicks a button on a smartphone.

The cacophony of sounds is silenced, but the images on the screens continue to flash. A bright spotlight illuminates the figure in the chair as well as a path to the podium.

I walk toward the chair like a lamb to the slaughter, but stop halfway to the podium. I always imagined the Shadow's deistic form to be something terrifying, but the strange thing is that this person doesn't have one.

It occurs to me that this might be the reason the Shadow has been able to survive wars, revolutions, and the collapse of civilizations. Without a discernible deistic form, the Shadow is truly a shadow, able to avoid a Descended life by hiding in plain sight.

Instead of someone imbuing evil, an elderly woman with a kind face rocks in the chair. She wears gray sweatpants and a yellow cardigan with a red carnation buttoned to the lapel.

She doesn't stand but gives me a grandmotherly smile. In one hand, she holds a pistol aimed at me, and with the other, she waves me forward. "Mattie, my love. Come closer. I wish to see your face one last time."

CHAPTER TWENTY-NINE

The Shadow

"It's been too long," she says, her voice amplified over speakers. Despite the woman's homely demeanor, her smile disturbs me; it's like a painted mask. "Closer. My eyes are bad. I wish to see the wife I love."

Keeping my gaze on the barrel of the gun. I don't budge. "I can't imagine any of my past lives loving you."

A pleasant grin emerges as she appears to recollect some distant memory. "Ah, but you did," she says, gently rocking in the chair. "We were very much in love. You don't remember. History is harder to recall the older you get. Our five-hundred-year marriage was one of the happiest times we've lived."

"Excuse me?" It's nearly impossible to mentally reconcile the idea that I was married to this woman *and* that we were together for five hundred years.

She nods. "Of course our bodies were different, but we ruled together for centuries. It was a time of great peace and prosperity. How could I forget our one-hundredth wedding anniversary? Ascended gods, both Mother and Father, came together for a month-long celebration and symposium. The spectacles were boundless—philosophers, jesters, contortionists, supposed shamans, and alchemists. The wonders of the ancient world were on full display." She stops rocking and muses. "Well, considering the amount of wine enjoyed, perhaps my memory is a little fuzzy about that particular episode," she adds with a wink.

I know I can't trust her. The scene she paints resonates. I was there. I was part of the celebration. But there's something she's leaving out.

"Do you remember our travels?" she asks. "We visited Ganesha in his opulent temples. Feasted with the Father Gods of the Han dynasty. Trekked through the jungles of the Khmer tribes to meet newly Ascended Mother Goddesses. Rode the last of the Syrian elephants." The Shadow's smile grows wider with each memory. "The world was smaller back then. Our friends may have lived great distances away, but we were connected by our immortality."

Behind the wall in my mind, I sense flashes of these memories. We did share these experiences, but I can't acknowledge them. That is what she wants.

"And of course, everyday I remember our children."

"What?" I ask, shock reverberating through me again.

"Are you surprised? What else are husband and wife to do? They were our everything. How fast they grew. How proud we were of their small triumphs. Often I will sit and recall small scenes, like the time I taught Tiberius to hunt wild boar, or the joy Caligula took in the theater, or Claudius's mischievous tricks. Their childhoods were but a blink of an eye in our lifetimes, but they outweigh the sum of millennia."

I remember what she describes. There I am, Gaia of Rome, cradling my newborn son, staring into his eyes, feeling his small heartbeat, consumed by all the hopes and fears of any new mother. A part of me wants to cry; I was so happy.

She shakes her head. "It's hard to believe, but we created mankind together. We were the first gods. When man emerged, he was nothing more than a primate, but I gave him tools and knowledge; you gave him love and humanity. I enriched his mind while you enriched his heart."

This explanation is too simple, too well rehearsed, too appealing. "You're not remembering history correctly."

"I remember a time when there was peace. When the world was in balance. It was a time before other gods. It was a time of just you and me." She pauses and stares into my eyes. "Mattie, we have shared lifetimes of joy. I know you remember them. The last thing I would ever do is cause you any harm. I have always been on your side."

Reality comes crashing home with that statement. I feel my cheeks growing red. "You're a murderer."

"Yes," she acknowledges, her face twisted in a complex mix of regret and shame. "The road to now has been long and difficult, fraught with suffering, but you should know that there is a reason for everything, and although every death was painful, it was necessary for the events about to unfold," she says, not revealing any more, still staring into my eyes. Her mouth trembles. "Please, come closer."

I need to face this monster—this woman who has sought to destroy my life. The person who is the reason for over a dozen murders of people I knew, including my best friend. This is not the time for cowardice; it's time to look the devil in her eyes and spit in her face. I'm tired of living in fear. I climb the steps to the podium.

The Shadow is small, skinny, and sickly. Her mottled, wrinkled face reminds me of the skin of an old apple sitting in the back of the fridge. Untouched, unwanted. Thin strands of hair barely hide her skull, while thick, bushy eyebrows sprout like swamp weeds.

"You're surprised."

"I expected you to be . . ."

"Younger?"

"No," I say. "More evil looking. You remind me of someone who wandered off from a nursing home."

She smiles and uses the butt of the pistol to scratch an itch on her cheek. "Expectations are set up to be broken in our world."

"Are you really the Shadow?"

She bristles and then shakes her head. "I don't like that name. It was given to me by those who never understood my true nature. I'm much more than a shadow."

"Then who are you?"

"I've known many names throughout history. I've always existed, along with you, for the history of mankind."

"What name do you prefer now?"

"Quite simply, I am the essence of the Father God."

"Pure evil?" I ask, my jaw tight.

"No, my love. You forget that the ethos of the Father Gods has become corrupted over the millennia. Admirable ideals that were exalted—intellect, logic, and wisdom—have been replaced by hate, anger, and tyranny, but I have always remained pure. I am facts and rationality. I am science."

"I've never heard of a science god before," I reply. "In fact, now that I say it out loud, it doesn't make any sense. Gods and science don't go hand in hand, do they?"

"Mattie." She says my name with too much familiarity for comfort. "You have never failed to be anything but perceptive. It's a paradox. How can it be possible? Where is the scientific explanation for who we are and what we can do?" she asks with a quizzical smile. "I have devoted my lifetimes to discovering the true nature of the Ascended and where they source their power, and you know what? I have failed. All the experiments and research has yet to explain why the Ascended exist. I still don't know why they're here."

"It doesn't look like you're done experimenting. I saw what you did to the Ageling. It was disgusting," I say, feeling a sudden urge to wash my hands.

"It is my nature to continue my studies, but the true purpose of that experiment you witnessed has to do with your final mission."

"Which is what?"

She leans back in her chair, assessing me. "I'm here to return us to the happy days we once knew. When we were tied together for the pursuit of knowledge but our hearts were bound by love."

"If you wanted that time and that love, maybe you shouldn't have killed all the Mother Goddesses."

She nods. "I admit it was a mistake. I acted rashly. You must understand, at the time, it was the most logical course of action. Although I'm not in favor of prophecy, Janus has never been wrong. I really thought that if I stamped out the elements of the Mother Goddesses, then humanity would be better. But I learned something. The more I tried to crush the spiritual, the more humans gravitated toward it. So I stopped trying to fight these elements. Instead, I've learned that we need to embrace and accept these qualities. It's the only way to solve the problem. You see, I was looking at the problem wrong."

"How so?"

"The problem was never you. The true problem is that the other Ascended gods spoiled our vision. They corrupted our influence. They sent mankind down a path to their own destruction." Her stare is fevered and intense. "Both the Mother Goddesses and the Father Gods are the problem. Both must be destroyed. So, in a way, although I didn't intend it, the Purging of the Mother Goddesses was the right step. Once the Father Gods are destroyed as well, society can be rebuilt. It might have taken two thousand years, but I finally understand. Humans need faith. They need one true faith. This is why I need you more than ever."

"If you need me so much, why do you want to kill me?"

The old woman's mouth falls open, and she recoils. "I don't want you dead. Just the opposite—I've been nurturing you, and I'm so proud that you have made it this far."

"What are you talking about?"

"I've been watching you for a long time. Ever since we discovered you in Salem, I've been impressed by your development. You have shown over and over again your ability to adapt and develop."

My eyes widen. "You've been watching me since Salem?"

"You are very important to me, but you were so young and unprepared. You had to learn the full might of your abilities. That's why I pushed you. That's why I sent the god of war after you and why I sent Pele to you. That's why I made sure you went to the Lyceum. If you didn't master your skills, you wouldn't be able to help us bring about the new world we need."

A wave of dizziness overtakes me. This woman has been an invisible puppet master. She's been a guiding force in my life. "What specifically do you want from me?"

Her eyes glimmer with the energy and knowledge of a woman much older than the one I see before me. "We are at the moment where history changes. Where the wheel will be broken."

"Stop speaking in metaphors."

"You," she says, pointing the gun at me, "and I were born to be queen and king for eternity. We were given the greatest gift and responsibility: to be stewards of mankind. Our children, the other Ascended gods, they were meant to serve us. But long ago, they rebelled, and from then on, it has been war after war after war. It was only in the past two millennia that I was able to gain control over the world. The missing piece is you. We must reunite to create a new world."

"I'll never do that," I reply, glancing at one of the muted screens, which displays a violent riot. This woman is a wellspring of pain and suffering.

"I know. Not yet. However, you will need to trust me. I have studied human societies as well as the rise and fall of civilizations. I know the secrets to creating perfection, but we can not achieve it unless we do it together."

I'm stunned by the woman's declaration. "If you know the secrets to creating a perfect society, then what about the deaths and horrors in the twentieth century? Who are you kidding?"

Her grin hides a lurking rage. "All deaths are necessary in the grand scheme of human development. This has always been your problem, Gaia. You love them too much. Especially the individual, as opposed to the group. You don't see them for what they are."

"What are they then?"

"Humans are the manifestation of the problem—like a disease that is the result of an outside factor. The Ascended have led humans down a horrible path. You witnessed the Lyceum? They have been corrupted by their own beliefs. They have lost their way. They strive to create an army, but where is the love that they stand for? It is absent."

A shiver runs through me. Despite everything, I agree with her on this.

"The Father Gods are no better. They were long ago corrupted. Their religions are hollow and filled with hypocrisy. They battle only for more power. I learned long ago that there are few gods worthy of existence. That's why I began the Purging, but I have not only been Purging Mother Goddesses. Father Gods too have been eliminated. This Purging needs to spill over. It must overwhelm the world. This is our last chance to save the earth and humanity before a great extinction."

I suddenly realize why Whiro met with Daichsun that night and why he would betray the Shadow. Whiro knew about the Purging of the Father Gods. But she's not just talking about Father Gods. "You want to kill more humans?"

"They are a cancer." She exhales and her face sags. "What do you do with cancer? You cut it out. You destroy it." Her voice is growing louder, steely and determined. "We need a great flood to cleanse the world and begin anew. Humans are a pestilence, a disease that feeds upon all other life on this planet. They are crowding out other species and causing their extinction. They are well past their tipping point, well past good intentions and the love you hope they can use to change themselves. No, now it is my turn to force change upon them."

"You're just as much part of the problem."

"Yes, but I will also be part of the solution when the last piece fits into place."

"What's the last piece?" I ask, feeling my stomach roll.

A thin smile emerges on her face. She raises her hand and hits a button on her smartphone; all the screens now show a timer counting down from ten minutes.

"What is it?"

"It is the answer to the problem, my love."

"Damn it! Just tell me."

"This is not the first time we have been forced into a desperate situation in order to save mankind from its own destruction. You mentioned the twentieth century, but there have been many wars, plagues, and famines throughout history. Desperate times call for desperate measures—is that what they say?"

The timers can't mean anything good. "You plan on killing people."

"I don't like to think of it as killing," she says, waving the pistol distractedly. "More like culling the herd."

"What will this culling entail?"

The old woman clicks the phone again, and up on the screens pop hundreds of pictures of humanity. A busy intersection in Tokyo. Refugee camps in Syria. People crammed into buses in Thailand. Surging masses of people. I'm reminded of a super hive of insects. "Look at that. An infestation whose population has gotten out of control. It is our job to decrease the population and save them."

"What does the timer mean?" I ask, my voice faltering.

"Around the world, I have planted gifts. These gifts are located in every city whose population exceeds two hundred thousand. Thousands of gifts to the humans, in cities ranging from Lusaka to Seattle and even Beijing. These packages are my gift to humanity. When the timer hits zero, the gifts will detonate. I estimate that a minimum of three billion people will die instantly. From the reverberating effects of food-chain losses, rioting, starvation, and disease, another three and a half billion people will die. Effectively, in nine minutes, we will reduce the human population to under a billion. The population will be what it was in 1800. Furthermore, because of the loss of medical facilities and knowledge, the average life span will be reduced to approximately fifty years. This is my gift to humanity—a great cleansing. In the end, there will be only true believers. You and I will create a new religion: a religion guided by rationality and logic, as well as harmony, peace, and love. We will do it together. We will wipe the slate clean and start over. It will be a utopia. We will finally unite the ethos of the Father Gods with that of the Mother Goddesses. We will create a new generation of Ascended, who will rule over humans and guide them along a proper course. This will be a race of pure believers."

I take in her little speech as if it's a whole bottle of whiskey. I'm stunned, speechless and shaky. Then the magnitude of the words rock me like a drunken roar, and I plant my feet wide, my pulse pounding in my ears. "You're completely insane! You're planning to kill most of humanity—how can this be a gift? How can you be happy about this situation?"

"I'm not happy about what I have to do, but it is inevitable," she replies, with the fakest of frowns. "We will soon get to the point where the earth will not be able to sustain life. Every day we destroy more. We crush nature. We kill the very thing we rely on to live. If we don't reduce humanity now, it won't have another chance. By killing billions in an instant, we will ensure that humanity will survive for another thousand years."

"This is not the role of the Ascended."

"My love, don't you see? We have always been the sheepherders, and right now, there are too many sheep. They consume all the grass in the meadow and all the water in the stream. To protect the herd, we must slaughter it."

"There must be another way."

The old woman shakes her head. "We have always been different sides of the same coin. As a Father God, I use war, disease, famine, and death to help man evolve. You, as a Mother Goddess, use love, compassion, and kindness."

"Why can't we use love? Why death?"

"Because death is the only thing that humans understand at this point. It will be simpler when only you and I are in control. Trust me—when we remake humanity, they will thank us for the great flood."

"Why do you keep saying 'we'? I don't want any part of this sick plan. I don't want the deaths of billions on my shoulders. I will not help you kill people."

The woman raises her hand and clicks the phone again. The timer is at seven minutes. With eyes full of sympathy, she says, "I know, my love—that's why I'm letting you decide their fate. You alone can avert their destruction."

"How can I stop this?" I ask, my voice trembling.

"Mattie, despite all the evolution you've undergone, you still don't realize your true purpose," the Shadow replies with a tinge of disappointment in her tone. "I need you at the peak of your abilities. That is the reason you've been put through so many trials. Do you remember Janus's prophecy?"

I nod, my mind scrambling to get one step ahead of hers. But all I can think about is the ticking timer and the deaths of billions.

"It took me years to ascertain the true meaning of it. Initially, I thought it was a threat to my power, which was why I acted accordingly, but it was centuries later that I realized I was interpreting it incorrectly. It was always necessary to perform a sacrifice."

The word sends a shiver of dread through me.

"Let me ask you a simple question. What is it that you fear most about the prophecy?"

I exhale slowly to control my rattling breath. "I'm destined to kill the man I love."

"Yes!" the Shadow exclaims. "That is also what I feared." The distress in my stomach grows larger. "Fortunately, when I finally found you, I knew what had to be done. You represent something incredible. You are hope and love. If we flood the world, I need my queen again. I know that we can only remake the world together."

I nod again, as I might nod to a ranting person, except this ranting person will kill billions with a press of a button.

"I've decided to embrace my greatest fear." Her corpse-like smile sends spasms down my back. She places the gun on a small table beside her chair and clicks her phone.

On the far side of the room, a door slides open and a chain of prisoners emerges: Enki, Jessie, and the Younglings, including Ganesha. Dozens of guards, led by Tatiana and armed with automatic weapons, flank the procession. But it's the sight of the last two prisoners that strikes me like a gut punch.

Jared and Daichsun.

They were our only hope of getting out of here alive. We don't have a chance.

The manacled prisoners line up against the wall of timers. Six minutes and counting. The sight of my defeated friends makes my heart drop to my stomach. My body tenses to fight, but I make no move. I want revenge against this old woman who has destroyed my life, yet there's nothing I can do. She sits, face calm, watching my reaction as everything falls apart.

Tatiana grabs a leash attached to a metal collar around Enki's neck and yanks him up to the podium. He stumbles forward with his wrists constrained by handcuffs.

Enki's usual hopeful, energetic attitude is gone. He's pitiful, and judging by his limping gait, his injuries extend beyond his bandaged hand and the bruises and cuts on his face. What did they do to break him?

"My love, time is running short," the Shadow says, nodding at the timers. My muscles clench. In five minutes, billions will die, and I have no idea how to stop it. "You must complete the prophecy. Once you do, you'll be free to help me bring peace and balance back to the world."

My breath seizes as I jump to the logical conclusion: I'll have to kill Enki. "I won't hurt him."

The Shadow graces me with a condescending smile. "No, I will not make you kill him."

Relief washes over me, but there must be a catch. "What do you want?"

"I need my queen, but as you've already said, you will not help fulfill my vision; however, I believe you will help your friends," she says, pointing to the Mother Goddesses, lined up against the wall like prisoners ready to be executed. "Quite simply, I require two tasks from you. One is an Ascension."

"Who am I Ascending?"

"Me."

I frown. "I don't understand how I can Ascend you when you're already Ascended."

"There are ways," she replies cryptically. "You see, I know you're not ready to commit to a union with me, even if that union could result in a peaceful world. Look at me," she says, gesturing to her shriveled body. "I am old. Death is at my doorstep. If I were in your shoes, I wouldn't want me either. But I think I would be more appealing to you if I were someone else. Someone you trusted."

"It doesn't matter whose body you steal—I would never share your vision of a 'perfect world.'"

She nods. "Maybe not at first. However, we live our lives over millennia, not years. What is repugnant at first might be appealing in another century or so. I believe you will come to share my vision. I believe you can love me again, especially if I am someone you may already have feelings for." Her gaze slides over to Enki.

My stomach tightens rock hard, and I feel my lips trembling. "You want me to Ascend you into Enki's body?"

"Yes."

"It's not possible. A person can't have two souls."

The Shadow's eyes fix on Enki. "Tell her."

Enki raises his head weakly, revealing bloodshot eyes. "It's possible. In a past life, I had two souls in me, but the Ascension process is incredibly difficult." His voice is strained. "You could end up destroying both souls during the ceremony. Also, it's not a symbiotic relationship. One soul is always stronger than the other. It controls both the body and its partner soul. The alpha soul dominates the beta."

"To paraphrase," I say, "I could kill you if I did this, and even if I succeed, you could be a slave to the Shadow. You could be trapped inside your own body without control."

"That pretty much sums it up."

"Why would I ever do this?"

"I'll kill your friends if you don't," the Shadow says, almost dismissively. Then she points to the timers. Four minutes. "And it's the only way to save billions. I see two paths forward. One is quick and chaotic, while the other is slow and deliberate. I completely understand if you don't want to Ascend me. If that's the case, I would rather save this world than continue to be in it. Admittedly, my gifts will be destructive, but over time, they will be appreciated. But if you Ascend me, as I would prefer, then this flood can be stopped, and we can work together to remake this world. It may take a thousand years, but it will be worth it."

I shake my head. This can't be right. It's as if there's one great scale. Billions of lives on one side, and on the other side, Enki. Objectively, I know that billions of lives are worth more than one, but why does that one have to be someone I care about? "If I Ascend your soul into Enki, he'll no longer be in control of his body. You'll own him. You'll be in possession of him."

The old woman smirks. "If you're skilled enough at conducting the Ascension, then that might not be the case."

"What do you mean?"

"I believe you have the ability to decide which soul will be in control of the body. Yes, both souls will be in one body, but one will be in control. You have the power to decide this. If you do it right, Enki will be the so-called alpha soul and will be able to channel me." She holds up her smartphone to reveal a password-locked screen. "He will simply need to enter the correct code and all my gifts will be disabled. The flood will be averted; however, it all rests upon your abilities."

"You're willing to be a slave to Enki?"

She grins. "There is no great reward without great risk. I want my queen back, and I believe that this is the only way to achieve it."

"But if I fail then Enki will be a slave to you."

"Maybe," she says, calmly. "It all depends on your powers."

I don't trust her for a second. I know she's hiding something. I need to think of a third option. There has to be a way to save billions of innocents and Enki as well as defeat the Shadow.

Sensing my hesitation, she continues, "You doubt yourself, but you have been trained well. You conducted an Ascension at the Lyceum. You can do it again."

I frown. "Wait," I say, finally seeing a flaw in her plan. This isn't the same as Jessie's Ascension. I remember Ganesha's death and rebirth as well as Caishen's in ancient Rome. To move a soul from one body to another requires a sacrifice. "You would have to be dead for me to transfer your soul, right?" There it is. The Shadow made a fatal mistake.

She's anything but nonplussed by my declaration though. "As you might remember, there are two things I need from you. The first is my Ascension."

"What's the second?"

Her eyes grow distant. It seems a memory has bubbled to the surface of her mind. "There was a time when I was the person you loved. Therefore, the prophecy must be fulfilled." She picks up the gun from the table. For a moment, I fear she'll turn it on me, but to my shock, she offers the weapon to me instead. "You need to kill me."

The statement works its way through me like an electrical shock. This can't be. It has to be a trick. She wouldn't allow this. Invisible lines of terror hold me in place. I can't murder this woman; I can't murder anyone. It goes against my nature. "No," I say. "I won't do it."

"You must," she replies. "A sacrifice is required to fulfill the prophecy."

"No, I won't."

"I'm not giving you a choice." I have no time to react to what happens next. The Shadow leaps from her chair and grabs my arm. I try to pull away, but she's stronger. She forces the gun into my palm and tightens my fingers around the grip.

"Stop! Please."

With one hand restraining me, she guides my hand with the gun and aims it under her jaw. I resist but her grip is like iron.

"No!" I scream.

She pauses, stares lovingly into my eyes, and says, "You will make the right choice." Without hesitation, she forces my finger to pull the trigger.

The gun explodes, and I flinch as pieces of skull and brain fly across the room.

The Shadow's lifeless body collapses to the floor. Her dead hand still holds her password-locked phone, which contains the only hope for humanity.

I stare in horror at the scene before me.

An uneasy silence fills the room, and I can feel everyone's eyes on me. Jared, Jessie, Enki, Tatiana, the Younglings and the guards—they stare at me, waiting for my decision.

But I can't turn to face them directly. Now, all I can focus on is the timer. The death knell for the lives of billions. If I don't make the right decision, the world is doomed.

And, I have three minutes to decide.

CHAPTER THIRTY

LIGHT AND DARK

"You heard my Lord," Tatiana says, breaking the silence. She doesn't seem shocked that her Lord committed suicide. "Do what she commanded." She nods at the guards. "Kill the Mother Goddesses if she refuses."

The steel-faced men raise their guns and point them at my friends.

Rivulets of sweat run down my spine. The seconds tick by. I know that the choice seems obvious. Billions of lives are worth more than one. Yet, I can't decide.

"Mattie, you don't have any other option," says Jared. "You have to do what she wants to save humanity."

"How can you agree with her?" I ask, looking at him with shock. "You hate the Father Gods. They murdered your mother."

"Because there really is no choice," says Enki, the man who helped me believe in myself, who taught me not to fear the person I could become.

"Not you too? There must be another way that doesn't involve losing you."

Enki shakes his head. "You won't lose me if you control the Ascension. I believe in you." He glances at the ticking clock. Two minutes. "You have to Ascend her soul into my body."

"I can't!"

"You must." This time it's Jessie. Anger swells up inside me. A part of me blames her for everything that has happened. It was her betrayal that brought us to this moment and my lose-lose choice. "The Shadow's Ascension is the only way. You know that."

Tears fall from my eyes. I turn back to Enki. "I'm afraid that I won't do it right. I'm afraid I'll mess it up and lose you. You'll be a prisoner in your own body."

"You have the opportunity to save billions. Don't worry about me. I'm only one person. What matters are the people who don't have a choice, who will perish because of the decisions we make now. I don't want their deaths on my conscience. I'm the one being selfish. I'd rather be a prisoner than know I somehow helped kill them." His voice hardens and his eyes narrow. "You're skilled enough. You can do it, and you can make the Shadow obedient to me. She made a mistake because she doubted your abilities."

"She's too strong."

"You're stronger. You will make me the dominant soul. I believe in you."

The room falls silent, and the realization hits me square in the chest. I don't have a choice. I'll lose everyone I love if I don't do this. This is the only way.

"Ascend my Lord," Tatiana says. There's urgency in her tone now. The clock is ticking.

"Don't do this for her," Enki says. "Do this to save billions."

I walk forward and place my hand on Enki's cheek. Then I pull him toward me and kiss him. I wish we could be happy together. I wish that we were far away, out of harm. I wish we were different people. But in one minute, nothing will be the same.

I step back and stare into his eyes. "Enki," I say quietly, "lie down next to the Shadow." I attempt to calm my hammering pulse but my anxiety only increases.

Enki lies parallel to the Shadow, his arm touching that of the corpse. "I believe in you," he says again, looking up at me.

I Descended Gurzil and Ascended Jessie. I have the power to do this, but knowing something conceptually is wholly different from actually doing it. I've never transferred a soul into another Ascended's body before.

Crouching, I place my hand on Enki's forehead. As soon as my hand touches his skin, I sense his soul—it beats strong and proud. A blue flame brightening existence. His soul provides me a sense of comfort and warmth that eases the tension in my chest.

With a gripping reluctance, I extend my fingers toward the Shadow. When I touch her already cold, dead skin, a sickening sensation floods me. Her soul is like a poison entering my veins. I push away the feeling of nausea and disgust, and in my mind's eye, I find her. Unlike Enki, she has no glowing, pulsing life force. No hope. No love.

Her essence is smoky, dark. A cloud of fear.

It waits for me, patiently. It knows what I must do, and that realization is more disconcerting than anything else.

As it has the other times I've Ascended, time stops. The state I enter transcends physical reality. It's the moment before the fusion of two atoms, the moment before a supernova, the moment before the Big Bang. It is the time before. When time did not exist.

In this timeless state, where I am the arbiter of all things, I realize that the Shadow is defenseless. I can enter her soul. I can find secrets hidden in her past lives. Maybe, just maybe, I can discover the four-number code that will prevent the flood *and* save Enki.

But what I find doesn't shock me. Inside her black soul is the demon that has haunted mankind since the beginning. The one that has called for sacrifices. The one that has called for blood and killings. The one great evil of the world.

I cycle through the Shadow's past lives as if they're my own; it's a montage of appalling scenes and horrible people—tyrants, dictators, ruthless and heartless leaders.

In her memories, I see camps filled with the hungry and dying. I parade by them. In her cold eyes, the final answer is death. Killing them will bring about a lasting good.

Battle after bloody battle. Millions slain, maimed, diseased, and abandoned. The carousel of misery spans millennia. It's incomprehensible, the amount of suffering that has been unleashed onto the world because of this one soul.

I'm sickened by what I see. She's the source of so much agony in this world. She's caused this suffering all in the name of progress. All because she believes her ideals are noble and good.

I calm these racing thoughts, focusing my mind to a single point. Somewhere the truth must exist. I must find her penultimate life, the one she just ended. That's where the code is—key to saving humanity.

But the more I search for it, the more her soul fights me. It knows what I'm searching for. How is this possible? As I creep closer to her penultimate life, memories emerge. Bloody massacres. Child sacrifice. Rape and murder.

The Shadow is fighting me with the only weapon she has: her endless reservoir of memories and all the pain and suffering they contain.

Each memory she shares brings me into the moment. It's as if I'm experiencing them. The torment, the anguish, the hopelessness.

I fight for as long as I can. I'm fighting humanity's fate, and I can't give up. The more I fight, the more pressure and pain builds inside of me. Each revelation is like a new wound in my mind. A knife cut. A broken bone. A death.

The harder I push, the more horrific and terrible the memories become.

Finally, I fear my mind will crack and crumble if I don't stop my pursuit. I back off. As soon as I do, the Shadow's memories disappear, and I can breathe again. I can feel hope again.

The thought of pushing again makes my insides twist. I can't win. So I stop. I can't overcome her.

I failed. I failed Enki, my friends. I failed myself. Somehow the Shadow knew she could stop me.

There's one last thing I could do—I have the power to extinguish her. I can take her soul and destroy it. With but a flicker of a thought, I could end her forever. Should I do it? Should I end this great source of misery once and for all?

But I'm reminded of the repercussions. Billions will die. The future generation of Mother Goddesses will die. I'll lose everyone I've ever loved.

I wish there were another way, but there isn't. I have to do what the Shadow wants.

When I will the Shadow's soul over to Enki's body, it moves without resistance. There's an explosion of movement. Light and dark battle one another. It's a swirling mess as the two forces push and pull. Enki's soul and the Shadow's battle each other for control. I'm at a loss as to how to help Enki. I thought I'd have the power to dictate the terms of this conflict, but I can't do anything. Their souls move too fast.

At one point, Enki's blue flame blazes bright. Has he defeated the Shadow? But the next moment, the Shadow's gray cloud rumbles and pushes back.

I pray Enki is stronger.

At last, the light and the dark merge. They twist and turn around each other like a raging candle. The light blinds my inner eye. An explosion knocks me back, and then the blue flame is extinguished.

There is only blackness and a lingering dark suspicion.

CHAPTER THIRTY-ONE

ALPHA AND BETA

I stare down at Enki clasping my hands together, my muscles quivering. Did I transfer the Shadow's soul into Enki? And if I did, is Enki the dominant soul?

I kneel and cradle his head in my arms. "Enki, wake up."

No response.

A chasm opens inside me. "Please, Enki," I plead. "Please wake up."

Still no response.

"Please!" My world shatters. I sense the ultimate futility of all our actions and the meaningless of our struggles. The full measure of my failure threatens to crush the last shred of hope I'd preserved.

Then Enki's eyes flutter and open.

The boulder pressed on my chest lifts.

He smiles. "Hi, beautiful."

I release a halting breath. Relief rushes through me, filtering away the darkness that was ready to consume me.

"Is it you?"

He nods wearily. "Yes."

But the affirmation doesn't dispel the kernel of doubt. Is it really him?

"Mattie!" Jared yells. "There's thirty seconds left!"

Billions will die in half a minute.

"Enki, you have to disarm the weapon."

He rises, unsteady, and then pries the phone from the woman's dead hands.

"Ten seconds!" Jared shouts.

"Can you channel her?" I ask.

"I think so." He closes his eyes, but a second later opens them wide. "I can't do it."

"Try again."

"Five seconds!"

I think of my mother and all the things I never got to say to her.

Four

"Put in random numbers!" Jessie screams with desperation.

Three

I remember all my regrets. I wish I'd done more for my friends and hadn't let them down.

Two

Enki's eyes flutter and his body shudders. "I have it," he says, and plugs in four digits.

One

The timers freeze on one.

I feel the explosions before I hear them. The entire room shakes, and the television screens fall from the walls and shatter. The floor convulses beneath me, and I collapse.

Then the sound hits. A cacophonous wave of power barrels over us, knocking down anyone still standing.

Several people scream. The smell of burning plastic hits my nose. The room continues to rumble as if we're in an earthquake.

The guards rush for the exits. Tatiana appears as confused as the rest of us. Wasn't this what the Shadow planned? "Come back here!" she screams at the guards, but it's clear we're all rats on a sinking ship. Tatiana pulls out a gun, seeking to rally her troops. In the chaos, Jessie leaps at her and, with a swift blow, knocks her to the ground.

Fire spews from one of the exits, engulfing several of the guards in flames. Daichsun and Jared round up the Younglings and lead them toward another exit. Jessie runs out a different door, likely in search of her family.

Now is the time to escape. But where can we escape to? The entire world is on fire. Billions are dying.

Another explosion rocks the room and pieces of the concrete roof rain down on us.

Enki rushes over to shelter me, but a hail of debris stops him in place.

Three explosions happen in quick succession and then there's silence. Now! I sprint for one of the exits, seeking cover. I run down the podium. I'm almost at the door when something hard smashes into my head.

I'm knocked to the floor. The room spins, and I fight to stay awake.

My vision wavers. Enki reaches out for me, half his face covered in blood. Tatiana emerges behind him. He doesn't see her. She holds a long blade, ready and poised. Deadly intent painted on her beautiful face.

I scream to warn him, but more concrete comes pummeling down. A piece crashes into his skull, knocking him out.

The next moment, another piece hits the back of my skull sending me into darkness.

CHAPTER THIRTY-TWO

JERUSALEM

I 've never understood why nations fight over Jerusalem. It's a city with little natural resources. For thousands of years, countless lives have been lost for the petty, meager ownership claim to this metropolis. The last time I was in the city was centuries ago, after I led a failed Mother Goddess peace contingent to resolve a conflict between the Romans and Parthians.

I never would have never ventured back here if not for my husband. I understand his reasoning for establishing his base in the city. From Jerusalem, he will be able to assemble, prepare and coordinate his armies for the conquest of the East.

Camilla and I slipped into the city under the cover of night, pretending to be a group of wool traders from Yaffo. Along the well-walked route from the sea, we observed more evidence of the fighting between Mother Goddesses and Father Gods. Much of the violence was fresh—maybe no more than a day or two.

I have noticed a change in Camilla. An anxious energy has been surrounding her since we left Alexandria. She's been more irritable than usual, if such a thing is possible. Several times over the dinner fire I've tried to ease the restlessness that is lodged in her mind, that eats at her with every passing thought, but she's receding into herself. I suspect she feels that we've already failed the Mother Goddesses.

But unlike her, I do not see all the deaths as evidence of defeat. The Ascended are not bound by mortality; we are not constrained by a single life. To die and be reborn is the natural cycle. Yes, many of our *sisters and brothers have perished, but they have not been lost. As long as the knowledge the Mother Goddesses have accumulated remains, we will live on. We will thrive and grow stronger.*

What Camilla doesn't know is that Gaia has powers that no other gods possess. Powers that the Father Gods can only dream of. All it will take is ten years, a mere blink of an eye in history, and the Mother Goddesses will be back to their full strength—and, dare I say, even stronger.

I've witnessed this in past Purgings of both Mother and Father Gods. There is the slaughter and then the rebirth.

The Mother Goddesses will rebound, but for this to take place, a sacrifice must be performed. A death will restore balance to the world. The moment my husband betrayed me was the moment he sealed his fate.

My grip tightens on Diamant's Dagger as the thought of that betrayal ricochets in my mind. For weeks now, I've been preparing myself for this moment. Finally, I'm at the precipice. The moment where everything is set right.

The tunnel is dark, long, and damp; the torch I hold in my other hand illuminates the smooth stone walls. It dates back to the First Temple, and the Mother Goddesses have secretly incorporated its design into the construction of the Second Temple.

I am alone, for this mission is too dangerous for Camilla. She is brave but foolhardy. It's her first lifetime, and if she is to live ten more, she must learn caution and the extent of her abilities.

Besides, the killing must be by my hand; it is the only way to fulfill the prophecy.

The flickering torch brightens a wall, which marks the end of the tunnel and the beginning of the next chapter in the history of the Mother Goddesses.

Surprisingly, the false stone wall slides open with ease. I'm near the Holy of Holies. My husband will surely be there.

Hearing faint footsteps approach, I spring to the opposite wall and hide within the shadows of a dark doorway.

Two Roman legionnaires pass me, oblivious of my presence.

After they turn the corner to go down a passageway, I creep down the hallway, passing windows. From the temple's commanding height, I see the orange glow of fires scattered around the city and hear the distant cries of distressed citizens. I fear Camilla might have been too enthusiastic in her mission of distraction.

As I approach the Holy of Holies, I do not see any more guards. I had thought I would have to fight to get to my husband, but the path appears clear. Perhaps my husband feels overconfident with the success of his Purging; perhaps he believes there is no one left to challenge him.

A heartbeat later, I'm at the entrance-way of the inner sanctuary. Where are the priests who attend to the business of the temple? They are like lice on a dog at most temples, impossible not to be found.

But these thoughts are cut short by my husband's sudden appearance.

He emerges from behind the veil of the Holy of Holies and walks to a gilt table in the middle of the room, and inspects a map displayed broadly upon it.

His back is to me. He doesn't know I'm here.

This is the moment.

I don't think; I don't hesitate for a second.

With Diamant's Dagger poised, ready to strike, I close the gap between us in a second. I ready my hand to deliver a death wound, but right as I'm about to thrust the weapon into the back of his neck, a blow to the back of my head sends me sprawling to the ground. My husband sidesteps my trajectory, I crash hard into the table.

I lie on the ground, pain reverberating through my skull. Scrambling to my feet, I receive another blow, this time to my temple, destroying any momentum I might have had.

As the world spins around me, someone pries Diamant's Dagger from my hand and relieves me of the sword at my side. Strong hands prop me up against the fallen table. I suppress the sudden urge to vomit from the intense pain and will myself to focus my gaze. What I see deflates me of all hope.

"Camilla, why?"

She stands over me, a fiery goddess, her aura blazing. She holds a long staff marked red with my blood. A pained expression flushes her features. "I am protecting the Mother Goddesses," she says simply, turning away.

"Look at me!" I cry, willing her to stare into my eyes. "How are you protecting them?"

Like the petulant child she is, she bites down on her lip. Maybe she's regretting her choices. "At first, I believed in you, Gaia. I followed you. I always did what you said, even when I didn't agree with you. But over the past few weeks, I have concluded that you are not the leader the Mother Goddesses need. You are weak. You have allowed the Mother Goddesses to be butchered. I am acting to save those who remain."

"Child, you betrayed your people."

"Stop calling me child!" she screams. "I am sick of your patronizing tone!"

"What else am I to call my daughter?"

"I may be your daughter, but I am nothing like you. You are the one who has betrayed the Mother Goddesses. Father was right. You brought about the Purging. You are the reason that so many have died. You don't see the truth. That love, mercy, and kindness you preach is hypocritical. You would have slaughtered the Father Gods just as quickly if you had been given the prophecy instead of Father."

"That's not true and you know it."

"It is true. I have read about the histories of past Purgings. More likely than not they were initiated by Mother Goddesses, with you often leading the fight."

"And I have paid for those sins and errors a thousand times over. Why else do I advocate mercy and peace?"

"More lies. More deception."

"He has poisoned your mind. He has led you off the true path toward a dark place. He has led you to an endless war."

"Just the opposite, Mother. He has promised an end to the Purging. I have come to an agreement with him."

"What is this agreement?"

My husband places his hands on Camilla's shoulders, and she doesn't flinch at his touch. In fact, she glances at him and smiles. How long has this deception been building?

He stares down at me, a shade of disappointment in his eyes. "I have announced that I will cease all hostilities against the Mother Goddesses. There will be no more Purging. There will be no more deaths. Peace will be maintained."

I snort. "The Purging has already been completed, hasn't it? You have succeeded in decimating the ranks of the Mother Goddesses in the West. That was always your goal, wasn't it?"

"You would have done the same thing if it were you who received the prophecy."

"That's not true," I say again. "You killed them, and this was always your plan."

"But I will not make war on any more Mother Goddesses. They will maintain their influence in the East."

"Your mercy is hollow. You never intended to invade the East. You knew you could never beat the combined armies of the Parthians and Hans. Your goal was always to consolidate power in the West."

"You may speculate however you wish."

"So, Camilla, what is it you exchanged for this false peace? What is it you sold for this genocide besides your betrayal of me?"

My husband smiles proudly. "She has agreed that I will be her new mentor. I will teach her lessons that you would have never had the courage to pass along."

"You will teach her to be a Father God. You will teach her to be corrupt."

"I will teach her to ignore the fallacies of emotions. To see through the lies of love. To value intellect and logic at all costs."

"You will teach her to be less of a human."

"This was your problem, Gaia," says my husband. "You didn't see the full potential of your own daughter. You didn't value her. You didn't respect her. I see her for what she is. A giant. A great one. Someone who will tower over her lessers. You thought your daughter had the soul of a Mother Goddess, but she was always a Father God in her heart."

I stare at Camilla. "I birthed you. I raised you and trained you myself. I am your mother. How could you betray me?"

"You trained me to be weak. I need a teacher to make me strong, and he was there."

"I trained you to love and have compassion."

"Your teachings are falsehoods. I am ready to build a new world with my father, my new Lord. Together we will create a new world, a better world."

"This world will be cursed."

"Then help us make it better," says my husband. "Swear your obedience to me and I will let you live. We can be a family again and create the world that was always meant to be. Help us."

"I would rather die than have my soul rot from the inside out. You will regret the decisions you made today. You will regret the innumerable lives lost today and those to be lost in the future. The day will come when I will be reborn, and on that day, I will exact my revenge."

"I did love you." He nods toward Camilla. "Kill her, but not with Diamant's Dagger. We may have a use for her soul in the future."

Camilla comes at me with my own sword. She places it against my throat. "Do you have anything else to say, Mother?"

"I'm sorry I let you down, Camilla."

"I am no longer Camilla. Father has renamed me. From henceforth, I will be Titania, old Greek for the 'giant, great one.'"

With my last ounce of strength and energy, I say. "I will return. It may be in ten years, or a hundred, or a thousand, but I will make both of you pay for the pain and suffering you will inflict upon the world. Mark my words. There will be a reckoning."

"And we will be waiting for you," says my husband.

The blade slides into my side. It's fast and swift, just as I have taught her. My life force spills out of me. I touch my wound and my hand comes away covered in blood.

Camilla smiles. "Goodbye, Mother."

CHAPTER THIRTY-THREE

WELCOME HOME

I t's as though I've been asleep for another two thousand years. Rubbing my eyes with my palms, I realize with shock that I'm alive. It's as if I died twice—once in Beijing and then again in Jerusalem. But I am most certainly not dead. I do have a massive headache, and my body is sore all over. I touch my forehead and find it wrapped in bandages.

As I survey my surroundings, the puzzle becomes only more peculiar. The most surprising thing, besides the fact that I am alive, is the green, dense forest of maple, fir and pine trees outside the big picture window at the foot of my bed. Sunlight filters through the canopy of leaves and needles. I hear birds call out, and a squirrel leaps from a branch.

The small room is comprised of only the bed and prints of seaside scenes, which hang on the log walls. "Where am I?" I ask myself out loud.

I hear voices, and it's as if someone has pushed the play button on life.

A Youngling from the Lyceum pokes her head into the room and yells, "She's awake!"

The room immediately fills with people. Jared, looking weary but happy; Jessic, smiling and radiant; and Daichsun, crossing his arms.

But someone is missing.

Before I can speak, I'm bombarded with questions about how I'm feeling.

"Whoa!" I hold up a hand. "Short answer, I'm fine. Can someone please tell me where we are?"

"Maine," Jessie replies. "Like way north Maine in the middle of the woods."

"Maine?" I ask in disbelief. "Why here?"

Jared sits down on the bed. "This is a Mother Goddess safe house."

"How long have we been here?"

"It's been a week since Beijing."

That's when I remember all the events that unfolded in the Underground City. "Oh my god! The weapon detonated. Billions died."

He shakes his head. "No, there was no attack. The weapon never detonated."

I blink. "What were the explosions?"

Daichsun raises his hand proudly. "That was me. Before I was captured, I set up explosives all across the Underground City. I might have gone a little overboard."

"The explosions helped us escape," says Jared. "We were able to get the Younglings out before the entire complex collapsed."

"How did I get out?"

"I saved you," Jessie says. "After I rescued my family, I came back for you."

My mind spins. I can't believe that all this happened while I was passed out. I swallow, not waiting to ask my next question. "Where is Enki?"

There's a long, painful pause, which is an answer in itself. Jared finally says, "Tatiana took him."

A pit of distress tears open in my stomach, but it quickly fills with determination. "We have to rescue him."

"We don't know where he is."

"Then we'll find him," I say, struggling to get up.

Jared puts a hand on my shoulder to stop me from getting out of bed. "Mattie, you have to rest and regain your strength. You were in a coma for a week."

"I'm fine now, and Enki needs our help. I can't rest here knowing that Tatiana has him."

There's another long, awkward pause before Jared asks, "Can I have a minute alone with her?"

"Certainly," says Daichsun tersely. He turns to me and adds, "It isn't horrible that you survived. I look forward to continuing to fight by your side." Well, if that was as warm as he goes, I guess I'd take it.

Jessie leans over and plants a kiss on my cheek. "I can't express how thankful I am. You helped save my family. I owe you a debt I'll never be able to pay back. I love you, and it's good to have you back."

She leaves as well, and I turn to Jared. "I know what you're going to say."

"Which is?"

"It's too dangerous to save Enki. You'll say that we can't risk losing me. You're going to convince me that he's not important enough to save."

"No, he is important," he says. He seems to be choosing his words carefully. "But we can't trust Enki anymore."

I frown. "Why can't we?"

"You Ascended the Shadow into his body. We don't know if it's really Enki in control."

"No," I reply, "he talked to me. I remember. It was definitely him. I know for sure."

"You don't know for sure. Nobody does. I was there, and honestly, it could have been the Shadow."

"But why did he stop the timer?"

"Maybe it was always the Shadow's intention to stop it. Maybe he wants you to think that Enki is in control. Maybe this is all part of his plan. The honest truth is we don't know anything for sure."

A sudden burst of weariness sends my head spinning. "I've heard enough," I say quietly. "Please leave."

"Mattie, we're here for you."

"Damn it, Jared. Please go!"

He flashes a frown and leaves. As soon as the door closes, the tears come, and for all my strength, I can't stop them.

CHAPTER THIRTY-FOUR

New Normal

F our weeks later, I'm limping through the woods with Jessie, following a winding path. I'm still weak, and after about half an hour of walking, I have to stop and rest against a tree.

"You're out of shape," says Jessie.

"No, I was in a coma."

"Well, as soon as you feel like it, I'm ready to go on our daily runs again."

"I'd like that."

She falls silent then looks right at me. "Mattie, I know I apologized before for what I did, but I'll never forget how you helped me."

"Jessie, you're my best friend. If I'd lost you, there wouldn't be much point to anything."

"Still, you trusted me again."

"You proved yourself. You saved my life. It's all water under the bridge, and you don't owe me anything. We're friends, remember."

"I really appreciate that," she says, wiping a tear off her cheek. "So what will we do now?"

"As the sole surviving members of the Lyceum, I guess we restart the school, but we'll do things differently. We'll teach them how to love first. We'll go back to the basics of what it means to be a Mother Goddess."

"Cool. I always wanted to be a teacher."

"Trust me, it's not all it's cut out to be."

The thought of all the work that's needed gives me a headache. "Listen, there's something I've been meaning to tell you." I relate to her my flashbacks of Gaia from Rome. After the last one, the one where Gaia died, I've yet to channel her. It's as though she's hiding, waiting. She gave me her message and disappeared.

"Sounds like she was a real badass. We could use her about now."

I shake my head. "I suspect that I may never channel her again. Yes, she was extremely powerful, but I sensed she was haunted by something. Her actions, her missteps, her mistakes. In the end, I don't think that she was much different from the Father Gods. Her visions were a warning to me. 'Don't become what I became.'"

"Well, look at the bright side—at least the Purging is over."

It's true. Ever since the events in Beijing, there haven't been any more killings. For the time being, there is peace.

"Was the Shadow serious about his new, perfect world?" Jessie asks.

"I don't know. It could all be lies. We'll know for sure by finding Enki."

"Jared doesn't seem too keen on that prospect."

I grimace, and my chest tightens. "I don't know what to do about him."

"You could always kick him out of the Protectors club. You're the de-facto leader of the Mother Goddesses. You're in charge now."

"True, but I don't think that would be the best thing." I could dwell and fixate on Jared for hours, but for right now, I don't want to think about him.

Instead, I focus on the light breeze swaying the maple trees that surround us. I listen to the forest as life chirps, squeaks, squawks. It's a new day. And it holds promise of a fresh start. I feel the sun warm my skin, and the sensation fills my heart with an unexpected eagerness. "You know," I say, "we have a lot of work to do, and I'm ready to get started."

CHAPTER THIRTY-FIVE

TRAPPED

Cold, cold, so cold. How long have I been in darkness? Time has lost meaning. I try to find peace in small moments, but hundreds of pains remind me of everything I've lost. The pains come in ever-increasing waves that drown any sense of control. Manacles bite into my wrists as I hang from the ceiling. Rats scamper over me. Gnawing hunger weakens my body.

I thought I was strong. I thought I could resist the torture. I was wrong.

Now I crave death at every waking moment. Death is release from pain. Death is escape from this wretched prison. Would Gaia be disappointed in me?

Suddenly, the door opens. Blinding light strikes my eyes.

It takes me a long time to focus, but when I do, I see a woman I vaguely recognize, as if she's from a dream . . . or a nightmare.

I want to curse her. I want to beg her to end me, but I have forgotten how to speak.

She walks up to me, leans close, and caresses my cheek. "Time to wake up, my Lord."

Then she rams the tip of the cattle prod into my chest. My body convulses under the electric burn. I twist, writhe, and struggle, but there is nowhere I can go.

After what seems like forever, she stops. I hang depleted and destroyed. Then she adds, almost desperately, "Come back to me, Father."

ACKNOWLEDGMENTS

There was a point when I thought that this book would never see the light of day. It felt like a mountain—a big, hulking pile of rocks, sitting on my shoulders. I was lost in plot lines that went nowhere, disliking paper-thin characters, and hacking my way through long, boring passages of description.

Despite this, I knew I owed it to you, the reader, to continue Mattie's story. To everyone that sent me praise, encouragement, and even criticism, I first want to thank you for keeping me writing.

Eventually, the story came together. Partially this happened because I refused to give up but mostly it was because of all the people who read early drafts and provided invaluable feedback.

This book would have been destined for the dustbin if it had been for the exceptional notes from two people in particular—Emily Frongillo and Thomas Finan. My deepest thanks.

During the depths of COVID, I was part of a zoom writers group who included Don Kaplan, Jenny Pivor, Felice Koslen and Steve MacKinnon—all of whom provided laughter, commiseration, and insightful critiques.

I am supremely thankful to a group of beta-readers who took their time and energy to read through the finished version and provide essential notes. Thank you Meyer Drapkin, Katherine Cocca Bates, Amy Smith, and Alexandra Arnow.

To my editor, Rachel Small, I owe you the stars above for your eagle eye and mighty red pen.

Lastly, to Anna, my love, my life, thank you for allowing me to disappear for hours at a time to the basement, to pound away at this story, despite a raging pre-schooler, a crying newborn, and a bathroom that still needs to be cleaned. Thank you for reading draft after draft. And thank you for your endless support and encouragement.

I truly hope you enjoyed the story. If you did, please share a review, , on Amazon and/or Goodreads it would make a real difference.

Lastly, I look forward to sharing the next book in the Ascended Series, GAIA STOLEN.

Subscribe to the newsletter to get a free story as well as stay up to date with all the latest news, sales, and promotions! If you're interested in the other books in the Ascended Prophecies Series, you can check them out at jrwalcutt.com.

You can also follow me on Amazon and get notified when I publish.

I love to hear from readers, and you can Email or reach me on Facebook, Twitter, and Instagram.

If you loved reading about Mattie and her adventures, the third book is coming soon. Turn the page to read the first chapter of her next incredible story, GAIA STOLEN.

GAIA STOLEN

(Coming in 2024)

I'm scared. More scared than I've ever been in my entire life, and I've faced down armies.

How does one prepare to meet a god? How does one dress and act? It's one thing to see his stone statues, pray in his temples, and make offerings during the festivals, but what should I do when I come face to face with my god?

When I received the summons, I couldn't believe it. Why would Pharaoh, our god, want to meet me, a simple soldier in his army?

True, I had shown bravery in battle against the Sea Peoples. I led a rally, when defeat seemed all but certain. This turned the tide of the battle, routed the enemy, and led to us recapturing the city of Ashkelon. My generals had praised me for my bravery and even promoted me to the rank of lieutenant.

Despite my accomplishments, it's still unheard of for the Pharaoh to meet a person of my rank, in his private residence no less. Yet here I am, in the glorious capital city, inside his royal palace.

The sun-dried earth bricks of the palace tower above. Along the walls, hieroglyphs, which I can not read, are clear to understand. They show our Pharaoh, in all his glory, crushing his foes beneath his chariot in battle. In another scene, he stands tall and regal with his wife beside him, their outstretched arms petitioning the gods to bring good fortune onto their people.

A faint breeze carries the smell of desert—baked sand with notes of Jasmine—into the palace's expansive halls. Outside the open *windows, the pyramids rise above the sands like great ships sailing on a golden sea. Faraway, slaves toil along their surface, appearing like crawling ants, hauling gigantic blocks of limestone up earthen ramparts.*

It's been centuries since the last Pharaohs were buried beneath them. Pharaoh, in his wisdom, has begun a reconstruction of the pyramids in order to bring them back to their former glory, and show respect to the gods who came before him. Once the reconstruction is complete, the pyramids will be capped with a gilded crown, pointed upward toward the heavens, painted an alabaster white, to reflect the light in blinding brilliance. The pyramids will carry their souls into the land of the dead.

"So, you're him," says a commanding voice.

I nearly fall out of my seat. When I look up, I see a beautiful woman, dressed in fine linen and covered in jewels. Her face is painted with purples and greens. I glance at the pictures depicted on the walls around me and suddenly realize that the image on the wall matches that of the woman in front of me.

"Your highness," I say, dropping to my knees in front of her. "Apologies, my queen."

The Pharaoh's wife looks down at me. She is shorter than I imagined. She has a pointed face, a regal nose upturned to an edge, teeth sharp as a leopard, and aristocratic eyes.

The queen reaches down and lifts my chin, until I stare into her immaculate face. "Tell me soldier, what do you see?"

A flicker of worry courses through me. "What do you mean, your highness?"

"When you look at me, what do you see?"

Is this some test? I have no idea what she means. I fear that the wrong answer may mean my own death, so I choose the most diplomatic reply, "I see you in all your beauty."

"Hmm," she replies, inspecting me for a long time. "Do you know the proper protocol for meeting Pharaoh?" But then she shakes her head. "Of course, you don't. Listen very carefully. If you don't follow *my instructions precisely, you may incur your king's wrath. He's been known to execute visitors who do not follow court policy."*

I gulp, feeling a shiver course through my body, realizing that my visit may be more dangerous than any battlefield I've ever fought on.

"You will wait outside the entrance of the central court," says the Queen. "When the court herald calls your name, you will enter the court. Never shall you make eye contact with your lord. Keep your eyes firmly on the ground. Approach until you are no more than ten paces from Pharaoh. At this point you will drop to your knees and present your offering. You did bring an offering, didn't you?"

"Of course," I reply, hastily, reaching into the basket which holds the stone carved sculpture of an Ibis. I spent most of my savings on the sculpture. My commanders had informed me about the importance of the offering to the Pharaoh. They stressed that I should spare no expense. To gain the Pharaoh's pleasure, would surely mean that my soul would find peace in the afterlife.

"If the Pharaoh accepts your offering, he may say a few words to you. If he does, remain silent. Wait until Pharaoh gestures for you to leave, at which point return the way you came. Again never make eye contact. Do you understand?"

"Yes, my Queen."

She nods firmly. "Follow me." She walks me down a corridor until we arrive at an entrance with massive double doors. "Wait here until you are called," she says, before disappearing through the ornately decorated doors.

I wait in the cool air of the palace, feeling my skin burn and heart race.

Eventually, the court herald gestures for me to enter. When I enter the sumptuous hall, I can barely believe my eyes. The walls are all painted in vibrant reds, greens and yellows. They depict the story of our Pharaoh and his conquests, building projects and glory.

"Lieutenant Ashkot, a soldier of the Northern Army presents his offering," announces the court herald in a booming voice. I keep my eyes fixed on the ground, remembering the Queen's instructions.

However, as I walk forward, a bright light draws my focus away from the floor. A burning image appears in front of me, as though the sun itself is in the room. Despite my better judgment, I lift my eyes to the source. It's a golden, glorious image of a woman. She's composed of fiery beauty, as if her skin is composed of flames. She walks toward me, the sun incarnate, majestic rays shooting off of her, illuminating the entire room.

An instant later, the light douses and the image of the fiery woman disappears. In her place, the Pharaoh steps forward, tall, barrel-chested, his commanding presence fills me with awe and impressiveness. His green eyes flicker with a strange familiarity, while he wears the beginnings of a smile.

It's at that moment that I realize that I've committed the gravest of errors.

I am looking my god right in his eyes.

I fully expect to be struck down by lightning. The Pharaoh will have me executed and have my corpse displayed in the streets as a warning to those who do not respect him.

But this is not what happens. Instead, the Pharaoh comes up to me, a smile forming on his lip, and he pulls me into an embrace.

"Here is our champion son, the soldier who single-handedly defeated the Sea People horde."

I don't know how to respond. I'm too shocked. I'm in front of my god. I can even smell his fragrant perfumes of myrrh and cinnamon. The Pharaoh stares at me for a long time. I glance around the court, and realize that beside the queen, who sits on her throne, we are alone in the room. "Your name is Ashkot?"

"Yes, my lord," I manage to say, nodding. I try looking away, but there is something arresting about the Pharaoh's image. What did I see before when I entered? Who was that fiery woman?

"Tell me about yourself," he says, his tone relaxed.

"I don't know what you mean, your highness."

"Tell me where you were born."

"Canaan."

"And who were your parents?"

"They were artisans. They made pottery. But they died when I was very young, from the plague."

Pharaoh's face becomes grim. *"Yes, that was a difficult time for our country. Many of our people fell to that disease."*

"I was raised by my aunt and uncle who were childless. When I reached the age of manhood, I entered the army and have been fighting with them ever since."

Pharaoh's eyes brighten. *"Fascinating. And you don't remember anything before your birth?"*

Shreds of doubt cloud my thoughts. *"Excuse me, my lord?"*

He smiles. *"Nothing. Tell me Ashkot, besides fighting, what do you love?"*

"Sorry, my lord, what do you mean?"

"Army life can't be your sole interest. What type of man are you?" Pharaoh says, his voice probing. *"Do you enjoy brothels? Or are you fond of wine? Maybe you prefer hunting? Or do you prostrate yourself to the gods? Tell me Ashkot, what is it that you enjoy most in this world?"*

I take a deep breath, and consider what would be the most diplomatic reply. Then I realize that the best reply would be the truth. *"I enjoy games, my lord."*

He smiles until his teeth show. *"Do you like Mehen?"*

I tilt my eyes down. *"I confess that I may be the best player along the northern border."*

The Pharaoh's smile becomes impossibly wider. *"Well, you are in luck because I am the best player of the upper and lower Nile, and I'm in need of a worthy rival. Would you be interested in joining my court and playing me when the need arises?"*

I'm speechless, and my mind spins. Why has Pharaoh favored me so? I am no more worthy than any other citizen.

"Come now, Ashkot," he says, *"It's no big thing. I will inform your superiors that I've assigned you a new post. What do you say?"*

"I would be greatly honored."

"You remember, my lord," the Queen interjects, *"For the next two months you are touring your building projects in Amarna, Luxor and Elphantine."*

Pharaoh waves his hand dismissively. *"The royal barge has more than enough room. Also, I'm sure Ashkot will want to meet my sister. She will be excited to meet you, I'm sure."*

"It would be a great honor."

Pharaoh nods. *"You must be tired from your travels. I'll have my servants escort you to the residential suites for you to rest, bath and clean. I hope that you will join me for dinner tonight."*

"I wouldn't want to intrude," I say in disbelief. *This can't be happening. Why does a living god want to be with me?*

"I couldn't think of dining without you," he says, *"I still need to hear the story of how you single handedly beat back the Sea Peoples."* He waves his hand, and a servant emerges and guides me from the room in a daze.

What just happened? Why has pharoah favored me so?

I'm walking down the same corridor from which I entered, when a bolt of shock ripples through me. I look down and realize that the Ibis sculpture is still in the basket.

I never left my offering with Pharaoh.

The Queen's warning flashes in my mind. To not leave my offering would be the greatest insult against him. I mustn't allow this slight to occur.

I explain the situation to the servant, and before he has time to protest, I extricate myself and rush back to the throne room. Maybe I can slip it inside the room without Pharaoh noticing.

As I approach the large doors of the throne room, I hear Pharaoh and the Queens' voices clearly.

"Can you believe it?" Pharaoh asks, *"It's her."*

"I must confess," replies the Queen. *"When our son said that he saw her true form, I didn't believe him. But he is indeed the lost goddess."*

"Not since the time of the first Pharaohs was she last seen."

"I heard that she built the first cities."

"In Sumer. She was their great king. Their god."

"Why has she been lost for so long?" the Queen asks.

"I don't know. I know she defeated him in battle, and then she disappeared."

"Well, she's returned. What should we do with her?"

"The most important thing is that we can't let him know about her. Her emergence would plunge us into war."

"Is it wise to bring her with you?"

"I'm not letting her out of my sight. We must Ascend her at all costs."

"Are you sure your sister knows the ceremony?"

"She had been the goddesses' handmaiden. She will remember it. Send her a pigeon, we will leave immediately."

"You will be gone for nearly a month."

"I trust that you will keep the empire functioning while I'm away."

"Should we tell the boy who he actually is?" the Queen asks.

"No, it must be kept a secret. His reality has already been shaken. The ceremony will allow him to know everything. He will travel with me until he is ready to Ascend."

Subscribe to the newsletter to get a free story as well as stay up to date with all the latest news, sales, and promotions! Interested in reading more? You can check out the other books in the Ascended Prophecies at jrwalcutt.com.

ABOUT THE AUTHOR

J.R. Walcutt is a former microfinancier, chicken farmer, and tarot card reader. He's searched for lost Native American tribes in the deserts of Mexico, hitchhiked in the south of Spain, worked as an aid worker in Mumbai, lived on a sinking boat in the port of Jaffa-Tel Aviv, and started an export business in Beijing. He lives in Massachusetts.